THE WAITING ROOM

THE

WAITING

ROOM

MARY

MORRIS

DOUBLEDAY

NEW YORK LONDON TORONTO SYDNEY AUCKLAND

All of the characters in this book are fictitious, and any resemblance to actual persons, living or dead, is purely coincidental.

PUBLISHED BY DOUBLEDAY

a division of Bantam Doubleday Dell Publishing Group, Inc.
666 Fifth Avenue, New York, New York 10103

DOUBLEDAY and the portrayal of an anchor with a dolphin are trademarks of Doubleday, a division of Bantam Doubleday Dell Publishing Group, Inc.

Parts of this work previously appeared in *The Ontario Review* and *The Nassau Literary Review.*

Library of Congress Cataloging-in-Publication Data

Morris, Mary, 1947–
  The waiting room / Mary Morris. — 1st ed.
    p. cm.
  ISBN 0-385-26169-1
  I. Title.
  PS3563.087445W35   1989
  813'.54—dc19   88-8025
                              CIP

Designed by Bonni Leon

ISBN 0-385-26169-1

To my daughter,

Kate Lena,

January 23, 1987,

and to the memory

of my grandmother,

Lena Malkov Zimbroff,

1882–1973

ACKNOWLEDGMENTS

I would like to express my thanks to the John Simon Guggenheim Foundation, the New York Foundation for the Arts, and the Friends of American Writers for their assistance in the completion of this project. I also would like to thank my agents, Lynn Nesbit, Amanda Urban, Suzanne Gluck, Heather Schroder, and Lisa Bankoff, for their support and enthusiasm. Various people offered their assistance in such areas as military history and medical research and I would like to thank Jim Shepard, Jonathan Cohen, and Geoffrey Amthor. I also want to thank Helena Bentz, John Harbison, Larry O'Connor, and Mary Jane Roberts for their careful readings and encouragement. A special thanks to my parents, Sol and Rosalie Morris, who were invaluable critics and loyal supporters throughout the years it took to complete this project. And finally no thanks can express my gratitude to my editor, Nan A. Talese, whose undying faith and endless patience saw me through many drafts.

CONTENTS

We are the only ones who are still waiting, in a suspense as old as time, that of women, everywhere, waiting for the men to come home from the war.

Marguerite Duras
The War

PART

ONE

HEARTLAND

Thunder Bay
Christmas, 1972

Dear Zoe, The sky is so blue it frightens me. I can't describe it to you, this blue. It's not the color of robin eggs or Naomi's eyes. It's not the blue of the lake or the old Chevy I fixed up back in '59. Remember that Chevy? When I found it in the junkyard and you said you're crazy, Badge, but I'll talk them into letting you keep it. How I'd let you ride around in it whenever you came home from college. And I always kept it so shiny, you could put on your makeup in its reflection. I've tried to pin this blue down to something I can actually remember. But it's not that way. It's not the lake we'd go to every day in the summer and it's not the blue of that dress you wore to prom. The one with the white and pink ruffles, a kind of ridiculous dress that crinkled and made silly noises while you walked down the stairs to greet your date, what was his name, that dumb, skinny blond boy you didn't even like, but no one else had asked you and they wouldn't let you go with Hunt, so you had to go with him. Remember that prom, how you hated having to wait for some boy to ask you out and you told Mom, I'm never gonna do this again. I'm never going to sit around until some boy calls me. But you went out with him and later you told me how he slipped his hand under that blue dress and you slapped him and said how can you take advantage of a girl who's drunk. No, it's not the blue of sadness. Or rivers or bluebells or blue jays when they rob from other birds' nests. It's more like the color when you look really deep into a crazy person's eyes. It just goes on and on. This sky makes you realize how small you are, how insignificant. How nothing matters. Sometimes when I wake up in the morning and go outside and there's not a cloud to break it up, I have to bury my face in my hands. It's the kind of blue I used to love in small doses, but not like this. You know they say the sky is blue because it reflects the ocean, but I don't believe it. I know different. This sky has a life of its own. My love, Badger

O N E

As the train moved toward the home she'd left behind, Zoe Coleman tried to remember when it was she'd fallen in love with distance. With trips across great continents and travel to the moon. With telescopes and marathons and the Midwestern sky. It was snowing as the train traveled up the lakefront and it was difficult for Zoe to believe how far she had come, through light years and galaxies, across borders and generations, to get back to this place she said she'd never come back to.

The train was a nice, neat Amtrak with scratchy red seats and little paper headrests. Zoe's headrest had an oil spot on it. A round oil spot from the head of a previous passenger. She pictured a middle-aged man, perhaps in a flannel suit, on his way to do business in Minneapolis. He would be the kind of man to share a train ride with. A sedate gentleman who'd ask her safe questions about vitamin therapy or bypass surgery. Someone who'd never say, "So what brings you here in this weather?"

Zoe sat by the window, looking at the sky. It was turning dark as she opened her briefcase. She took out a book on neurological disorders. She took out a copy of *The New England Journal of Medicine.* She took out a notebook. She put the book on neurological disorders back. She tried to decide which book would help her think about Badger less. She opened her little plastic tray table, but it had a big coffee splotch on it and some cake crumbs. She put the plastic tray table back.

Someone tossed a bag down on the seat across from her. She'd seen him before. He'd stood in line behind her at Union Station. He'd said, "Do you know what time the train for Green Bay leaves?" She'd wondered then if this was a come-on. And now he sat across from her. There were plenty of seats on the train, so she decided he was following her.

Zoe looked away, at her reflection in the glass. Her long, dark hair was pulled back severely into a ponytail. She wore a beige khaki shirt and green army pants; she looked ready for combat. Once Badger told her this joke. He said what do King Kong and Che Guevara have in common? She was never very good at guessing his jokes, so he told her right away. They're both urban guerrillas.

She laughed out loud, then caught herself. The man glanced at her. She thought how Badger always had a good sense of humor. How he'd gotten her through whale and grape and Polish jokes. She wondered if he'd make it through light bulbs.

The North Side zipped by. The red and black rooftops. Abandoned buildings and railroad yards. The sun peered over the buildings. In the glass she saw the reflection of the man who sat across from her. He was looking her way. She saw his mustache, his pale-colored hair and eyes. Zoe turned to an article about a part of the reptilian brain. She didn't feel like reading about her specialty. She had only recently decided upon it, but already she was thinking about taking off. Going to work in a jungle somewhere, just disappearing for a while.

There had been so many parts of the body to choose from. Some parts she'd liked better than others. The eye, for instance. She'd always been fond of the structure of the eye. She liked the way it sat so obediently in its socket and the way it came in colors. She liked the fact you could see all the way to a person's brain. But in the end some of the problems of the eye upset her. Once during her ophthalmology rotation, she tried making dinner with her eyes closed. She'd made frozen vegetables, mashed potatoes, and chicken. Her old boyfriend, Robert, had complained about the way the meal came out. And another time, she tried crossing a street with her eyes closed and someone had actually helped her get to the other side.

She couldn't stand depending on anyone. She rejected the

heart and the brain. She rejected the eye and the bones. She settled on flesh. Surfaces interested her. She didn't want to go deeper than that. Skin-deep was deep enough. Not farther than adolescent pimples, blackheads and pustules, reactions to strawberries, and minor bouts of skin cancer. You don't see many fatalities of the skin. Not like the heart. She didn't want to go deep. Just wide. The skin is the largest organ. It's a little like the Midwest where she's from. Open and even, only of interest if you've been there for a while. Or are returning, after a long time away.

But then if you understand it well enough, the skin has its interesting side. Everything shows up there first. A teenage girl's first blush over love, the twitches of a nervous student, herpes for the promiscuous lover, Indochina itch for the exotic traveler, hives from stress, the liver spots of age. The skin is an honest organ. It tells no lies. It has no place to hide.

Her mother used to say that Zoe wore her feelings on her sleeve. But June should talk. Zoe remembered when her father came home from the war. He was only back a few weeks when June began to break out in those big red welts on her arms and legs that made her soak in all kinds of special baths. She'd say it was some fruit she ate. But her grandmother, Naomi, knew and told Zoe that the only thing June was allergic to was her own husband.

Badger always had baby-smooth skin. No matter how much older he got, his skin stayed the same. Smooth and pink, unblemished. Even as a teenager, when his friends came over to toss a football around, and they all had acne which they tried to hide with Clearasil and those fuzzy mustache hairs, Badger's skin was flawless. He had angel's skin. And sometimes when they were small, Zoe would touch his face and he'd smile and look at her and Naomi would say how he was just a little angel.

But there was something else about Badger. His eyes. The eyes didn't go with the skin. He had dark, deep-set eyes that were never wide like a child's. Badger's eyes always took in a whole room with one sweep. He had the eyes of someone older. Someone who'd already seen it all.

Once Zoe read that there were only ten faces in the world and the rest are variations. But Badger seemed to have all the variations. He was like one of those dolls where you keep changing the features until they match, only Badger's never did. Mr. Potato Head.

From the time he came home from the hospital when he was born and their father began taking his picture, Zoe remembered how Badger stared into the camera. He blinked, but that was all. He told you nothing with his eyes. If Cal said "cheese," her brother would never smile. In all the pictures, he is staring. Or if Cal would scream at them and Zoe left the table in tears, Badger wouldn't move. He'd just sit there and not move. It bothered her more than anything else in her family. The way Badger could just stare their father down.

The man who sat across from her hadn't taken his eyes off her. Zoe didn't know how she knew this. But she did. She wondered about the eyes. She wondered how it is that you can feel when someone has his eyes on you. She began highlighting with a yellow marker. She underlined indiscriminately. She highlighted things she didn't even want to remember. Things she'd never need to know. She liked the squeaky sound of the yellow marker across the page. She managed to center her attention on the sound and the yellow marker as it moved across the page, but she had no idea what she was reading.

She scribbled in the margins of the book. She wanted to look as if she was doing something important. She wanted to impress the man with the important work she was doing.

After a few moments he leaned her way. "Excuse me," he said, "but do you mind if I ask what you're reading?"

Zoe looked at him. She performed a quick anatomical assessment. He was about her age. Perhaps two years younger. He had a nice mustache and blue eyes. It was a three-hour ride, but she didn't feel like talking with anyone. She wanted time to think about what was happening to her. She decided to put him off. "It's an article about the locus coeruleus and the biochemical impact on the function of certain neurological responses . . ."

"Yeah," he said, "drug withdrawal." He smiled at her. He had a very boyish smile and his brown hair fell across his brow. "That's that blue spot in the back of the reptilian brain," he said, tapping the spot at the back of his neck.

It was dark as they pulled out of Waukegan and Derek got up. "Would you like to get a drink?" he said. Zoe nodded and closed her book. She had read three sentences since they pulled out of Chicago. She'd read those same sentences about four hundred times. She had counted the lights on the road as they sped along and she'd tried to count the snowflakes as they stuck to the glass.

In the several times that Robert, the man she'd just stopped seeing, had gotten Zoe high, he'd once gotten her high at Disneyland. They'd dropped acid at a small drinking fountain for kids and watched alligators come out of the water. They'd watched Indians shoot from behind trees. They'd taken a ship navigated by Donald Duck, and had lunch in Cinderella's Castle, and finally, the biggest thrill, they had entered the crystal of a snowflake. They got into little cars and the little cars had gone into a tunnel and there was some deep voice that told them all about the snowflake and the crystal. It had been that deep, reassuring voice of a man. You could almost picture him, tall and fatherly, the kind who'd never let anything bad happen to you.

But then they went into the snowflake. It had been a gorgeous white crystal with lines and sharp edges, and Zoe had felt as if she were going right into Middle Kingdom, into the Underworld, to the center of the earth. Into some place where nobody had ever journeyed before, and not on some Disney ride that people take a million times a year. She'd felt as if she were actually going into the crystal of a snowflake, but then the acid,

or Badger, had gotten in her way. She knew she was just enter-
ing a U.S.-approved, homogenized, prefabricated, all-purpose,
All-American snowflake.

But now, as the train made its way through the Midwest,
Zoe, trying to read three sentences on the part of the brain where
drug withdrawal occurs, actually entered the crystal of one of
these snowflakes. She did on this train ride what she wasn't able
to do on acid with her brother or her lover. It was much easier
than she imagined. The snowflake landed on the window and she
fixed her gaze on it. It had frozen right there on the window
under her gaze and she'd gone inside.

She'd made herself small enough, the right size and texture
to go in. All you have to do is relax, breathe deeply, and never
take your eyes away from the crystal. And you will grow smaller.
You will shrink in size. You will become nothing. Your being will
become nothing. You will grow so peaceful, you won't notice the
cold. And then it will enter you. You won't have to do anything.
It will come to you. It will be an act of love.

Derek held the door as Zoe moved between cars. The cars
rattled back and forth. It was dark out now and she wished she
weren't getting into Brewerton so late. She wished she'd taken
an earlier train, or even flown. She'd never trusted herself very
much at night. She was capable of anything in the dark. And
now she'd only have a short time with Badger. And then she'd
have a long night in her hotel room. Perhaps she should have
stayed with her mother, but it seemed better this way.

They moved shakily between cars and finally reached the
club car. She saw little bottles of liquor all lined up, the cans of
soda. The little trays of fruit and cheese. The sandwiches. Ham
and cheese, egg salad, sliced turkey, all in white boxes, wrapped
in cellophane body bags. They ordered ham and cheese sandwiches and little bottles of white wine. Carefully removing her
sandwich from its cellophane, Zoe told Derek how the wrapped
sandwiches looked as if they're in body bags. Derek thought this

was very funny. Bits of sandwich clung to his teeth as he laughed.

Zoe told Derek how one summer when she was in medical school, she'd worked for the city morgue and dated the coroner. They'd met over a knifing victim and the first thing he said to her was, "An autopsy's tough no matter which way you slice it." He was a dark, lugubrious sort, not given to bursts of laughter. "Deadpan," she said. Derek laughed again. Zoe could tell he thought she had a great sense of humor. She said how she and the coroner talked about undertakers a lot. She'd learned how there was a whole profession called mortuary science. She named classes you can major in and Derek kept laughing. Embalming I and II, The Funeral from Flowers to Grave, Makeup for Eternity, All Dressed Up with No Place to Go.

Derek was doing research in genetic engineering. He was trying to come up with bacteria that would keep citrus fruit from getting frostbite. "I'm a little worried, though," he said, "that if it escapes, it'll melt the polar ice cap." He knew a lot about medicine. He told her about castrating his first cat in comparative anatomy and about the cadaver of an old woman who turned out to have this calcified fetus inside of her. "It was perfect, like an ancient stone carving," Derek said. "Little hands. Little feet." And they laughed over that. Everything was funny. They got back to their seats with an extra bottle of wine and when that ran out, Derek went back and got more wine.

When he returned he said, "So, why're you going all the way to Brewerton just to see your baby brother?" Zoe thought there were lots of ways to answer this question. There were all kinds of answers. She could even tell him the truth, but it would probably ruin the fun they were having. But before Zoe got a chance to answer Derek started talking about his own brother. How he was a cabinetmaker in Eugene, even though he was pretty smart. "I guess I got all the breaks," Derek said.

"Yeah," Zoe said, "I know what you mean." But she didn't want to turn the conversation around onto herself. She saw in fact that it was quite easy to keep herself out of the conversation altogether. Derek liked to talk. He was a good talker. He was the kind of person who talked in such a way that it made you feel as if you were talking too.

Derek leaned forward after a while and Zoe felt his breath against her face. "I've got a joint," he said. "You wanta smoke it?" He pulled out the joint and showed it to her. She wondered if smoking a joint was a good or a bad idea. She'd just entered the crystal of a snowflake with no problem. That was far enough for her for now. But she was having such a good time, and the wine had made her giddy, and she'd even forgotten what it was she was doing here in the first place.

Zoe pulled on a sweater because she knew it would be cold between cars and followed Derek outside. They peered through the window of the door. The sky had that deep, bright blue that comes with the cold. Zoe saw snowflakes, hitting the glass, crystallizing. So many snowflakes, falling by the wayside. "I've got a sister too," Derek went on. "She's a great kid, wants to be a magician. She hangs out at some store on the South Side all the time. My parents are beside themselves. She tried to make our golden retriever disappear last week."

He passed the joint to Zoe. "My parents," he continued, "they like to show me off at parties. Good schools, medical research, you know. But Lisa, that's my sister's name, she's the really talented one. She tears my Dad's newspaper to shreds every morning and then hands it to him in one piece."

Zoe laughed again, then they were quiet. Outside they saw the amber lights of towns flash as they passed through those towns where people lived and they saw the amber light illumine the snow as it fell in heavy, wet clumps. The train rocked back and forth and the coupling between cars pulled at itself like an accordion.

Derek put his hand on the window and Zoe read his skin. She saw in his hand the place where he was going. She saw ski slopes. She saw him aging badly, loving many women, never quite having what he wanted. She saw him at the peak of his life right now, at that moment, at a high point from which he could only go down.

Derek let his hand fall from the window onto Zoe's shoulder and pulled her into his chest. He put his lips into her hair. She felt his lips as they brushed her hair. He kissed her hair, her neck. He turned her toward him. He kissed her throat. He cupped his hand under her throat and she felt his tongue in her mouth.

Zoe wasn't sure how long he kissed her. All she knew was the endless motion of the train, a motion she didn't want to stop. It cradled her to sleep. She'd always felt the most alive on trains and in cars. Ever since she was a girl and she and Melanie would drive around sometimes for hours in Melanie's father's Buick, which they called "the green bullet," Zoe had known her life would be intimately connected with machines.

When she was a girl, her favorite place to make out was in the back seat of cars. She enjoyed the difficulty of it, the impossibility. Those passionate, endangered embraces. That lovemaking that always had a specific limit. Those limits based on the great American sport. First, second, third, home. She'd never gone to home. Or even to third. Not in a car. She'd go to first, to second, but she'd always known when to stop.

To sit in a parked car with a boyfriend had been heaven to her. And to some of her friends it hadn't even mattered much who the boyfriend was as much as it mattered what kind of car it was. Station wagons and Lincoln Continentals, though big, weren't cool. Mustangs and VWs, though cool, weren't comfortable. But an old Chevy like the one her brother had, that blue Chevy he'd lend her whenever she asked, now that had been a good car to make out in. But usually it was in VWs or Mustangs. She could still feel the bucket seats, the gearshifts—the real standard kind, and not some fake automatic posing as a standard —the steering wheels, pressed into your spine. Legs intertwined around the emergency brake. The tumble into the backseat. The way the seat sloped forward and you had to dig your nails into the upholstery so you wouldn't fall.

Derek kept his mouth on Zoe's mouth as he moved his hands up and down her ribs. He worked his hands under her sweater and his hands felt both warm and cold. But suddenly the motion stopped. The train stopped. The doors opened and outside it was winter. The conductor came through, announcing the stop. "Listen," Derek said, "we'll be at my stop in fifteen minutes. I want you to get off this train with me. I want you to come home with me. Call your brother. Tell him you'll be there tomorrow."

Zoe looked at him dumbly. She couldn't call her brother. That was completely out of the question. "No," she shook her head, "he wouldn't understand."

"Tell him you were delayed."

She shook her head. The train lurched forward, the doors closed. The cold air was gone. He led her back to her seat. Zoe looked into Derek's eyes as he kissed her again. Now in the light of the train, she saw him better. She saw something in his eyes she'd seen before. Something she couldn't quite place. Zoe pulled away, but Derek whispered into her ear. "I want you to get off this train with me. I want to spend the night with you."

Zoe shook her head again. Derek grabbed the paper headrest where Zoe imagined the distinguished middle-aged gentleman had sat. He wrote his phone number on it. "Call me," he said. He's gathering his things. He's leaving the train. He's going to leave her there, incredibly cold, stuck in a time warp, in the center of a snowflake.

T W O

The Heartland Clinic is located on the lake road on a rolling estate on the outskirts of Brewerton. The Hyde family, one of the wealthiest families around, whose daughter is Melanie Hyde, had donated it to the town several years before. Though Zoe had never been inside, she'd always understood it to be a place for borderlines. For hopefuls. For those who might get well. This is where you come to rehabilitate when you are on the mend. After the accident, the stroke, the breakdown. After the worst has happened to you. There are other places nearby for those who will not get well. It is a form of triage. You separate the dying from the wounded. You don't do much for the hopeless cases.

Zoe paid the taxi and was struck by the night air. It was cold and she took a deep breath which made her feel lightheaded. Naomi used to say that the people who lived in Brewerton went through life a little bit tipsy. The Colemans hadn't lived that far from the breweries and there was some truth that the malt and the hops that entered the air produced strange impact on the inhabitants. Now she was surprised to smell the beer in the air. She had never smelled it, not once in all the years she was growing up, yet it was always there. And she wondered how it could have eluded her.

Brewerton was unimaginatively named for its breweries, its only industry, which was now in the process of failing. Unlike the other towns and cities in the state, which had Indian names like Menomonee Falls and Winnebago, Brewerton had simply adopted the name of its primary industry. It had once had an Indian name which meant "Home of the Great Water Chief," but during the industrial era its Indian mounds had been dug up and paved over, its winding rivers and surrounding lakes turned into industrial waste disposals, and its name changed to Brewerton.

It was a town that had betrayed its past, and superstitious people felt, when the breweries began to fail and leave, that it got what it deserved. But underneath, it was still all there—buried beneath. She thought how she could feel it as if she were a student of geomatria, the study of the vibrations that flutter through the earth.

Brewerton is a grim town that besmudges the edge of a Great Lake. The inhabitants say that when the wind comes down from the Arctic the first place it hits is Brewerton. But it all looked beautiful and clear to Zoe as the taxi pulled away and she paused to look at the stars. It was a cold, wintry night, but her body still felt the warmth from Derek, though she could feel it dissipating in the winter air. The stars were so bright they seemed fake, like the stars on a planetarium sky.

There were things that came back to her now, like the shock of cold air and the clarity of the sky. Zoe couldn't remember when the last time was that she'd bothered to look up and see the stars. Since she had been in the East, she'd hardly looked up at all except to see the clock above her bed in the on-call room at the hospital. But now she took it all in. The stars, the night air, the smell of beer.

Some people know the places of their past by sight, but Brewerton is a place you know by smell, depending on which way the air is blowing. If it's a northwest wind, you'll get the pungent odor of industrial wastes, of chemical plants, and if it's from the south in the summer, you'll get the dead fish who've died from the chemical waste. If it's from the west, you get beer. But if you are lucky, you can get that pure wind that comes down from the north, from the land of sky-blue waters, where the sturgeon are still clean and everything is pine forest and the deer and the bear roam as they did during the time of the Chippewa. It was that northern wind with a little beer mixed in that greeted Zoe as she walked toward the clinic. And she was filled with a rush of love for this place, sheer, unutterable love that made her wonder how she ever could have left it behind. So, Zoe thought, taking a deep breath of the cold air off the lake, I've come home.

The building in front of her was solid and large. It had a sense of certainty about it. A purpose. Zoe read the plaque at the entrance. It said how the Hyde family made this clinic as a place of hope, for those who will surely get well. Zoe found it odd that a hopeless family like the Hydes would build a place of hope. But what seemed stranger still was that not only was Melanie Hyde Zoe's best friend when they were growing up, but she was also the girl Badger had chosen to love.

Zoe had watched their love blossom, flourish, and fade and now her brother was entombed in the Hyde family's biggest tax shelter. The irony seemed remarkable when she thought about it, but she didn't wish to think about it for long. Besides, she liked the feel of the place. It was sturdy and strong, though the building itself was dark. Unnecessarily dark. A place of hope should be cheerier. There were only a few lights on. In one room above she saw shadows moving.

As Zoe walked in, the sound of her heels on the marble startled her. A hard, clicking sound. The small, elderly night nurse, dressed in conventional nurse attire, who sat at the receptionist's desk, looked up. She seemed stunned, as if she wasn't accustomed to seeing people at all. "Excuse me," Zoe said, "I'd like to see William Coleman." The nurse looked as if Zoe had asked her to fly around the room. "He's my brother," Zoe offered by way of explanation.

But the night nurse shook her head and said, "It's Sunday night and there are no visiting hours until ten o'clock tomorrow morning. No one ever visits on Sunday night."

Zoe listened patiently. In the past several months, she had acquired a great deal of patience. She explained carefully how Dr. Sharp had left permission for her to go up when she arrived. "His assistant called me earlier this week. He said it was urgent."

"Now, dear, it can't be that urgent. We're not that kind of a place, you know."

This woman, Zoe thought, is being condescending to me. She was not in the mood. "I've come an extremely long way." As she said this, she felt fatigued.

The nurse smiled sympathetically. "Well, then, why don't you get a good night's rest and see him in the morning. I'm sure it can wait until then."

But Zoe knew she must see him now. She must see him right now. She stood up very tall. "I am a doctor and I would like to see my brother."

"I don't care if you're Albert Schweitzer," the nurse, now losing patience, said, "you can't go in until tomorrow morning."

Zoe leaned forward. She got a very good microscopic look at this woman. She saw coffee stains on the teeth. She saw liver spots on this woman's cheeks. "I'm not sure you understand," Zoe said. She leaned closer until she smelled the old nurse's breath. It was that kind of staid breath of people who haven't been kissed in this century. Dying breath. Zoe thought perhaps she should say how she's just graduated from a prestigious medical school, how she is planning on specializing in tropical dermatology, how she's been on a train with a man who'd asked her to spend the night with him and how she hadn't spent the night with him because her mother had pleaded and her grandmother had phoned and because—something she had not even admitted to herself as yet—because, two nights before, her father whose breath smelled sweet as honey and who still had plenty of spunk in him had come to her in a dream from that place between heaven and hell where all souls must wait and make their peace until they are ready to enter the next realm and had appeared before her at the foot of her very own bed and told Zoe to pull herself together and out of the doldrums and make this trip.

Badger had always been just like their father. But Zoe hadn't. Zoe hadn't been raised by her father. She'd been raised by her mother, June, and by her grandmother, Naomi, in the plaid rooms and blue corridors of the Home on the Road Motel while her father was away at the war. The start of her life had been at an entirely different place. What saved Zoe, and Zoe knew it, was that when she was conceived her father had been one man, and when Badger was conceived he had been another, and the war lay in between. June used to say that—how their father wasn't the same person when he came home.

Cal had gone off to war when Zoe was an infant and she'd spent the first three years of her life in the company of women. She'd spent years with Naomi and June, watching them clean and cook and let time pass as if each day, each hour, did not make the time a little closer when Cal would come home. They perfected the art of doing what Naomi said women had always done best. Carrying on while their men were away.

During the war, Cal Coleman had been an aerial photographer over enemy territory and the experience had left him bald, among other things. Every day for months Cal leaned over the edge of the open bomb bay doors while two men held onto his legs so he wouldn't fall. He felt the sting of cold air on his face, the blood filling his brain as he snapped pictures of German installations. The munitions factories, rail junctions, bridges, supply lines.

Cal always wore his helmet on those aerial missions. He seemed to think that if his friends let go of his legs and an air pocket bounced him forward and out of the bomb bay doors of their B-26 bomber, his helmet would somehow keep his brains from splattering across the pine needle floor of the Black Forest.

One day after a mission that was no more eventful than usual Cal removed his helmet and thought a furry animal lay sleeping inside. Then he realized that all his hair had just fallen off his head; only the fringe would ever grow back. His commanding officer said he'd seen things like this happen before.

Cal had been in combat and he'd seen shattered limbs and starving faces, the way most soldiers had. He'd seen the fighting on the ground, but it had not done to him what the view from the sky had done. From the open bomb bay doors, he had watched the little smoky fires of battle. He saw the smooth, dark green rising clusters of trees, the occasional castle sited on a hill, the gentle slopes with sheep grazing along the side. When he got back, he tried to tell Zoe and June how beautiful the enemy had seemed from the air, but the words wouldn't come.

Cal had gone to war a young man and had returned, only a few years later, old. His teeth would begin to rot soon. Zoe was an infant when he left and she had only a vague recollection of someone tall and burly tossing her into the treetops and catching her before she crashed to the ground. She was frightened and annoyed by this bald, aging stranger who suddenly moved into her mother's room, rambling through the house, taking showers in a locked bathroom, a room that had never been closed to Zoe before.

Even June had trouble recognizing Cal when he came home. She remembered her husband as a powerful, sturdy man and this one seemed ancient and tired and full of fear. But Naomi, who'd never liked him in the first place, and had never approved of the marriage, told June not to worry. "That's him all right," she said as she made the firm decision to go on living in the room above the garage she'd moved into when Cal went away.

He slept on the floor for the first month he was home because he couldn't stand the softness of a bed. He complained that everything itched and he had crusty scabs on his elbows and hands from scratching himself everywhere for no reason. He became convinced danger lurked in every object, behind every curb. He could take a cotton ball, an extinguished match, a melting ice cube, and turn them into lethal weapons.

June nursed him. She made him hot baths and cooked him special soups. Once she'd felt a great passion for him, but now she took him upon herself as she'd taken her housework. Cal became a chore. Taking care of him was like folding the shirts and dusting the shelves. He became her work.

He wasn't any trouble, really. Mostly he just sat. The man who'd once photographed General Patton and performed danger- ous aerial reconnaissance missions over enemy territory now sat in a stuffed armchair, leafing through picture books and maga- zines, staring oddly at the photographs. Sometimes he glanced at his watch and he often looked like a man waiting for his bus to arrive.

Sometimes he reached down and touched the photographs he was looking at, as if they were real. As if he could poke an angelfish or stroke a llama in *National Geographic*. Or feel a raging fire in *Life* magazine. For hours he sat in a dim corner by the window, leafing through these magazines, checking his watch. And Zoe would sit on the floor near him, quietly wonder- ing if he'd ever toss her in the air and catch her again.

Even though she wasn't fond of Cal, Naomi sat with him every afternoon as well. She thought that if her daughter insisted on being married to this man, he should get back to work and make himself a useful creature. Naomi sat beside him and talked. She talked about anything that came into her head, any- thing except war. Sometimes she brought him pictures she thought he'd like. Usually old family portraits, pictures from the family album. She'd show him photos of himself as a child. And when he grew weary of these, she'd go to libraries and bring home all kinds of pictures. Pictures of cows in fields. Pictures of beaches, of China, of snow.

Naomi spent months in the rocker in the afternoons, talking to Cal and dozing. Cal didn't seem to pay any attention to her or to anyone else. Then one day, for no reason in particular, he got up and got dressed. He walked the few blocks from his home to his old studio and opened his darkroom. He took apart his en- larger and cleaned it with fine brushes. He took apart his camera and did the same. He washed his developing tanks and chemical vats. He threw out all the old paper and bought new paper. He bought lollipops and stuffed animals, rocking horses and scenic backdrops, a bird bath and a portable waterfall. Then he settled

down to work. The man who had photographed generals and
invasions and enemy territory opened his studio and set upon
what was to become his life's business of photographing babies
and weddings.

At first June was pleased to see him getting up early and
heading out to the studio without any breakfast. She was glad
when she woke up in the mornings to find him gone and glad
when he wouldn't stumble home until after dark, and then col-
lapse on the bed and sleep as if he were drunk. She was glad
when he started jabbering away about his old negatives that he
was now cleaning and sorting through. She was glad when he
talked about new sepia paper stocks or mixing his batches of
chemicals the way an alchemist might talk about his prepara-
tions for producing gold.

She was glad to see signs of life coming from him again. He
was productive. He was working hard. A little too hard. After a
few months, she realized she never saw him. "Well, now the
darkroom is set up, maybe you should take it easy."

But Cal told her he'd just begun. He had so much shooting
to do, so much printing. He had a great deal to accomplish.
Instead of slowing down, he worked even longer. By day he did
his weddings and babies, the joyous events of life, but by night,
when most men are home with their families, having dinner, Cal
was working on something else. Something he couldn't discuss
with anyone.

Sometimes when June went by the studio, she'd find him
reading books on mathematics, great discoveries, and theories of
perception. Sometimes she'd find the darkroom with its door
open, like an abandoned shack, and she'd come upon Cal pacing
outside in the moonlight. He would look up at her and say,
"Leave me alone. I have work to do." When he'd crawl into bed
at dawn, June would ask what he was working on, but he'd never
tell. No one would have believed him if he'd said he was figuring
out the way to photograph what was not there, what cannot be

seen. But that is what he was doing. Ghosts, secrets, memories, the invisible—those were the subjects of his night hours.

One day when he'd been back for over a year, he brought Zoe to his studio and made her sit while he snapped her picture. Zoe had almost no idea who this stranger was, she had spent so few hours with him. He had her sit still and turn to the right and the left. He gave her a lollipop and a teddy bear and dabbed Vaseline on her cheeks. Then he went to work and the flashing lights stunned her.

The next day he brought her back again. He led her through the studio with the bright, hot lights that he'd shined in her face and took her into a small, sulfurous-smelling room. For a few moments Zoe stood awkwardly in the dark with her father. The sulfur smell made her uneasy, yet she recognized it as her father's smell. It was the way she'd learned to recognize him, by an odor that was always on his hands, in his clothes—an odor that sometimes came into her room while she slept and made her wrinkle her nose.

Suddenly he flicked on a switch and the darkroom turned a deep shade of blood red. It was dark still but Zoe saw her father's face. It was all fiery and his eyes had little red circles in them and the whites seemed very white and his bald head shone like a fireball. When he smiled his eyebrows raised and Zoe thought how he looked just like the devil she'd once seen at Halloween.

She started to cry but he picked her up. He said to her, "Don't cry. My little girl is brave and doesn't cry." She felt comforted by his smell and his arms and by the way he repeated her name over and over again softly. Then he put her down and had her sit on a stool. He took out a thin slip of dark film and put it into a machine. A strange image was reflected onto white paper. He took the paper and dipped it into one vat of chemicals. All the time he spoke to her and she would never forget the sound of his voice. He spoke soothingly about things she'd never understand. He told her how the light exposed the silver in the paper. He told her how the light made the paper dark and how a dense negative made the paper very light.

He spoke to her in long words and she could never seem to reach the end of the sentence. He talked rapidly and then gently. Zoe thought perhaps he was speaking a language he had learned in the war. And yet it was soothing to listen to him, though he went on for so long that eventually she wanted him to stop.

She looked at his face as he talked. His whole head was dark red and shadows. His baldness was red. He smiled and his teeth gleamed. He turned over the paper that he had been moving from vat to vat as he spoke and she saw the face of a startled, terrified child with the kind of smile you see on a child's face just before it bursts into tears. "There," he said, holding it up proudly for her, "that's you."

It was almost midnight when Zoe got to her hotel. She had argued with the nurse for half an hour. Then she had argued with the resident on duty for about as long. And then it had taken some time to get a taxi. She had no idea how she was going to make it through the night. With Derek she would have made it through just fine, but now some eight hours stretched before her.

She thought of calling him. She had never been the kind of woman to wait for a man to call her. But it was late and she didn't really think she should call now. She knew she had to call her mother. June would be up all night, just sitting by the phone, wondering when Zoe would call. She'd call later, she decided. First she'd take a bath, have a drink from the mini-bar in her room. She'd relax, watch a little TV. She wouldn't call her mother until she had to.

Zoe was glad she'd chosen to stay at the Holiday Inn. She didn't want to stay at home with her mother. And she didn't want to stay at the Home on the Road. She could have stayed at the Home on the Road for free. She preferred the invented intimacy of the Sheraton or the Holiday Inn, where the clerks are trained to learn your name the minute you check in, but they're also trained to learn nothing else. At the Home on the Road it was the opposite. The guests were known only by their numbers, not their names, but Naomi had known everything about them, and Marvin, the desk clerk, knew even more. Naomi would say to Zoe when she was little, "Room 4 hasn't eaten a thing since he got here." Or later, when Zoe was older, "I think Room 35 is sleeping with Room 51."

She didn't feel comfortable with memories. The Home on the Road had too many of those. The blue-gray walls, the cobalt-blue carpeting, the swimming pool that always had a circle of algae around it and dead bugs floating on the surface. The plastic lounge chairs with their webbing missing. And the desk clerk, Marvin, whom Naomi hired so long ago, he'd recognize her and ask questions. And he would remember what had happened so many years before, the thing they had never spoken of. He'd say nothing, but she'd be able to tell in little ways that he still held her in scorn for what she had done.

Zoe had spent most of the first four years of her life at the motel, while her father was away at the war and June worked at the radio station. And June had grown up at the motel. It was her home. Her father, Ralph, had bought the motel during the Depression. June had always hated it. That had been a theme of Zoe's youth. How much her mother hated growing up in the motel. When June was young, it was her job to change the beds and some days she changed as many as fifty. When Zoe was growing up, June always made her change the beds at home.

When June was a girl, her friends were people who stayed more than two nights. But nobody ever stayed a week. Her friends were traveling salesmen, business people, or wives having affairs. They'd come for a few nights, then move on. Then they'd come back in six months or a year. When June got married, she told Zoe once, she'd made a decision. She decided she'd live in a house where people slept in the same sheets for a week at a time and used the same towels. Where your friends had houses and thirty-year mortgages which meant they'd be around for a while.

June knew, once she was old enough to understand such things, that she wanted something permanent. She used to tell Zoe this. She used to say, "Have something that's yours. Something nobody can take away."

Zoe eased her way into the bathtub. She pictured her mother and she knew exactly what she was doing. She knew her mother sat near the phone, wrapped in her nightgown, in her dustproof, climate-controlled house, smoking a cigarette. She probably had the television on and a glass of brandy by her side. The back of her hair was set in little pincurls and she had a full ashtray near her.

Zoe had perfected the act of torturing her mother. She had certain favorites and this was one of them. Say you will call at a specific time on an important subject. Make sure you are unreachable. Don't call at the specified time, but don't forget to call either. Occasionally Zoe underestimated her mother's tolerance for such experiences, but she knew her mother was probably going mad now, waiting to hear from her.

Zoe was not a mean person. This tiny act of cruelty wasn't typical of her. It wasn't a way she liked to be. She would not do this to her friends back in Boston, even to her old boyfriend, Robert. But now it made her feel powerful. It made her feel more powerful than her mother. June still had great hidden reserves and inner strength. Zoe knew that. Zoe had carried her mother's secret around for all these years. Zoe knew about her mother's reserves.

Zoe got out of the tub. Propping herself up on some pillows, she dialed her mother's number. "It's me," she said, "I'm here." She yawned and stretched. It was dark outside. June had picked up the phone on one ring. Why couldn't she have let it ring twice, just to make it more interesting?

"I've been worried sick," June said.

"I got in late. I thought I'd call in the morning."

June sighed. "Did you see him? He looked terrible when I saw him."

"No, they wouldn't let me." Zoe heard her mother pack a cigarette and light it.

"I think it's ridiculous for you to stay in that hotel."

Zoe shook her head again. "It's better for now, Mom. I've got a lot on my mind."

June breathed into the phone and Zoe thought how she'd always loved the sound of her mother's voice. "I guess things have been rough for you."

Zoe sat up a little. "Look, let's talk about it tomorrow."

"When will I see you?" June asked, her voice shaking a little.

"I'll call you in the morning."

"I love you," her mother said.

"Me too," Zoe replied, thinking she had to say something.

She hung up and lay there for a moment, wishing she were somewhere else. She decided to call Derek and tell him to come over. But he wouldn't come over that night. He'd say it's too late and he'd say I thought you were going to be with your brother. She'd tell him to come over the next night. My brother was busy tonight, she'd say. He had things to do. She decided to call room service and order a drink and then she'd call Derek if she still had the nerve. She scanned the phone for the room service number. This time she looked at the phone. At each number there was a little symbol for guests who do not understand English. The number six had a man, his face black, carrying luggage with a bell going off in his head. Four was a waiter with a white face, holding a tray with one hand. Three, a woman, definitely Hispanic, dark, Third World, her head wrapped in a bandana, in a little black and white uniform. The maid.

Badger would have enjoyed these, Zoe thought. She started to lift the phone, then put it back in its cradle. I must tell him about it. He'd say, hey, look, even on our telephones, we're exploiting people. Everywhere you look, we're fucking muthafuckas. That's what her nice middle-class white brother would say. But he wouldn't say it with his mouth. He'd never open his mouth and say anything like that. He'd just let you have it with his eyes.

T H R E E

Gabriel Sharp was the last person Zoe expected to find working on her brother's case. Zoe had known him vaguely in high school when she was photographer for the yearbook and he had worn his Coke-bottle glasses, greased his dark curly hair down flat and parted it in the middle, and spoken in a deep, sonic-boom voice. When she'd taken his picture, the flashing glare in his lenses had made him look like an alien. The staff of the yearbook had called him "the Martian." All he needed, the girls would say, were antennas.

But Melanie had called him Clark Kent. She said if he ever took off his glasses, he'd be terrific. To Zoe in high school he'd always looked more like a geometry problem than a person. With his baggy pants and glasses, everything about him had seemed square or round.

But as he walked toward her, it came to Zoe slowly that she knew this person. Contact lenses had replaced the glasses. Salt-and-pepper curls bobbed on his head and the chunkiness of a high school halfback had stretched itself out. All the lines had lengthened. The man who came toward her now did so with a confident spring to his step. Zoe never would have recognized him, but it had taken three tries to get his yearbook shot straight and you don't forget someone that easily.

"You're a long way from the kennel," Zoe said as he approached the reception desk where she stood. He looked at her oddly as she extended her hand. "Gabe, it's Zoe Coleman." He still did not seem to recognize her. "We graduated from Brewerton High together."

He stepped back a little. "My god," he said, "it never oc-

curred to me that William was your brother." He whistled
slightly through his teeth. "You've changed," he said. He didn't
say how, but immediately he regretted what he'd said. And he
knew he'd made Zoe feel bad. But she had changed.

Once she'd been the most beautiful girl at Brewerton High
and Gabe remembered when half the boys would have lain down
on the tracks of the Milwaukee Road to take her to a matinee.
But now she wasn't spectacular. She wasn't even particularly
special. She still had the lovely green-and-orange-flecked eyes,
the squared cheeks, but the rest of her had somehow hardened
around her lines, and she didn't have the soft, sensual look she
had in her youth. Yes, he thought, she's lost her looks. It was the
first time he had thought this about anyone he grew up with and
the thought alone made him feel old.

He collected himself. He wondered what he was going to
tell her. What would he say? He was good at small talk. He
could invite her to Shelton's for an ice cream sundae and they
could talk over old times. But then they hadn't really had any
old times. Instead he leaned against the receptionist's desk. "I'll
take you to see him. You're a doctor now, right?"

Zoe nodded. "I haven't done my internship. I've been kick-
ing around for a while. It took me some time to make up my
mind. I think I'm going to be a dermatologist."

"Zits," Gabe laughed, which annoyed her.

"Tropical dermatology," Zoe said.

"I always thought you'd make a great ob-gyn."

Zoe nodded. "You're—"

"A shrink. I specialize in burnt-outs. Mainly drug cases.
Somehow I just couldn't keep up my interest in hormones for
milk increases. I attended one meeting of the local chapter of the
American Association of Bovine Practitioners. That was enough.
God help me, I turned to people."

His eyes were charcoal and opaque. Zoe wanted to know
what he knew. But she also knew that she'd know soon enough.
"Can I see him now?" she said in a soft but impatient voice.

"You know," Gabe said, "there'll be a lot of people anxious to see you. Have you told anybody you're in town?"

"This isn't a social visit," Zoe said wearily.

"Of course not. I'm sorry," Gabe said, wondering why he kept saying the wrong thing.

"I've come a long way." She was amazed at how tired her voice sounded.

"Yes," Gabe said thoughtfully. "When was the last time you saw him?"

Zoe sighed. "It's been a while."

"Well, he's probably changed a great deal. These drug flashbacks, they have taken their toll." Gabriel paused. "You might not recognize him."

Zoe had not expected this. That he might not recognize her seemed all right because of his condition, but how could she not recognize him? How could you not recognize your own flesh and blood?

He was leading her toward the waiting room. "I'll take you to see him myself," he said. "But I need ten minutes to finish some rounds. Is that all right?"

"That's all right." Suddenly she wasn't in such a hurry.

"You know," he said, "I have no idea why I didn't think William was your brother."

"We've always called him Badger."

Gabe took her by the arm. "After the state animal?"

She shook her head. Badger was Badger because he bothered people. He was a professional botherer. He had a talent for questions. At the age of five he'd ask them in an endless stream that made little sense. How come a radish doesn't come up when you plant a carrot? Why are grains of sand so small? Why won't water sit still?

Nobody ever called him William. They called him Pest and Menace and Big Pain, but not William or Bill or Willy. Cal just called him Badger one day. He said hey kid, you bug me. I'm gonna call you Badger, and that was it. He was in the way and they'd let him know it.

He made himself in the way. He built huge cities in the middle of the living room and he gave them names like Kittentown or Limabeansoupville. He constructed them out of pieces of wood and turned over chairs and blankets: mammoth villages with churches and hospitals and schools and prisons and residential neighborhoods. Each town had its own urban design and it was impossible for anyone other than Badger to know what the design of any given city was. If you tried to get from the dining room to the kitchen, he'd say, "You can't go in that direction. That's one-way." Or if you wanted to change the station on the TV, he'd say, "You can't cross there. You've got to cross at the intersection."

They tried to redirect his efforts to the basement—which he refused because his citizens would not live in a dank underground—or to the spare room upstairs which he said was for mission control, or to his own room, which was necessary for the early planning stages of new villages.

It was a phase, the building of cities, though Zoe could not help but think that her brother would have made a brilliant architect, a planner of great metropolises. But he'd gone on into other modes. He had a French Revolution phase where he walked around swinging a yardstick, saying off with your head, until Naomi could stand it no more and made him relinquish the yardstick. Then he settled into his most benevolent period of being a polisher of stones, a maker of bits of jewelry.

He could do anything with his hands. He was precocious and gifted and doomed. An eccentric child, he loved to hug, but he wouldn't kiss. He didn't sleep in sheets, but instead rolled himself into a kind of cocoon of blankets as if his body could never get warm. In the morning they didn't wake him; they unraveled him.

Zoe knew her brother was special and she tried to do him in. She was always the one in control and she loved the power games. Cops and robbers, cowboys and Indians, doctor and patient, and a game they invented called Mata Hari and the Spies. Zoe was always the cop, the cowboy, the doctor, Mata Hari. She always got her own way and nothing, no one, could stop her.

The waiting room itself was predictable enough. Big leather chairs and a red leather sofa give the place a feel of authority, as if she were walking into a professor's study, though some of the chairs had puncture wounds, places where the stuffing was coming out and she could see a spring sticking out from under the couch. The usual white walls. A picture of hunters, gun raised, as a flock of ducks flies toward the sky. Others of thoroughbred horses, legs raised, perfectly poised. Prints of athletes—runners, chests pressed to the finish line, swimmers about to take the plunge, cyclists coming around the bend. All the pictures on the wall were of winners. Thoroughbreds, hunters, athletes. No endangered species, no dead Indian chiefs, no underdogs here.

She noticed the plants. The pothos and philodendron, suspended from large plastic pots in the windows. Their tentacles reached down, then wrapped themselves up the rope of the macramé hanging. They intertwined, as if in a lover's embrace. These were good plants, hard to kill. There were no delicate African violets, no seasonal ferns, nothing that would shed or yellow or get picky if it were neglected for a day or so.

When Gabe left to finish his rounds, the young nurse, named Julie, had directed Zoe, with a gentle wave of her hand like a tour guide indicating some minor point of historical interest, toward the waiting room of the Heartland Clinic. "We're sorry you were inconvenienced last night, Dr. Coleman," Julie had said. "That Nurse Burlington, she's such a hard-nose." Now Zoe had made friends here, she thought. Now she had pull. And Julie had told her in a comforting voice that Dr. Sharp wouldn't be long and then he'd take her to see her brother. It was a normal, straightforward procedure. There was no sense of urgency in her voice. No life-or-death situation here.

But now the normality of it all was beginning to make Zoe nervous. The nurse's uniform was so white it almost hurt her eyes. And suddenly Zoe realized that the nurse was wearing one of those little pointed white hats. She kept a pen attached to her clipboard with a small silver chain and the chain dangled from the clipboard as the nurse walked. She was too efficient. Too cool and crisp for Zoe's taste, and it suddenly occurred to her that the nurse knew more about Badger than Zoe knew. "Just have a seat," the nurse said. She seemed to float away as Zoe glanced around.

When she sat down the sofa made a little noise, but nobody looked up. There were a few other people in the waiting room. They'd seen her come in, but then they'd looked away. They were preoccupied. She wished she were dressed differently. She wished she were wearing her doctor's coat and a stethoscope around her neck so that these people would realize that she's a winner too. That she knows what's going on and is privy to private information. She wanted to impress them with her importance, but these people were not about to be impressed. A black man sitting near her nodded, then turned away. A young man stared out the window, tapping a finger against the pane. A woman flipped the pages of a magazine at evenly spaced intervals of about one a second, so that Zoe knew the woman couldn't be reading, or perhaps even seeing, the page.

Zoe decided to look occupied. She looked through the magazines piled on the end table near the sofa. *Time, Newsweek,* some home-decorating magazines, fashion magazines. Nothing to really sink your teeth into. Literature for those with a short wait. Or with little power of concentration. No Kierkegaard or Tolstoy here. The magazines were tattered and worn and old. No surprises. No shockeroos. Just old news. What you already know. What you expected. Zoe picked up an old *Time*—circa Nixon's resignation—and pretended to be interested.

During her early training, she used to glance into the solariums and lobby areas, the cafeterias and waiting rooms, where loved ones of patients milled around. She'd look into those sun-drenched rooms where people looked bleached out, those rooms that always had the pothos and philodendron, the Formica tables and plastic chairs, the winners on the walls, rooms that feigned a certain durability. Like an observer of some obscure tribe, Zoe had recorded in her mind the way people handled their grief.

There were the pacers, the readers, the talkers, the ones who harassed the nursing station, the ones who just sat, staring, doing nothing, the knitters, the letter writers, the criers, the moaners and groaners, the nervous laughers, the people who thought money would buy what money couldn't buy. There were the ones who went into the smoker's corner, leaned forward, elbows resting on their knees, smoking as if they didn't care what happened to them. There were the people who waited in the clinics, and the ones for the private rooms, and then there was that whole special breed for emergency, the ones whose lives had been normal until a moment or two before—those hysterical mothers screaming over an injured child, and the wild, hysterical children screaming over an aging parent whose heart had just missed a beat or two; the ones waiting to see if the accident victim, the robbery victim, the lover who made a suicide attempt, would live.

Zoe had watched them all, as they waited for those deci-sions that would determine their lives, shape and color the next twenty years or so, remold the way they saw themselves, resolve whether they'd grow old alone or with a mate. She'd seen them cry and plead and pace and flip through magazines and slam their fists into a wall, and now she was suddenly one of them.

She decided she was the distracted reader type as she flipped through a women's magazine with many human interest pieces in it. About a woman and her husband who taught a bird with half a wing to fly. About what kind of lingerie will really turn a man on. And then there were recipes. An entire sixty-minute gourmet section. Stuffed crab au gratin with an avocado salad in sixty minutes, not including shopping. She started to write the recipe down. Then she lost interest in it. She went to the window and saw the dead trees outside. She looked at a woman sitting across from her, wringing a handkerchief in her hands. Now the black man stared at his shoes. The young man who had been at the window twisted the wedding ring around on his finger. He had dark circles under his eyes.

The perky optimism the nurse had instilled in Zoe was fading. At first she had felt superior to everyone in this room. Better informed. More in control. Privy to private files. She assumed they would let her see all. She has access. Professional privilege. Her training has made her immune. But now, as she looked around her, she understood that nobody was here for any good reason. Zoe was a doctor in her normal life, but now it didn't matter as she stood on the other side of grief.

F O U R

Badger wore tattered jeans and a T-shirt depicting the Milky Way with a swirl of stars and planets and an arrow pointing to somewhere in the middle which read, "You are here." He'd lost thirty pounds. He was covered with scabs from where he'd scratched himself but these were bandaged and his hands were wrapped in white gauze gloves so that now he couldn't scratch himself. His eyes stared straight ahead.

Zoe sucked in her breath as if she could take in the whole room. She noticed the brightness. She couldn't believe how bright it was and then she realized there were no curtains, no shades, just raw windows, with bars. Everything in the room was white. Though she had known the whiteness of hospitals before, she was amazed at this. She tried to think what it reminded her of. The whiteness of paper, of eggs, of gleaming statues like the Pietà, of light at midday. But it was none of those. It was a whiteness not found in nature. "Badger," she said. "It's me. I know I should've come sooner, but I couldn't get away until just now."

She looked to Gabe for help. His eyes were concerned, but he said nothing. She was going to cry. She was going to lose it right there in front of a Brewerton High former halfback and her freaked-out brother. She decided to make a joke. "Bad trip, huh, kiddo?" He didn't laugh. He didn't speak.

"Some days he just refuses to speak. Some days he'll write things down on this slate. Others he'll talk a blue streak." Gabe said. "He understands what you say . . ." He hesitated. "He only speaks in baseball terms—for now."

"He loves baseball," Zoe said.

"He thinks he is center fielder for the Milwaukee Brewers. The problem is he's got all the players mixed up." Gabe put his hand on Badger's shoulder, giving him a strong shake, "But he's doing better. He's graduated from being a vegetable to more of a house plant, haven't you, kid?"

He gave him another strong shake and this time Badger seemed to smile.

"May I examine him?" He nodded, handing her his stethoscope and small hammer. She opened Badger's eyes wide and shined a small light in. She touched his neck. She felt under his arms. She took the small hammer and banged on his knees and elbows. She examined the sores on his neck and hands. She felt his belly and let her hand feel his groin. She took a pin and ran it along his arms and feet. There was minimal response. Gabriel Sharp shrugged, indicating he expected no more.

Zoe thought of all the things her brother wouldn't say. All the things he couldn't say. The feelings he wouldn't express, the longing, the desire, the ambition, the greed, the lust. He had answered all the questions for himself now in his own mind. He had no reason to answer to anyone. His isolation was complete. But she didn't have to accept this. She wanted him to talk to her about baseball. So she asked "Hey, Badger, who is President of the United States?"

It took a few moments, but slowly he wrote down the words, "Mickey Mantle."

"And how many people are in this room now?"

He wrote, "Two men on base."

"Who's pitching?"

Zoe smiled. She was enjoying this. Her brother was talking to her. He raised the chalk and began to write, but seemed to change his mind. She thought she detected a smile in his face as he turned to her. She looked at her with their father's dark gypsy eyes and the eyes twinkled now. He opened his mouth and spoke the first words she had heard him speak in two years, the first words Gabriel Sharp had heard him speak in weeks.

"Hunt Fisher," he replied.

Zoe stood still, not quite believing what she'd heard. This name had not been spoken between them in a decade. It was their understanding that they would not speak this name. Somehow even Gabe understood and turned away. But he couldn't hide the look of surprise on his face and Zoe thought that somehow he must feel sorry for her. She turned to Badger, angry and annoyed with him now. Why would he mention Hunt? Why would he do this to her? He would only do it to hurt her, that's all. Flustered, she decided to change the subject. "If you could do anything in the world right now, what would you like to do?"

He smiled straight ahead, toward the window. "Steal home," he replied.

Her brother had been beautiful. Not the way Zoe was beautiful, but in an interesting, exotic way. Zoe had wanted to be exotic, but hers had been a classical kind of beauty, the kind you find in magazines. But Badger was different and Zoe had known it, even when he was born. He was dark in a Moorish way and had an ease about him, a languid look. Jet-black hair, onyx eyes, skin pure and smooth as milk. He was mysterious, like an Arabian prince, and people were drawn to him for his mystery, the way they were drawn to his father.

She had always been jealous and she tried to get rid of him. She used to take him into the woods even though Badger was allergic to everything. He was allergic to the dust and the weeds, to the grass and the animals. To mushroom spores and to the pet dog. Her brother was allergic to the world. And he was allergic all over his body. Except his face. For some reason his face always stayed smooth and pink. But in his lungs he was allergic and they'd fill up with liquid and he'd gag and cough and all kinds of humidifiers and expirators had to be provided. His eyes would swell like golf balls and wet snot would seep out of his nose. He'd gasp for air. He would gag.

But Badger had beautiful skin and even as his eyes red-

dened and swelled and welts broke out all over his body, none of
it ever touched his face. The skin on his face was always white
and unblemished. Never a pimple, or a mark. Zoe longed to have
his skin. Instead of her face with the mole her mother called a
beauty mark, her oily skin subject to breakouts always before
proms and important social events, the open pores on her nose,
the freckles that matched her bronze-flecked eyes.

One day when they were about nine and four, Zoe took him
into the woods to play cowboys and Indians. He was the Indian
and she was the cowboy and Zoe captured him and she took him
out into the woods where she knew he shouldn't go, but she did
this to her brother. She took a rope and tied him to the tree. It
was her favorite tree. The old one the Indians had bent back to
mark the trails.

So she tied him to this tree. A tree with sap and spores and
pine needles and grass and dust and animal hairs and lichen and
mushrooms. His eyes were already weeping as she tied him. His
skin was already swelling and she could see the hives starting to
break on his hands. Then she said okay count to sixty and he
counted to sixty, the way they always did, and he said, now all
right, untie me. But she didn't untie him, not at sixty, or at a
hundred, or at two hundred.

Instead she retied her knot, a careful double-stitch she'd
learned at Girl Scouts. Then she left him tied to that tree and
wandered home, stopping to look at birds, to pick up horse
chestnuts, to admire the changing colors of a leaf. When she got
home, she sat down and talked to her mother. She had milk and
cookies and she didn't think about him, not even for a moment
did she think about Badger tied to a tree with all those allergies.
As it grew dark, her mother began to go to the window and stare
out. It was always the saddest time of day for June, just before
dusk, and she'd just sit at the window and stare. "I wonder
where he is," she said. "I wonder why he hasn't come back from
playing."

And just then when Zoe thought it might be time to go and

get him, except by now it was very dark, and she had her own
fears of wandering off into the woods alone, just then he came
back, with the rope in his hands. He came back with his eyes
swollen shut and mucus running down his face, his lungs gasp-
ing for breath. He came back covered with great red hives that
reached up toward his cheeks but never made it to his face. He
had blood between his nails from scratching at his hands. June
made him his special bath and she had shots for him by now and
she put her arms around him and said who did this to you, tell
me, who did this to you.

But his lips were sealed. He never spoke. If he told anything, it was only with those eyes of his. He made it clear to Zoe
with those eyes that even long after they'd forgotten the incident,
he'd never trust her quite the same way again. He'd look at her
from then on with the stare she knew only too well, the one he
always used to stare their father down.

Zoe never knew why they wanted him. She told him the day
before his physical to run ten miles through the woods and no
one would ever take him. She told him to go roll in the weeds
and play with the dog. She'd said she'd even tie him to a tree
again. And he just gave her the stare. The one that said he'd do
exactly the opposite. That he'd do the contrary of what she'd told
him. Instead he got dressed, took a shower, and rode the bus.
Badger had been as calm as could be. He was calm when the
doctor took out a stethoscope and put it to his chest. And when
the doctor said breathe, Badger had breathed.

It is said that there is more magnetism on the shores of
Lake Michigan than anyplace else in the world, except the North
Pole. Zoe read this once in a book when she was young and she
never forgot it. Compasses along the bluff refuse to point north.
Ships have been known to set their sails straight for the beach.
The best navigators have been thrown off course and had to turn
to the stars for guidance. Sometimes, along the lake road, people
say they can see the bows of ships that have run into the shore.

Zoe does not believe this, but she believes in the magnetism. She had come back despite herself.

Now as Zoe drove along the shore to meet her mother, she knew she was going to stop. She had a specific place where she wanted to go—a place she had always known. Even though she knew she would be late to meet her mother, even though she knew she should not go there, something drew her back. She went to where two rivers flow into the lake, where she could sit high on a bluff and look down at the waters. Zoe thought how she'd know this place anywhere. She'd know the water, the light.

It was the place she used to go to meet Hunt. He chose it for them because the Indians who lived on these banks, the Chippewa, say it was a place of special powers. Of hidden dreams. And he chose it because it was beautiful, high above the lake, with the bluff below.

Zoe had not been back since Hunt went away, but before then she'd come here and wait for him. She'd stand leaning against a tree, listening for the sound of his footsteps, for his breath as he came up behind her. Somehow he always knew when he'd find her there and he'd come softly, as the Indians would come upon this spot. It was here that she learned to listen.

Now she stood again motionless. She could almost hear the footsteps, feel him moving through the bushes to the place where she stood. She felt the tree to her back, the wind to her face. She shut her eyes as if his hands were going to reach around the tree, his arms fold across her chest.

PART

TWO

HOME ON
THE ROAD

Saskatoon
October 15, 1967

Dear Zoe, Canada feels too big. The roads are too long. There is too much space between houses, too little space between the trees. There are never enough people in any one place. The sky is farther away here than back home and there's nothing I can touch.

I've been traveling with this guy named Whittaker Jameson Peters, the Third. His friends call him Whit. He comes from a rich Boston family and he has long blond hair. But actually Whittaker, he's a great adventurer. He's done vine diving on Pentecost Island, the only white man ever to vine dive, and he's found the biggest cave in Java, and he's skied the Matterhorn. He chews tobacco and spits like a grasshopper. He hasn't changed his clothes since I hooked up with him. He has taught me how to carve seals and caribou and narwhals out of wood for tourists. I'm good for an animal every two hours or so.

Whittaker and I, we keep moving. We've gone from place to place, carving out these animals. Funny thing is I've never seen a caribou or a seal. Let alone a narwhal. Have you ever seen even a picture of a narwhal? They call them unicorns of the sea. But to the Eskimos they are magical creatures, these whales whose single twisted horn that extends from their head serves no purpose as far as anyone can tell. But I have heard that if you are in water touched by this horn, then you become blessed and pure and protected by the Great Spirit.

I carry pictures around of these creatures and carve from the pictures. I also carry pictures of you and Melanie and Mom and Dad and Naomi and even Puzzle. When I feel lonely, I try to make carvings of all of you, so I can have something to carry around with me, but so far you come out looking like seals and caribou.

We've crossed Canada two or three times. I wish I could give you a place to write to me, besides general delivery here and there, but I'm always on the move. Eventually if you write, one of your letters will catch up with me. I'm not sure why that is, but for some reason I can't stop and neither can Whittaker, so we keep going.

Do you ever feel that way? Like something, some animal has gotten inside of you, gotten under your skin, into your veins, and it just won't let you rest. Maybe you don't. You always had that incredible ability to sit still for hours in the same place with the same book. Something crazy like advanced physics or medieval history. I used to watch you sitting there. You had these nervous little habits. You'd tug on your hair and twist it around your finger like a noose. Or you'd shake your leg like an engine starting up. But you never got up. You never moved. You had the power of concentration. Me, I keep moving.

Maybe it's a bad thing for a restless person to have too many places to go. I can't seem to get a grip on things. I paused in one town in Alberta where we lived for a few weeks with two French girls. I was with this girl named Marie-Elena, but she only made me think of Melanie more. She was terrific in bed. I probably shouldn't say this to you, but she was. But I had nothing to say to her and I was sad after intercourse. I was sad in the morning as I sipped my coffee. I am lonely without love.

I feel like an island, adrift in a sea, with no other islands. Once I flew over the Caribbean with Melanie and we saw a million bridges connecting a million islands. It all seemed warm and friendly. But here there are no bridges. Everything—the people, the places, the trees, the sky—it is all too far away for me, beyond my reach. Including you.

If only I could stop, sit still. Do you know who I remind myself of? You know, the one person in the world I swore I'd never be like. And here I am crazy and alone, just like him. Your brother, Badger

F I V E

It was June who suggested Jojo's. Jojo's was in the middle of a mall in the middle of the Midwest in the middle of Nowhere. The smell of french fries and coffee could have come from anyplace. It was the kind of place where great leaders could sign a peace treaty or drug dealers could do business. It was neutral territory.

June hadn't wanted to meet at the hospital. She'd preferred to meet at Jojo's which was only a few blocks from the radio station. June thought they could meet here, have a cup of coffee, chat, catch up on a few things. Then they would slowly take a drive and see Badger. June had her own routine for going to see him. She always went right after lunch. She took a normal lunch, maybe did some shopping. Then drove to the hospital and sat with him for half an hour. June pretended all of this was perfectly normal. The lunch, the shopping, the visits to the hospital.

June loved her job at the radio station where she'd worked since the war years when she had begun doing spot ads. June had a deep and sultry voice and it was perfect for getting people to do what they didn't entirely want to do.

It was not the music of her voice that made people listen. Rather, it was what she could do with it in dark corners, in undefined moments. It was what she could do with it in the park at dusk or in bed on a Sunday morning. It was what had made Cal fall in love with her. June's voice was rich and subtle and even Cal, when he was off in a bunker in England, when he would dream of June and long for her, it would not be for her doe-like eyes or for the soft curves of her body, but rather it was for her deep, yearning voice which would call to him across the vast desert where he dwelled.

June had tried other, more lucrative work over the years. She was good at numbers and had worked in a bank. She sold insurance and had dabbled in real estate, but what she really liked was to put her lips to the microphone and convince people of things. She had begun with ads and could convince men that beer made you manly, women that makeup made you young, pills made you healthy, deodorant made you popular, toothpaste made you lovable—all in a nameless, faceless voice. She did so well that eventually her boss gave her a small spot called Advice from June and she told women how to stay desirable to their men, she told men how to make their women feel loved. She told people all the things she could not tell herself and after a while she grew dreary and depressed. How can I help people when I can't help myself? Sometimes she tried to take her own advice. She tried a certain perfume, changed the lighting in the bedroom, made special meals. And when it all failed, she turned to her boss one day and said, "Just let me do traffic and weather. That's all I can really handle."

In the end it was the weather reports she liked best. She liked to say there was a cold front coming and warn her listeners to bundle up, or that a warming trend was expected. She loved to picture the faces of the thousands of people who listened to her, to see them pausing for an umbrella or taking off a heavy sweater with a smile as they walked out the door.

In the beginning she knew nothing about the weather. She just read from the sheets of paper in front of her. The only thing she knew was that the weather was one of the most difficult things in the world to predict because there were too many variables. A front could blow in from across the sea. Pressure could shift in the southern hemisphere and all the weather reports of the world would have to change. But in the end she acquired a sense of the depth and bulk of the clouds. She knew what a change in the breeze meant and she could convince people with her voice that what she said about the weather was real, and when they listened to her they felt the winds in her sultry breath, in her cold, harsh words.

Now June could predict the weather better than she could predict her daughter who was already twenty minutes late. June told herself she would say nothing about this. Her lips would be sealed, but still Zoe was late. Typical, June thought. Just like her. June knew that it was Zoe's destiny to be late. It was in her nature, her fate. But the last time they'd seen each other was two years ago in Boston. How could you be late after two years?

Zoe had always disappointed June in all the little imperceptible ways that no one but a mother would see. Zoe never lost her temper or said mean things. But she did it just enough to let you know it couldn't be an accident. The way you had to pry information out of her. How she could be late. How when you held her, she seemed to pull away.

Zoe kept this space between herself and the world. When she was an infant, just a tiny thing, you couldn't hold her unless she wanted to be held because she'd cry until you put her down. But if she reached out to you, if she extended her arms, you had to pick her up. But there were times when it made June angry even when Zoe was a baby, the way she had to have it, even then, on her own terms.

Sometimes June could sense when Zoe was near. It was just a feeling when her daughter moved toward her, closer to her. When she was on her way home from school, when she was moving from her apartment over the garage that she shared with Naomi to June's kitchen. Before she could hear her, June could sense her.

June glanced across the parking lot. Cars sped by. It was just a big parking lot out there. America was just a big parking lot. America was just Sears and J. C. Penney and E. J. Korvette's and cars and streets and parking lots and somewhere out there in the heartlands, her only daughter roamed.

It was five years since Zoe had set foot in Brewerton and June pondered her daughter's return. Nothing had made her come back since Cal died. Not June's late-night frantic pleading, nor Naomi's gentle prodding. She wondered if Cal had visited her as well.

Occasionally he'd come and stand in front of June, blocking out the light of the television or at night at the foot of the bed. She knew him by his smell of chemicals and the oranges he sucked on as he ate and moisture on his skin from the lake where he loved to swim. In truth his presence bothered her. His dampness filled the room and left a mildewed scent to the chairs where he'd sit, the bed when he decided to lie down. June knew he wanted what she didn't have to give. He'd tried for years to win her back before he died and now he still kept trying. It was useless, but he'd linger and June was beginning to lose her respect for him. She decided she could tolerate anything except being haunted by an obsequious and apologetic ghost.

Though Zoe would never tell this to her mother, he'd been to see her as well. He'd come in the night a few weeks ago as she'd sat curled up, hot chocolate by her side, a book open in her lap. She must have been dozing in a vulnerable state, for her father, a man who'd always wandered, had wandered comfortably into her dreams. As always, his smell preceded him and she woke to oranges and hypoclear and her skin drenched in the wetness of the lake he carried within him.

He stood at the edge of her sleep and she expected him to tell her how he'd come to make his peace. Instead he told her what she already knew. That her place was a mess, her life in shambles, and it was time she went and did something for somebody else. Unlike her mother, Zoe had been saddened and impressed by the deep, desolate look in her father's face, by the burden of the loneliness of his later years. "You did this to yourself," she said to him. But it was she he had clutched to him as he died and she could not bring herself to turn him away.

But now as she approached Jojo's, Zoe thought that perhaps she had not understood his message correctly because everything felt wrong. She knew she was doing the wrong thing with the wrong attitude and, worst of all, she was dressed wrong to see her mother after two years. She should be wearing anything—a kimono, a muumuu, a kaftan, a sari, a dashiki, a grass skirt—anything other than jeans. They were, of course, good, sturdy Jewish jeans. Levi Strauss jeans, the kind that would survive an Outward Bound test or a limited nuclear attack, but they were still jeans. Jeans for June weren't clothing; they were a political affront.

But there was no turning back now. June, who sat in perfectly matched green, spotted her. She waved and smiled. In her mind Zoe dared her mother to look natural as she moved through the odor of french fries and coffee, the sound of Muzak playing "You Are the Sunshine of My Life," past the gingerbread house all done up for Christmas, a kind of Hansel and Gretel house. Nazi houses, Badger called them. He used to say it's right there in their fairy tales. The way they cook the wicked witch in the oven. His theory was that the wicked witch was a Jew; the oven was the first crematorium. Badger knew how the world worked even then.

"You're late," June said as Zoe bent down to kiss her, wondering why she had said the very thing she swore she would not say. Zoe kissed her anyway, thinking how her mother stank of Lucky Strikes and Repliqué.

"Sorry," she said. "Traffic was bad."

June smiled dumbly. There was no traffic in Brewerton. There never had been. June did the traffic reports and she knew. "No problem, dear."

"We should've met at the hospital," Zoe said. "It would have been easier."

June did a quick assessment of Zoe's alpaca sweater, the jeans, her hair pulled back, her face pale and white like a hardboiled egg. Zoe's eyes gave her away. They were green as prairie grass. June saw the softness in them. And Zoe couldn't hide her surprise at her mother's white hair—as white as the rooms they kept Badger in.

They hadn't seen each other in two years and both decided, incorrectly, that they didn't look like each other anymore. June knew that Zoe thought she looked older and fatter and Zoe knew her mother thought she was messy and unsophisticated. June thought how she should have gotten in shape, lost ten pounds for this meeting. Zoe thought she should have plucked her eyebrows, put on lipstick and a skirt. She curled her fingers into her palms so her mother couldn't see her bitten-down nails.

Zoe felt bad about lying to June about her lateness. Her excuse sounded feeble, so she expanded it. "Oh, and then I got lost. I've never come here on the new highway."

"Yes, they've done a lot of building since you left. This mall is where Shady Oaks Stable used to be."

Zoe looked around. "This is where I used to ride horses?"

"Yes, it's hard to imagine you, riding off across that parking lot, isn't it?" June said wistfully. Then she collected her things and picked up the check. "Well, let's get going."

"I'm famished," Zoe said.

"You haven't eaten?"

"Well, no, I thought we'd eat something."

June sighed, "Yes, dear, but it's so late now. But then if you're hungry, you should eat. Why don't you have an egg salad sandwich? You like egg salad."

But Zoe signaled the waitress. "I think I'd like to see a menu."

"Well, it's just a standard menu. You know, hamburgers, eggs . . ."

Zoe ordered a turkey club with cole slaw on it and a glass of milk. June lit a cigarette. Zoe fanned the smoke away as she ate and her mother kept trying to hide the cigarette under the table. "Mom, that's just the worst thing you can do to yourself."

"I don't do anything else."

"But that's the worst thing."

Zoe hated Jojo's. The bread was stale, the turkey was dry. Her mother stared at her as she ate.

June nodded. "So," June said, "you look well. How are you?"

Zoe shrugged. "Well, all things considered, I've been better."

June leaned back, pushing the ashtray away from her. "So've I. I don't know what to do about it."

"What to do about it? I don't think there's anything you can do."

"Oh," June said. "There must be something. How did he seem to you? I mean, you're the expert now, right?"

Zoe wished more than anything that she were not the expert. She wished she were as ignorant as a newborn. "I'm not sure he's going to change very much, Mom. I mean, he'll have good days and bad, but it's just not clear . . ." Zoe wondered at herself for saying this. She wondered how it was that she could be so clinical about her own brother with her own mother.

"Well," June blurted, "some days he's better than others. You never can tell. Some days it's one way. You're probably seeing him at his worst."

"But that doesn't mean he'll get better."

June nodded, taking a sip of coffee she didn't want and didn't need. Already she felt jittery. "No, I guess it doesn't." She sighed. "But he's your brother," she said almost to herself.

"I know he's my brother." Zoe couldn't hide the annoyance in her voice. "But what do you want me to do about that?"

"He's all you have," June said, looking away.

June Fyer, the only child born late in life to Naomi and Ralph, grew up at the Home on the Road Motel which her parents ran, and she'd assumed she'd wander its rooms forever. When June was little and the motel was on the main road to Chicago, her mother had decorated a room for her. But as she grew older and the highway was diverted, she lived in whatever room she pleased. She had a room she dressed in and a room she danced in. A room she read in and another she hid in. She was a nomadic child, roaming from place to place like a Bedouin, packing up her things and moving on.

Most of her friends were traveling salesmen—men who'd stay a few days at a time a few times a year. Sometimes she thought she'd marry one of them, but mostly she thought she'd grow old within the confines of the motel until one day when Ralph went looking for her. He found her in Room 27, her study room, where she sat in blue pajamas, hair pulled back into a ponytail, reading a Victorian novel. She was eighteen years old and while not exactly what one would call a beauty, there was something mysterious and compelling about the girl with the jet-black hair, the dark skin, the green eyes.

On this day when her fate was to be sealed, her father looked at her carefully. He could not help but think how odd it was that he would produce such a child who bore no resemblance to him at all, who only seemed to take after her mother, except for her height. To Ralph, June was still a little girl, though she was eighteen years old. It wouldn't have surprised her father to have come upon her sucking her thumb, for in the lonely rooms of the motel, without siblings, where time had not mattered very much, no one noticed if June was growing up or not and in a sense her age had been forgotten and she'd remained a child.

But now he looked at her carefully and found a woman peering up at him. He thought that perhaps Naomi had done the right thing in tracking Arthur down. He took a breath and said, "Get dressed. We're going to the train." He paused. June glanced up from her book and looked at his large head, his broad belly, and the cigar he chewed between his teeth. Her look told him she did not intend to go with him. "We're going to pick up your brother."

"I don't have a brother," she replied, turning back to her book.

"Yes you do," Ralph said, walking out of the room. "Now get dressed."

June would always recall that icy morning of her brother's arrival at the end of February. It was the kind of day that had once made Brewerton the ice export capital of the world. Sometimes when it was this cold, cows froze to death standing up in the fields and you could see them there like statues, white and glazed. As they drove through the side streets of Brewerton, June sat huddled in the back, indifferent to the purpose of their journey, picking out giant birds and monsters and beautiful women in the ice formations they passed. She did not ask questions as she watched the ice, but as they approached the station Naomi said, "I'm going to explain something to you now. It's what you need to know, so listen carefully."

June kept staring outside while Naomi spoke. Ralph, Naomi explained, had been married before, briefly, to a woman from the East, and they had had a son. Ralph had left the family when the son was three years old, though he sent checks regularly. But he had not seen this boy, named Arthur, who was by now a man of twenty-five, in more than twenty years.

But one night, a few weeks before, Naomi had had a dream that frightened her. As she spoke of her dream, June turned toward her mother and now she listened. "I dreamt," Naomi said, "that you had gone East on a journey and there you met a man and you fell in love with him. In the dream as you stood at the altar, wearing a beautiful peach chiffon dress, you were so tall and slender, and I saw the man you were marrying. It was your own brother." Naomi told June how she tried to scream at her from the borders of sleep, to reach her in the dream and stop her before it was too late, but no matter how hard she tried, she could not make herself heard.

Naomi had woken, shaking, from the dream and told Ralph, "You must find your son and bring him here to meet June, or else something terrible will happen."

At first Ralph resisted. He saw no reason to cater to his wife's superstitions—this Russian peasant who hoarded stones and bits of clay for luck, spit in the air to keep evil spirits away, and who believed in the message of her own dreams. But Naomi would not relent. The dream stayed with her and every night she pleaded with him. "Something terrible will happen," she said, "if you don't find your son."

Finally they began their search. They contacted various people in the East. They ran ads in *The Jewish Forward* and in the Yiddish papers. And then one day a letter arrived from Ralph's former wife, saying that their son, Arthur, would arrive on a certain train.

They reached the platform of Union Station, Brewerton, and waited for the Milwaukee Road to pull in. Arthur, her father told her, had traveled from New York on the Broadway Limited and now he had come on this train, and he was going to stay with them for a while, so that June could get to know her brother.

They waited and waited on the freezing platform until in the distance they saw the train. It was two hours late and their fingers and feet were numb from standing in the cold. But as it appeared, June could see it. A beautiful silver train, frothing like a serpent on that frigid morning. It pulled in and came to a halt with a great crunching noise. Slowly passengers began to exit the train. People who came from the bigger cities, like Chicago.

They got off one at a time, and June and her parents scanned the crowd.

At last a young man stepped down. He had a head of dark hair and pale eyes that met hers. He had dark, almost gypsy-like skin and something melancholy about him. But it was the kind of melancholy June liked, the kind she'd seen in the eyes of the gentle creatures who were her friends, who earned their way on the road as traveling salesmen. He had the face of one who is looking for a home. He was struck by the cold and he put a scarf quickly around his face.

June knew as well as she'd ever known anything that a terrible thing had happened to her. She realized that despite herself and the warnings of her parents, she was drawn to the stranger who stepped off the train—drawn by some inexplicable force to her own brother. And though she did not believe the superstitions of her mother, she felt there was nothing she could do to stop it.

But the man who rushed toward them with open arms, waving, was not the same man she'd been watching as he stepped off the train. The man who rushed to them looked like Ralph. Thick, bullish, but with thin blond hair, a flushed and poky face that reminded her of a pie set on the window to cool. He wore bottle-thick glasses like Ralph. June was glad, seeing her brother, whom she now recognized as being her father's child, that she took after her mother.

He ran to his father and embraced first him, then June. Feeling the sharp edge of his glasses, June was surprised at how weak his embrace was, how moist his cheek against hers. She had expected someone more solid. Then he introduced his friend. "I brought someone," he said, pointing to the dark man June had noticed getting off the train. "He's a photographer who works with me at the paper." Arthur said, "This is Cal Coleman."

·   ·   ·

It was no problem finding space for both young men. The motel was nothing but rooms and not very occupied ones at that. They moved into adjoining ones, 52 and 53. They were planning on staying a few weeks and they wanted to see the city. Arthur was going to be a journalist and he and Cal had met at a paper where Cal was becoming a photojournalist, a new profession he claimed would become very important in the newspaper world.

During the days Arthur and Cal went sightseeing while June was in school, but in the afternoons they waited for her at home and they went to the movies or to a museum. But as February turned into March and the weather improved, they went to the beach or to an amusement park. The three of them would go everywhere together. They seemed to have so much fun that for a time Naomi forgot her fears.

But one afternoon when the weather was especially nice Arthur wasn't feeling well, so June and Cal went for a walk in the park together. It was different being alone with him. When they were with Arthur, the three of them made fun of one another, told jokes, and never talked about anything serious. But now as they walked, Cal talked about himself and June listened carefully to his every word.

He told her how his parents and a sister had been killed in a train wreck not far from Brewerton. He had been an infant at the time and was found alive in the backseat, where his mother had flung her body across his. He had been sent to live with an aunt in Oklahoma and his aunt had given him his first camera. He told June how the first picture he'd ever taken was of Black Thunder, that rolling ball of dust that swept through five states. His aunt had died of it and *Life* magazine had published his pictures of Black Thunder and of his aunt on her deathbed.

And then June began to talk of her life at the motel, of her growing up in the lonely rooms with Ralph and Naomi. As she talked, Cal listened to her voice. It was not her eyes or her soft features that would capture him. It was her voice, so filled with longing, as if it came to him from across a vast sea. As she spoke he snapped pictures of her, hundreds of pictures it seemed. She teased him about it, but he only said softly, "I want to capture you in the late afternoon light—always." But in truth he would never be able to capture her voice, the one thing that had truly beguiled him.

When they returned it was past dusk and Arthur was sitting at the window, waiting for them. His face had a pinched look, as if he'd eaten something bitter and there was a tone to his voice June did not like. "So," he said, "where'd you go?"

"You weren't feeling well," June replied, defending herself too quickly. In the afternoons that followed June felt her half-brother's presence as an intrusion. She found herself turning more to Cal, laughing more at his jokes, making time for him when she could not find time for her brother.

Arthur sensed he wasn't wanted and began to find excuses not to go with them. He would sit and read the paper and like a dejected parent tell them to run along. And if they did, he'd rumble around the motel, much the way his father did, and when they returned he had that look in his eyes, and some nights he would not even talk.

But sometimes June found him dressed up in a tie and jacket as if he were trying to impress her. June began to feel that Arthur looked at her in odd ways. They had, after all, just met and it was not normal that they would feel about each other as a brother and sister felt. Sometimes June felt uncomfortable when he gazed at her. Sometimes in the corridors of the motel at night as they'd pass each other on the way to their rooms, she'd feel his arm as it brushed past her, hear his breath as he walked down the hall.

Whenever they could, June and Cal sneaked away to walk in the afternoon in the park until the chill of the evening air brought them home. The first time he kissed her was the first time anyone really kissed her. But it was a moment imprinted in her mind, the way the death of her brother would be imprinted. In the years when Cal was gone or when she was alone, it was

what would come back to her. The breeze of spring, his arm
across her back, pressing her to him, the wind in the trees. His
mouth landed smoothly on hers and he pressed her slowly to him
and she felt how love was smooth and easy and how it was hers
for the taking.

Naomi could not hide her concern. In a matter of weeks her
daughter had turned into a creature she hardly recognized. She
walked with a lilt and held her breasts high. She wore bright
colors that brought a blush to her cheeks. The child who had
always run to Naomi when she saw a frost pattern in a pane of
glass or a small animal in the yard was now disappearing into the
afternoons and evenings and out of Naomi's life.

She would sit in the office of the Home on the Road, among
the alchemy jars, the objects for predicting the future, the broken bits of porcelain and the handful of soil from Russia in
which she could get nothing to grow, among the canary named
Banana, the cat named Saturn, and the remnants of dead things,
including a bone—large, white, and dusty—which Naomi
claimed was the leg bone of a woolly mammoth and which was
the only real tourist attraction of the Home on the Road, and
here she would try to imagine what her daughter was doing on
those late afternoon walks with Cal that extended themselves
into evening when the cold breeze blew off the lake.

She sat at the check-in desk, sleeves rolled up, tapping a
pencil on the sign-in sheet where young lovers, tense and embarrassed, often signed invented names. If Naomi said to them,
"Mrs. Johnson, please sign here," the young woman would look
at Naomi blankly, not remembering that her name was "Mrs.
Johnson." Or as Naomi made up the endless succession of beds,
the sheets still warm and moist, where sometimes legitimate cou-
ples but more often lovers spent a few hours of intimacy away
from the world of their jealous wives or fathers who would go
insane at the thought of where their daughters might be, she
wondered where June was.

Her life had acquired a certain pointlessness. She had not crossed the ocean, fled to a new world, endured the banality of a loveless married life to see her only daughter wind up with a penniless drifter, a would-be photographer, a Yankee and a Protestant. While she was not religious, she was superstitious and she believed no good would come from her daughter's marriage to a man who was not of her persuasion. But beyond this, Naomi sensed that it was too early to have June wrenched from her, and that her daughter was about to make one of those mistakes for which she'd pay for a lifetime.

At first Naomi tried talking to June and convincing her that Cal wasn't the right person, but June would sit with a hazy look in her eyes, her gaze going above Naomi's head, her lips slightly parted, and Naomi knew her daughter was not hearing a word she was saying. Then she forbade June to see Cal in the evenings after dinner, but all her deterrents were doomed to fail. June and Cal slipped in and out of rooms, sneaked out of the motel, ignored her warnings, defied her punishments. They hid in any of a dozen or more rooms where they would speak in whispers until all hours of the night and Naomi could do nothing to keep them apart.

When logic and persuasion failed, when discipline and punishment were no use, and she knew she could not banish Arthur with his friend from his father's motel, Naomi resorted to the wisdom of her ancestors, a concoction whose recipe her mother had once taught her. It was a potion of wood betony, saltpeter, lavender, and chamomile, intended to ward off wayward love. She made the drink and added it to June's nightly glass of milk, but all it did was make June sleep better and wake in the morning with a long stretch and a yawn of one who is completely untroubled by her dreams.

Realizing that her daughter was slipping away and that she herself was somehow to blame, Naomi returned to the old habit that Ivan, the only man she'd ever loved, had cured her of when she arrived in America. She repeated that gesture that had marked her earliest years and that had only returned with the death of the man she loved, but then she had cured herself. She picked at the walls. She dug her nails into the wood of chairs and tables. She scraped, sometimes for hours, at a shred of wallpaper, a fleck of paint, a chip of wood.

At dinner Ralph and June would watch as Naomi would at first surreptitiously begin to pick at some small scrape on the wall and soon she would have her nails into it, removing paper, paint, whatever stood in her way, until her fingers bled and her nails were broken in horrible ways. Ralph asked her to stop while Arthur and Cal pretended not to notice, but she could not stop. It was what she had learned to do in the grave her mother had buried her in. It was what she did whenever she grieved.

This scraping began at the turn of the century as their ship crossed the Atlantic and Naomi Mayashinsky kept her eyes on the sea, never noticing how she was breaking the hearts of men, all the time digging with her nails into the wooden bench upon which she sat. She did not know that the first mate had fallen in love with her or that the man who'd arranged passage for her had not kept his eyes off her, or that a young Russian man was in his own way watching out for her. All this was lost on Naomi as she stared at the sea and scraped with her nails.

She was fifteen years old then and she had tasted death. When Naomi was smaller, her mother had dug graves in the backyard. When the cossacks rode into town, Naomi and the other children went to their graves. Their mother put reeds in their mouths, covered them with dirt, and left them there until the trouble passed. Under the earth Naomi tasted filth. She felt worms crawling across her mouth. She lived in dread of the reeds being wrenched from her mouth. She dug herself deeper into the ground with her nails and, for the rest of her life, when she felt trapped she'd try to dig her way out.

From beneath the ground she could hear the stomping of horses. One of her small brothers pounded his fist against his grave and she pounded back. Once she heard the sounds of her

mother being raped and those sounds would ring in her ears
forever, so that sometimes when June, and then Zoe, were growing up, Naomi would say to them, "Did you hear that scream?"
and she was always surprised when they had not.

She had tasted what the end of her life would be. When she
came out of the ground, she spit it out. All of it. Nothing would
stop her. When her father said he'd gotten passage to America,
Naomi said take me with you. She was the oldest and her parents
knew that she was beautiful and that the next time she might
outgrow her grave.

Her mother would stay behind with Naomi's brothers and
she would make the trip later. They would come to America after
Naomi and her father were settled in with a distant relation in a
place called Milwaukee where Naomi's father, a respected
scholar of Talmudic lore, was to work as a bottler in a beer
factory.

When they were ready to leave, Naomi's mother clutched
her to her in a way that made Naomi feel she'd slipped back into
the tiny grave her mother had dug for her. She felt stifled in her
mother's arms and couldn't breathe. Naomi knew she would
never see her again. She recalled nothing of the crossing, except
for the water. She had never seen so much water. For five weeks
she stared at the sea and ate bits of bread that someone kept
handing her. She did not recall the filth and the rats, the stench
of excrement, the outbreak of disease. She never saw the bodies
of small children tossed overboard when they died or the men
and women who made love under blankets at her feet.

Some said the sea had entered her. In truth she simply felt
as if she'd traded graves. She was, and would always be, a creature of the land. But the first mate who could not take his eyes
off of her was certain she'd gone mad. He came and sat beside
her every day. He put his hand under her chin and lifted her
eyes to his. He looked at her blue eyes more deeply than he had
ever looked into a woman's eyes before. One day she spat in his

face and he slapped her. The women around him laughed and he laughed too.

All of this was being watched by a young man who was traveling alone. He had decided to take care of Naomi and he did this without saying a word to her. For the rest of the journey he silently brought her water and extra pieces of bread. He left them at her side. He never spoke to her and she never looked at him, but she took whatever he offered. While the first mate pined away, then made insulting comments, the young man from the Ukraine did her small favors, asking nothing in return. But when they reached Ellis Island, he was the one who escorted her, along with her father, off the ship to the customs officials. While the first mate told the customs officials that this girl was crazed from having looked too long at the sea, the young man said he was wrong. She was simply tired. So the officials let her through.

She was separated from her father and the young man and sent off with the women. She was told to bathe. They made her scrub her skin raw with a sharp pumice stone and they poured lye over her head. Slowly the lice were killed, the dirt fell away. Her hair acquired its former sheen. Her clothes were washed and she was told to sit on a bench among the other women. She sat and stared ahead and the only signs of life in her was the digging of her fingers into the bench, until splinters embedded themselves beneath her nails. She sat there on that bench in immigration, frightened, unsure, and the first thing she said out loud in America was, "I don't even know his name."

When the immigration officials called her, Naomi did not respond. They sent the matron to get her. When she stood in front of them, she took the babushka off her head. Thick black hair tumbled to her shoulders. She stared at the men with her icy blue eyes and the blond men looked back at her. "May I go into America now?" she asked and they laughed. When they asked her her name she said, "Call me what you will. But my first name is Naomi."

So one of the men shrugged. "We've got a wild one here,"

he said. "Let's name her Daring." And that was her name, which she would keep, through two husbands.

Then they gestured for her to pass, and as Naomi Daring stepped into the Port of New York, she found her father and the young Russian man waiting for her.

Together they went to Milwaukee where Naomi and her father moved in with her cousin and Ivan took a room in a boarding house. Every Sunday Ivan sat with Naomi in the cousin's parlor. They talked quietly about their lives and soon they began to talk about their futures. They took walks in the parks, much the way Cal and June took their walks, and he entered Naomi's mind the way the sea had.

Ivan never left Naomi's thoughts, not for a single waking moment. In her eyes, he was all she saw. He was always there in the back of her mind, no matter what she was reading, no matter what she was doing. For ten years he was there. He would arrive every Sunday. And when she was twenty-five and her father despaired of her ever marrying, Ivan told her that he had money and he could marry her now.

Ivan told her that when he arrived in America, he had lent a friend of his family's almost all the money he had. He told her how the friend had gotten involved in the wrong crowd and had begged for the money. Ivan had given him two hundred dollars and now, ten years later, the friend had returned the money with interest, and Ivan now had two thousand dollars.

They planned their wedding. They wanted to make it simple, but they planned it carefully. And they took a small flat which Naomi decorated with pink lace and white pillow shams. One day in the apartment, Ivan pulled Naomi to him and tried to make love, but she pushed him away. She said they had such a short amount of time to wait now.

On the day of their wedding Naomi picked out her husband's coffin. Only hours after the wedding and before the marriage was consummated, some men shot Ivan in the back. The police said that the man who'd given him the money had swindled it. The police said the killers made a mistake. Instead of going on their honeymoon, Naomi went to Appleburg's Funeral Home, still in her wedding dress, and picked out a sweet-smelling pine coffin. Then she went to the Ridgelong Cemetery where she selected a nice piece of land. The coffin made her shudder because it recalled the time she had been buried in the ground. Then Naomi went home. She put on black and went to the funeral as Ivan's wife.

For a year she mourned. She stared out the window and moved lethargically through the house, picking at food when she found it on a platter, but never really sitting down to have a meal. She was inconsolable and her father feared she would never be right again.

But then one day the great Houdini, who was becoming an internationally famous escape artist, returned to play his hometown of Milwaukee and Naomi's father got two tickets to see him. At first Naomi had no interest in going to see this young magician who could pick locks and find his way out of a box dropped into the sea. But since her father had tickets and begged her to come with him, Naomi went along.

She watched as Houdini wrapped himself in chains, slipped easily out of them, how he could be put in a straitjacket, with more chains, inside a locked safe and soon pick his way out. She was unimpressed.

Then the entire theater was invited to walk down to Lake Michigan, a distance of only two blocks or so. It was a lovely spring afternoon and so everyone enjoyed the outing. At the lake there was a boat waiting. On the boat there was a pirate's chest where Houdini was again put into a straitjacket, into the pirate's chest, the chest wrapped in chains and then flung over the side of the boat into deep water.

Now Naomi watched intently as she recalled the time she'd spent buried in a tiny grave and suddenly she was consumed with admiration for this man who could get out of anywhere. For what seemed hours but was only a few moments, Naomi kept her eyes fixed on the spot where the chest was hurled, and she breathed with great relief as Houdini surfaced, jubilant, to great cheers.

Her father managed an introduction, and when she met him she was touched by his soft brown eyes, but she also recognized a certain sadness there. A sadness she had seen in the eyes of many. The eyes of those who always have to be ready to escape. Only a Jew, Naomi thought, could be the great Houdini.

He was the only man besides Ivan who would ever impress her, and she would think about him almost as much as she'd thought about Ivan. And even as Ivan began to drift into memory, the great Houdini stayed fixed in her mind, and whenever Naomi felt stuck somewhere, she thought to herself how all she had to do, really, was escape.

The day after she met Houdini, Naomi took off her black and put on a red dress. She took off her wedding ring. She found a jar that had once contained marmalade and washed it. She washed the jar carefully and let it dry. She put her wedding ring inside with a shiny new dime and a note that read, "Finder's Keepers. May your luck be better than mine."

Then Naomi went down to the lake. She went to the spot where the two rivers entered the lake, the place where Houdini had been tossed from the boat the day before. She stood high up on the bluff and hurled the jar into the water. She watched as the current picked up the jar, carrying it down the stream. She watched as the jar bounced and turned and suddenly, when it was too late to do anything about it, the jar slipped behind the waves, heading out into the lake. Naomi was sad. What if the jar broke and no one would find it? But as the ring disappeared, Naomi knew all that was behind her now and whom or what she loved would not matter to her anymore.

She could not stay at home forever, so she married Ralph. He was fifteen years older than she and he ran a motel, the Home on the Road. He was a good man from a nice family, and

Naomi would never be unkind to him, though she would never care about him either.

It was not long before Naomi began to run the motel and it was the one thing that would keep her sane. She managed the books, organized the staff, and ran the kitchen. But still her life was filled with a great emptiness that even the birth of her daughter would not fill. All the rooms of the Home on the Road were exactly the same. There was blue carpeting with green bedspreads and the same blue tweed chairs and blue-green plaid curtains. There were fifty-three rooms and they were all alike. In the worst years of her marriage, when she still longed for Ivan, Naomi would go from room to room, leaving her impression on the beds, trying to find a room that felt or smelled differently from the ones before it. But she could not tell them apart, no matter how she tried; like the years, they were all the same.

Naomi had accepted this. She had accepted all of it. But she wanted something different for June. She wanted more. Naomi had stayed married and worked so that June could go to school, have something she liked to do, and eventually marry well. And now this man had stepped off a train and changed it all and Naomi knew she had no one to blame, not a soul but herself, for listening to her own dreams.

Naomi felt a resentment growing within her. Every afternoon she watched as June and Cal walked from the parking lot of the motel, heading toward the lakefront or the parks of Brewerton. She wondered what it felt like to June when Cal touched her body. When Naomi had been with Ivan, she loved it when their bodies were near each other. When she had been with Ivan, Naomi had felt ready and open for whatever happened to her. But with his death, she closed herself off and her wound healed with a harsh, ugly scar. She did not even remember what it was like to be with him. She had an amnesia about love.

When she married Ralph, she learned to hate the feel of a man's body close to hers. She'd found herself cold and hard, like a stone, in bed with him, and though Ralph tried, and though he did seem to know what he was doing to please a woman, Naomi could not warm her body with his. She grew to hate his touch and to imagine all touches hateful. Lovemaking, it seemed to Naomi, was for the lower beasts who did not care who their companion was and who only made love when it was their season.

Naomi could not bring herself to admit that the longing she saw in June was really a distant memory within herself. She was like one of those magic oriental flowers, kept in plastic capsules, that only need be dropped in water in order to spring to life, but there was no one left in Naomi's case to do the dropping, and so she was enclosed, self-contained, as if she'd lived her life as a monk. And now her daughter was making her remember a part of her that she'd thought was long dead and she was enraged at June for bringing back to her in this way what she'd imagined gone.

Despite Naomi's concerns, June and Cal usually weren't doing anything more than walking through Brewerton, unaware of the smell of barley and hops that permeated the air, thinking it was love that made them a little tipsy. He would hold her hand in the light of dusk and take her picture dozens of times, making her pose. She felt she had something special when Cal kissed her and ran his hands up and down her ribs. And once, as they kissed, his hand grazed her nipple and a feeling ran through her that reminded her of when she'd stuck a bobby pin into a light socket in one of the rooms of the motel.

June felt lucky. She had spent years listening to Naomi whisper curses under her breath as she made the bed of lovers when she herself had to crawl into the bed of a man she did not even care for. She had grown up with a dread that her own life would be like her mother's. An endless stretch of time that lay before June to which she would always be deferential—dividing it into little units, into hours and afternoons, days and years. Chopping it into smaller and smaller segments, manageable, bite-size pieces. But now this would stop. June knew that her life had finally begun when this man, brought to her by her brother, had stepped off the train, just as Cal knew he had come to stay.

She could not help herself and soon they went off alone in the afternoons without even bothering to ask Arthur. Arthur began to go to bars and drink until evening. He left in the afternoon and disappeared until sometimes late in the night. He made some friends whom he went out with at night and he dressed up before going out. At times Cal went looking for him, but mostly he stayed with June. He thought Arthur could take care of himself.

One night in the spring, Arthur and Cal had a terrible quarrel. Arthur wanted to get back to New York, but Cal tried to talk him into staying longer, and Arthur shouted, "You can stay, but I'm going." All through the motel June had heard the sound of their shouting. Arthur yelled that Cal had betrayed him, that he'd been a traitor to their friendship. And then he shouted words June would remember all her life, "It's better for you if I'm gone anyway."

But then the fight seemed to be forgotten and a few nights later Arthur invited them to go with him to a beer-chugging party on the enclosed roof terrace of one of the breweries. At the party he laughed too much. Whenever he could, he grabbed June for a dance. Cal stood back, trying not to lose his temper. June would sneak away to be with Cal, but Arthur kept pulling her back. When the roof races began, he chugged a pitcher of beer and whispered into June's ear, "Winner gets you." She felt her brother's breath hot against her ear.

He took off his thick, wire-rimmed glasses and handed them to June. "Hold these for me," he said. She put them in her purse, thinking how will he see. He puffed up his face, smiled at her, then raced across the roof. When he reached the other side, he hit the plate-glass window that enclosed the roof. For an instant when he struck the glass he lay still, pressed against it like an insect struggling in a spider web. But then the glass shattered and he sailed off, out into the sky, into nothing at all.

June wondered what he'd thought when he realized what he'd done. What ideas rushed through his head. Perhaps he thought about something he'd never get a chance to do. Or maybe his mind went blank and he thought nothing at all. But June would never forget her brother scrambling like a cartoon character, trying to get back onto the building, then disappearing, six floors below.

After the funeral, Cal kept talking about going back East, but he didn't go. June knew he wasn't leaving. She understood that somehow their lives were inextricably tied as if bound by blood. But Naomi thought it was different. She thought Cal's staying was the realization of her worst dreams and if they were bound, it was by nothing good.

Four months later they were married in the game room. Ralph pushed the billiard table, the card tables, the bingo scoreboard out of the way. He had the cook make cheese puffs and watercress sandwiches. June never felt more beautiful than she did in the apricot chiffon dress she'd wear once and never again, though she'd sworn she'd bought something practical. She didn't mind the fact that the game room was dingy and cold, that the guests were few, or that her father kept complaining about the cost of the champagne. June was happy. She was just nineteen years old and she had married the man she loved.

They drove to the Dells and stayed in the Chippewa Hotel. They checked into the bridal suite which had a king-size bed, champagne in a cooler, a huge vase of yellow roses, and a drawn curtain. But the plaid spreads, the dark carpeting, the piles of clean sheets and towels in the housekeeping carts in the halls, the maids who scurried about, the sound of a radio coming from the next room—it all felt too familiar to June.

How many times, she thought to herself, had she and her mother made up a room just like this one for some couple who closed themselves away after dinner and did not emerge for hours, days, and their meals would be left at the door and the empty trays picked up later, and they would enclose themselves in darkness as if they were prisoners in solitary confinement? And then every time Cal came near her, it was not his face she saw or felt, but rather it was the round, soft cheeks of her brother. When Cal pressed his face to hers, she felt her brother's damp face as he'd embraced her when he descended from the train. And when she closed her eyes, she saw once again the spider-like splintering, her brother trapped in the web of glass.

June could not make love to Cal on their wedding night. They kissed and hugged and groaned in each others arms. He held her and trembled and for the first time, except for once briefly in the park, she felt him hard beside her. He was hard half the night but they stayed in their pajamas and in the morning, after twelve hours of trying to make love, Cal was exhausted. June explained to him that it didn't feel as if they were on their honeymoon. It felt more as if they'd sneaked into one of the rooms of her parents' motel and she was now one of those guilt-ridden anxious lovers, always looking over her shoulder, signing the name Smith or Jones. She didn't mention seeing in Cal her brother's face.

That day they went to the dinosaur museum and the petrified forest and rode the water slide. They walked in the woods until it was almost dark and they ate dinner in their hotel. After dinner, they went to see an Indian performance. It was dark and a huge fire blazed. At first June's attention was on the flames, rising and falling as the Indians moved. She watched as they dropped handfuls of colored sand on the ground, their torsos gleaming in the heat of the fire, faces contorted as if in pain.

June put her knee on Cal's leg. She put her hand on his thigh. She looked at the Indians, dancing, their bodies glistening in the light of the flame. Cal put his arm around her and whispered into her ear, "I want you."

June wasn't sure what she wanted, but she let herself be led away. In the car Cal pulled her close as he drove silently to the hotel. She let him take her to their room where he undressed and she touched his skin for the first time. It was smooth and white, like milk, in the moonlight. "I want you," he said again. The memory of her brother's face and all the motel rooms of her youth faded. She wanted him too.

S E V E N

One day Mrs. Margolis took her husband to the train, kissed him good-bye, and never saw him again. That was thirty-five years ago. Now Mrs. Margolis moved with her walker from the patients' upstairs solarium to the downstairs waiting room where the families assembled. Zoe had heard of Mrs. Margolis in her youth because one of her boys attended Brewerton High School when Zoe did. That is, Zoe had heard of the man who kissed his family good-bye, boarded the 7:58, and was never seen or heard from again.

Zoe didn't know how she knew about Mrs. Margolis because no one ever spoke of her directly, at least not to the children of Brewerton. Rather it was implied, whispered in kitchens, on back porches, at dinner parties when the children were tucked away. For the women of Brewerton—and June was among them—those women who sat at their Formica tables with egg-coated dishes piled high, steamy cups of coffee in their hands, hair in little pin curls, facing the long day ahead of running small errands, throwing in loads of wash, those women who let the TV play low in the background all day, never quite watching it but never quite having the courage to be alone without the sound either, to those women the fate of Mrs. Margolis became their fate. It threatened them like some dark and rare disease, never seen before, that seemed capable of moving from house to house, neighborhood to neighborhood.

The women of Brewerton never kissed their husbands good-bye, took them to the depot, or stood waiting for a train to arrive without wondering, "Is this the last time?" Would he never appear again? No women ever watched her husband gaze off contemplatively in the direction of the lake or pause with a sigh from mowing the lawn without wondering was this it, the sign they'd dreaded, the symptom they had to watch for. And at times the women stared out the window themselves wondering if that kiss had been the final kiss, that touch the parting caress.

The men of Brewerton—many of whom had ridden the train with Mr. Margolis, and had even shared a hand of gin or a stock tip—publicly criticized him for his failure to accept responsibility, for getting involved with the mob, for embezzlement, for falling into the trap of mindless love and disappearing with a woman he thought he loved, for flinging himself into a part of the lake where the currents would not carry him back to shore, but instead would hold him, pulling him down into the deepest parts of Lake Michigan. There were various theories and explanations—all of which was rumor and none of which was ever proved. But through the bleakest, coldest days of winter, staring into the industrial landscape, in their private moments—while shaving, reading the newspaper, clipping a hedge—the men paused to think of Mr. Margolis and were filled with awe and wonder at what they imagined he had done. They pictured him on a tropical isle, sipping coconut drinks, a bronzed woman at his side. Or in Portofino, painting seascapes. They saw a golf course, trimmed and green all year around.

The Margolis family lived in a cul-de-sac in a housing development on the other side of town from the Colemans, but no one in Brewerton would ever look at their children again, tossing a ball on the way home from school, or see Mrs. Margolis in the market squeezing a melon without saying to themselves, "This is the family that will never be the same." These are people to whom something irrevocable has occurred.

Mrs. Margolis, who had been an attractive woman in her youth, who was tall and stately with soft reddish-blond hair, spent her days staring out the window of her house, day and night, year after year, anticipating her husband's return. The house was unkept, children's meals went uncooked. At first there were the police searches, the FBI investigation, the scanning of the books, the bank records, the closets, the drawers, for some clue, some hint—money withdrawn, an object missing, a note scribbled in a strange hand—but there was nothing at all.

At first Mrs. Margolis was moved by the search, the quest, and this is what gave meaning to her life. Once a body was found in Waukegan with the hands chopped off and for a week or so police thought it might be him, but analysis of bone tissue proved it was a much younger man. And another time Mrs. Margolis herself came upon a receipt in the bottom of one of her husband's pockets from a lingerie store. But when she called the store to inquire, she realized it was for a robe he'd bought her for Christmas. And then after that there were no clues. Not even hints at what had happened. The case was closed, and Mrs. Margolis had nothing left to do with her life.

In the process she became an observer of the neighborhood. She watched the arrivals and departures of husbands, the good-bye kisses of wives, the release of cats and dogs, the children wandering to bus stops with small lunch pails in hand. Mrs. Margolis could tell before it happened when something was wrong. Like a barometer, from the slight changes she detected in the air she knew when Mrs. Rothschild's marriage was on the rocks because she stopped getting dressed to drive him to the train, when the Barnett boy was in trouble because of the way he drove out of the driveway, when Mr. Sampson was drinking too much.

But mostly life went on without change as she watched the amazing consistency in the lives of others, their incredibly pre-dictable domestic tedium as they lived out the length of winter days, the delivery of large household appliances, the planting of annuals, without a change. As she retraced, every day in her mind, her husband's final steps the last day she ever saw him—the tie he put on, humming to himself, the sip of coffee he gulped down, the quick kiss as his train pulled in—she was amazed at the ordinariness of it all, how but for his disappearance her life would have gone on as well. And now her life stretched itself into an eternity like a book that does not end, a song with no final bar.

And now as Mrs. Margolis wandered the Heartland Clinic, a woman who has lost her thread, who can no longer find the names of her children, her own telephone number, a woman still expecting the story to make sense and her life to come to its natural close, she had become a woman with a vision. She saw what no one else ever saw. She knew what no one else ever knew. She whispered into the ears of patients. You will go on a journey, she said to a bedridden man. A new love will come your way, she told a boy paralyzed in an accident. Two people will come in a car this afternoon, she told Badger.

Julie, the day nurse, recognized June and Zoe right away and motioned for them to go up. Now, Zoe thought, we're getting somewhere. We are becoming intimate with this place. When they see us, we can just go on up. It was nice to feel as if you belonged. But just as they were about to reach the elevator the nurse caught up with them. "I'm sorry," she said. "I forgot. He's getting his bath. He won't be ready for a few moments."

The day nurse pointed in the direction of the waiting room and reluctantly June and Zoe headed that way. Zoe felt a tightening in her chest. She wanted to get this visit over with. To see her brother and be gone. Instead they went into the waiting room. The small plastic couch had a seat available and there was another plastic chair, so June and Zoe sat almost across from each other.

A few of the regulars were there. The man who twisted his wedding ring sat beside June on the sofa, staring into space. The woman who flipped through magazine after magazine but never read anything was there. The man with the wedding ring got up and offered Zoe his seat so she could sit with her mother. Zoe preferred sitting across from her mother, but since the man had gotten up Zoe took his seat. The man went to the window. The other woman flipped through magazines. But the moment Zoe sat down, June got up and began walking back and forth.

Zoe thought her mother must be thinking about Badger, but it was Zoe June couldn't get out of her mind. June remembered when she conceived her. She recalled the actual moment when conception occurred. Not the night, not what happened in the night, because then all the nights were the same. Each night, then with Cal, had been perfect and right. What she recalled was the spring day when she rode on the bus.

It was a beautiful day and she'd gotten a seat. She was sitting there when suddenly she felt a warm rush course through the center of her being, as if her blood was flowing backward. She felt it go through her muscles and bones and into her fingertips. It was the way she imagined radio waves were beamed from the station where she worked, her voice traveling out across Wisconsin, all emanating from her center. She felt it ripple through her and she knew then that she was going to have a child.

She'd loved being pregnant with Zoe. It had been the happiest time of her life. It was her happiest time with Cal. Her last happy time with him and the time she still held on to. In the summer during her last months she and Cal used to lie in bed and make love and he would photograph her belly and he would set up the camera and take pictures of them together, pictures she'd long ago hidden away and forgotten.

She'd loved the changes her body had gone through with Zoe. She'd been careful about everything she ate and drank. If she drank coffee, she felt the baby grow restless inside. If she drank wine, she felt the baby grow sluggish. She'd stopped coffee and wine. She only drank fresh-squeezed juices, mountain spring water. She did everything for the child. She did everything to make it peaceful and quiet in the womb.

Naomi said it was a girl. She had said you are carrying a girl. Boys you carry high, but this one was low and it's a girl. So June had named her Zoe while she was still in her womb, because Zoe meant life and June had never felt more alive. And then she was born. June and Cal had gone to play cards that night and Cal said to her why did you play that hand? She didn't know why she played it, so she left the card game in tears. She cried all the way home and she went upstairs and sat on the bed and cried and Cal had knelt down at her feet and kept saying, "I'm sorry. It was a fine hand. There wasn't anything wrong with that hand."

But June just kept crying and it took a while for either of them to realize that her water had broken.

She hadn't really minded the pain. As Cal drove her to the hospital, she hadn't minded it at all. She'd even asked the doctor not to use ether, but he'd gone ahead and cupped it over her mouth.

From the moment she was born, they'd understood each other. They'd been close. Zoe always used to curl up in her mother's lap to go to sleep. But then something had happened and June had never been able to pinpoint it. But Zoe had drawn away. Not the way children naturally draw away, but abruptly, suddenly. Zoe had a secret. June knew that. Zoe was hiding something. June didn't know what it was, but she knew it had changed things between them.

What June didn't know was that Zoe's secret shaped her entire life. It gave structure to everything she did. She didn't even think about it. It was just there. Like a strawberry mark, or some scar you've grown used to, Zoe hardly thought about it at all anymore, but it would always be there between them.

June finally sat down not far from the woman who flipped through magazines. After a few moments the woman with the magazines came over and leaned into June's face. The woman was not very old, perhaps only forty-five, but everything about her was white and felt old. The woman said, "I'm so sorry about your boy. My son was in Vietnam too."

June nodded, but then shook her head. "Oh, I'm sorry

about your son, but I'm afraid you've made a mistake. My son didn't go to Vietnam."

"Oh," the woman said, "I thought he had." The woman sounded very perplexed. "My son went and was very brave. Then he came home and went nuts." June looked at the woman. She didn't know what to say. But the woman went on. "I thought the same thing happened to your son."

June shook her head. "No," she said. "Not quite the same thing."

The woman extended her hand. "My name is Mrs. Alexander." June shook hands with the woman and the woman shook hands with Zoe. "My son came home and he was fine. Then one day he plucked out his eye. He said he couldn't stand what it kept seeing."

June and Mrs. Alexander kept holding hands. "He was fine. Then he plucks out his eye." The woman shrugged and went back to sit down. She picked up a magazine and flipped through as if she were looking at a book of animation.

They were relieved when the day nurse beckoned to them. "You can go up now," she said. Zoe watched how June punched the elevator buttons with authority, as if she worked there. As if she had to wait for these slow elevators every day and she could smile at her coworkers with the same exasperated smile every morning. Such things bind the workers together, the slowness of the elevators, the quality of cafeteria food.

But then this wasn't a place where anyone was going anywhere fast. This wasn't a place for emergencies, life-and-death situations. This was a place for slow elevators and regular hours. Naomi would have categorized it a low-turnover motel, a place where the regulars stay awhile and usually come back at least once a year.

Zoe would have walked the two flights. The Heartland Clinic only had four stories. Zoe had to walk five to get to her apartment in Brookline. Two was nothing. But her mother was not a woman to walk stairs. She was not the kind who would walk to the corner for her own cigarettes. June's favorite mode of transport, she told Zoe once, was the escalator. She loved to take the kids to the mall in Milwaukee and ride the escalators. If June could have her way, Zoe believed, she would simply live on a moving staircase. She liked to get places without doing the work.

June punched the elevator buttons, breathing heavily. "Ridiculous," June said. "A place like this. You'd think they'd have elevators that worked."

"What's the rush?" Zoe said.

"There can be emergencies. Things can happen." But in truth nothing much ever happened at Heartland. It was a place for slow rehabilitation, questionable comebacks. A place for stroke patients to learn to talk and amputees learn to walk and where kids who've dropped one too many try to find their way back into the world they wanted to get out of.

Badger sat in a puddle of sun—the only sun in the entire room, in the entire clinic, in the entire Midwest, it seemed, and Badger sat right in it. Like a lizard by the side of the road. He was dressed in jeans and a red sweatshirt and he didn't look bad. He just looked smaller. As if he'd shrunk in the wash.

He looked pale there and the room was too bare. It was just plastic-covered chairs and Formica tables and no plants or magazines. Nothing the patients on this level could toss about. The bars on the window cast an eerie shadow and he played the part of prisoner well. "So," Gabe said, "You've got visitors today." And Badger, without looking, turned his back on them.

He faced a tree that stood, devoid of leaves for another few months, a dreary, dead-looking tree, and he fixed his gaze on that. June sat in one of the chairs that made a squeechy sound and Gabe leaned against the wall. She blamed herself for her son's condition. Zoe was her love child, born of her happy years, but Badger had come from another time, another place. He was the child of her desperation and she had raised him as if he were the illness between herself and Cal, as if he were sick and frail and soon to crumble.

But he was also her child. Yet somehow she had grown used to seeing him like this. It amazed her how you could get used to anything. Once she'd read about a woman who'd seen her child burned all over his body except his feet and he'd hug her with his toes. How could a mother not go mad? I would kill for my children, June thought. I would steal, rob, walk through fire, tear a man limb from limb, for either of these children. But now somehow I've gotten accustomed to seeing him like this.

When he was little, she never got used to seeing him come in the door or leave for school. He always surprised her, as if she never expected him to be there at all. He was so alone, she ached for him. How can mothers stand these things? It is as if it were happening to her, not to him. She thought of her friend Margaret, whose daughter Debbie, a fat, dowdy girl, hanged herself on the clothesline in the basement when Margaret went to the store for hamburger meat. When she came home, she made hamburger patties. Then she went downstairs to throw the wash in the dryer. She found Debbie hanging there. After that Margaret was always short of breath and the doctors gave her medicine for asthma, though she'd never been asthmatic before.

Why do people become mothers, June asked herself sitting there now, looking at Badger. She hadn't really cared much about the last war. Badger had gone to Canada and she had lived through worse, much worse. She had been on rations. She had given up her stockings. She had suffered alone. But then one picture had come screaming at her out of the news. One picture that raged inside of her—the open mouth of a child racing toward her, arms open with burning holes, devastation behind her, and June had longed to reach out and take this child in. Comfort it, heal its burns. This picture had made her a mother again. And then there was no turning back.

But somehow she had grown used to this, to seeing him. If she thought back to the night when she made him, she could see it wasn't a night when she was thinking with the rational part of her brain. One child with Cal would have been enough. But she wanted this one. She'd wanted Badger more than she'd ever wanted anything. She'd thought this was the child that would bring them back together again.

"I don't want to live in Texas," he said when he noticed them sitting there. "It's too big and hot."

"You can stay right here if you want," Zoe said.

"I gave my best years to this team. Me and Hunt, we gave our best years, didn't we?" June looked quickly at Zoe and Zoe looked away. She couldn't believe he was bringing up Hunt again. "I could've gone a dozen times, but I stuck with you. I had the most R.B.I.'s in the division when we were low man on the totem pole, but I stuck around. And now, when I'm having a bad season, you want to trade me."

"Darling," June said, "nobody wants to trade you."

He stared outside at the tree so Zoe said, "Nice tree, huh, Badge?"

"Mrs. Margolis told me you are living a secret life," he said directly to his sister. Then he lost interest in them all. "I want to be out there." He pointed to the tree. "I want to be that tree. I want to look just like that tree." Zoe looked at the tree, leafless, barren, in the dead of winter.

He'd never had any understanding of winter. He used to sit by the windowpane and watch as the snow fell hour after hour. If the weather report said they expected two feet of snow, Badger would rush inside. It took years for June to make him understand that it would fall slowly, fluttering down, and not all in one big swoop. He was afraid of being engulfed, buried, taken in. While Zoe was outside building a snowfort, fortifying it with snowballs, constructing giant, monstrous men, Badger would be in the living room, nose flush to the window, examining the frost, those silken patterns like the webs of spiders, entrancing him, and in them he saw maps of towns and valleys, other countries, places he would visit someday.

June always pleaded with Zoe—take him out to play, be nice to him, help him make friends. So Zoe would take him out and pound him with snowballs or bury him in the snow. She'd say let's play Frosty and she'd pack snow around his body until his teeth chattered and his lips turned blue. Or she'd say you be the prisoner in the fort and she'd encase him in the snowfort until once his nose turned white and she feared it would drop off.

Or sometimes, and this was the game he liked, on a very cold winter's day, Zoe would say let's play doctor. And they'd go upstairs to the cedar closet. He liked to go up there because they could be warm. That closet that smelled so nice of red husky cedar trees, a deep, sweet smell, and in the dim light of the cedar closet, in the light amber glow, they'd take off their clothes, and she'd examine him for broken bones and an appendix or tonsils or a tummyache, and sometimes when she was in the mood, when she felt like being good, Zoe cradled him as if he were her own baby, naked in her naked arms.

As they were leaving, Gabe tapped Zoe on the shoulder. "Could I have a word with you?"

He sounded very serious and professional, so Zoe didn't hesitate. "Of course," she replied, motioning to her mother that she'd just be a minute.

They walked to a corner and for a moment he looked at her very oddly so that Zoe expected him to utter some terrible prognosis. But then he cleared his throat and stammered. "Uh, I hope you don't mind my asking." He waited for her to say something, but she said nothing so he went on, "But would you have dinner with me?" Her face remained blank, as if she hadn't heard him. "Would you have dinner with me tomorrow night?"

"Tomorrow night?" Zoe said slowly as if she were a person with important plans. In fact she had nothing planned for the rest of her life. She wanted to say no, but she could think of no real excuse. "Yes, dinner. I suppose we could have dinner."

"I mean, if you have no other plans . . ."

"No, I have no plans. We could talk about my brother."

This was the last thing Gabe wanted to talk about over dinner. "We can talk about anything you like. I'll pick you up at seven." Already he was regretting having asked her.

"Seven is fine."

"You know," he hesitated, "there's a lot of people around here who would like to see you. I could arrange a little something."

Zoe shook her head. "This isn't a social visit."

"Well, maybe it should be." He walked away. "Seven," he called back, his head receding.

June was standing around the corner, waiting for Zoe. "I want to know everything," she said. "What did he say?"

"Nothing, Mom. It was personal."

"How personal could it be?"

"He asked me to have dinner with him. Let's take the stairs."

June groaned, pushing the elevator button. She put her face to the elevator doors now and sucked in her lips. She was a beautiful mother, Zoe thought. She had been a beautiful mother. She was tall with thick dark hair and green eyes and there had been a time when people said how she and Zoe looked like sisters.

They had gotten their height from Ralph. Otherwise, June used to say, they looked like Naomi, the Russian peasant, with their high cheekbones and flashing eyes. Still, they liked to believe they were opposites. Zoe wore blue jeans and alpaca sweaters and June wore matching green and a broadcloth coat. Zoe rushed from place to place and June was the essence of patience. But she looked less patient than she had before. Now she rocked on the balls of her feet, like a person about to be introduced to give a big speech. Like someone about to be made head of the women's auxiliary. June never complained when Cal was at war and she'd never complained when he came home. And even now, she didn't complain.

E I G H T

When June and Cal returned from their honeymoon, they put a few hundred dollars down and bought a house. A small, wood-frame house with an apartment over the garage. And Cal bought a small cottage a few blocks away where he had set up his darkroom. For June this was the beginning of her adult life. She had a place that was her own. She didn't live in a motel anymore. She didn't roam from room to room. She had a home and a person she loved and those were things no one could take away.

Every afternoon for three years June and Cal took long walks at the end of the day and at night they would be coy about coaxing each other to bed. June would put on jasmine perfume and cream on her cheeks and they would sit after dinner, their feet touching, delaying as long as they could the moment when the other would rise to go to bed. They toyed with their desire, making it long and drawn out, sipping it slowly like a strong drink in summer.

When Zoe was born, they would place her between them in bed. They'd touch across their daughter's sleeping body. They placed kisses on her head until their own tongues reached for each other. But Zoe would have no recollection of them being happy. One day before she even knew him, her father went off to war.

He enlisted shortly after Pearl Harbor and asked to join aerial reconnaissance. Focus cats, they called them. He told June he'd be safe in the air. The day he left, they stayed in bed all morning. It was a warm autumn day, Indian summer, and the leaves were a yellow-orange, and they'd just stayed in bed, staring at the giant sugar maple outside their window. They didn't make love, but they touched, ever so carefully, each part touching, as if hand was saying good-bye to thigh, face to breast, arm to leg. As if their bodies were learning how to be apart, learning how to say good-bye.

Even though Cal didn't want her to, June drove him to the train. It was the same train he had arrived on five years before that would now carry him away—the train he'd come on with Arthur. The train was late and it made them both irritable. Cal paced up and down the platform and June just sat with Zoe huddled against her. "Why don't you just go," Cal said over and over again, but June shook her head.

Despite herself June started to cry. She knew it would annoy him, but she couldn't help it. She couldn't stand this time before having something and then not having it. Cal looked at her crying, then turned away. "I guess we'd better go," June said.

Just then the train appeared. It was the Milwaukee Road and it would take him east to his base camp. Then it would be a month before he'd ship out, but they wouldn't see each other again. Suddenly tears came to Cal's eyes and he buried his face against her breast. "I'll be back soon," he said, "as soon as I can."

Then he grabbed his duffel and slipped away from her. His fingers from her fingers. Lips from her lips. He climbed the steps of the platform, onto the train, and they didn't touch again.

A few days after Cal left, June went out and purchased giant stretchers which she assembled in the basement of her house, and all kinds of cloth, and cotton batting, and she began the avocation that would occupy her spare time and get her through the next few years. She set about the task of making quilts for all the beds in her house. She began with Zoe's room. For Zoe she made a quilt with bears and flowers and stars and assorted beasts and small fish and she made pillow shams and curtains to match.

It took her over a year to make the quilt for Zoe and when she had completed the task, she was surprised to find that Cal still wasn't home from the war.

She went on to the next room. For Naomi she made a blue bedspread covered with waves and clouds and ships to match her dreams of the sea, the sea that had entered her when she crossed it to come to America. She made billowy curtains like waves and a dozen pillows of the same cloudlike images to prop her up as she embarked upon her nightly voyages across water she would not cross while awake.

And when Cal still had not returned and the letters came with less and less frequency, with no more pictures of him, and she felt him growing remote from her, slipping farther away, June moved on to other rooms. But not her own room. That she would not touch. She refused to change one light or chair or knickknack from their room, because she wanted Cal to return to life as he'd left it. So she began decorating the extra bedroom as a room for a boy child, the one she knew she'd have when Cal came home. At night, long after Zoe and Naomi were asleep, June's fingers would work, making a bedspread of battleships and dogs and soldiers and baseball bats and ponies. Things she thought a boy would like, not knowing that the boy she'd have would collect such things as colored shells and bits of polished glass, delicate fabrics, furry beasts. But she knew she'd have a boy child and so she prepared herself in this way.

And when Cal still wasn't home, June went on. She thought of giving up the quilting, but found she could not stop. Even though her fingers ached and her back was sore, even though she had to work all day long and would stay up till all hours quilting, she found she could not stop. It was only during the quilting that June forgot about time. She forgot about the moments, the hours, the days passing.

And when she had made a million more stitches, when she had upholstered every inch of furniture in their house that could be upholstered, except for their own room, when she had remade the curtains, the pillow shams, when she had filled the rooms with ships and trees and animals and clouds and angels, she received word that her husband was coming home from the war.

She put away the stretchers, the cotton batting, the bits of cloth. She made herself a red silk dress because it had been his favorite color. She polished her nails for the first time in three years, nails that had been chewed and bitten down to the quick. She had her hair done the way it had been before he left, and she dabbed on the perfume she knew he liked. Then she went back to the train station where she'd left him three years before and she picked up a stranger.

The man who got off the train bore little resemblance to the man who had gotten on it. Her husband had left as a virile, athletic young photographer and this pale man with almost no hair had returned. He tried to act natural, but there was something about him that was not natural. The first thing June did was touch him all over. She touched his arms, his legs, his face, his chest. He was all flesh, not wood. But there was something strange about him.

He would not speak, except to answer in brief monosyllables. He would answer questions, such as if he was hungry, but he would not offer information. Not about the war, not about himself. If June talked to him, he seemed to listen but he did not reply. She was as alone with him as she had been without him.

But in the three years of his absence June had learned patience. She had waited for him to come and now she'd wait for him to get well. But this was worse than anything she had experienced before. Now he was home and she could not quilt. There was nothing left for her to cover.

For almost a year June nursed him. She brought him food, sat with him. She tried to piece together what was wrong. As she thought back over the years she had known him, there had been things that were strange. A moodiness she couldn't quite put her finger on. A drifting in and out. He could turn on her suddenly and for no reason, and then he would come back an hour later as if nothing had happened. But now she saw that he was in retreat and he would stay there for as long as he liked.

No one could help Cal really or understand just what it was that had been done to him. For Cal's difficulties had begun before the war, but the war had brought them back. Cal was a man whose memories of his life went screaming through him as he slept in the form of a train whistle screeching to a halt and though he could recall nothing of the accident or recall his parents or anything about the way they had died, he could still hear in the night that whistle of the train.

He had been an infant when his parents packed up their belongings, put them in a trailer, left their farm in western Wisconsin, heading to Seattle to start a new life, only to get as far as the first hundred miles, the fartherest west Cal Coleman would ever travel, and be struck broadside by a freight train of the Union Pacific. He had been asleep when his father, tired from the long day's drive and unsure of the life that lay ahead of him, missed the signal of the blinking railroad light and drove across the tracks in search of a place for his family to sleep for the night.

It had taken the rescuers hours to pry the wreck of the car from the front of the train, to pick apart metal, limbs, bits of flesh, to pry and pull and unfold the accordion of a car, only to uncover what none of them could believe. They found Cal's mother, bloody and dead, who had flung herself across her sleeping child, and saved his life. What they found was a living infant who had made its way into her clothing, burrowed its face in, and was suckling contentedly at his dead mother's breast. It seemed a terrible omen to the rescuers. They pried the infant, now an orphan, from its dead mother's breast and listened to its cry, the loneliest cry any of them would ever hear.

Though Cal could never and would never know anything of this, the sounds and sensations of that evening found their way deep into some part of him and buried themselves there, like a larva that could lie dormant in the ground for decades or a quarter of a century and then come out like a plague on the earth. The screams, the halts, the fumbling in that womblike wreck of a car for his mother's breast, it was all there within him, and in the war, in the cries he heard, the sounds of metal crushing, the accident came back to him, night after night, but in the war there had been no warm woman to soothe him, no breast to suckle. He was left with the raw experience of his life—the terrible accident he could not recall and the wrenching away that shaped everything that had transpired.

He was destined to be a man without a family. For a time, with June, and then with Zoe, he had forgotten that. But in the war, on those daily missions or alone at night in the barracks, he remembered in some deep part of himself who he really was. When he returned home, it was as an orphan. Troubled and perplexed by those who floated around him, Cal was unsure of what to do with himself. He knew that he would never belong anywhere and that no one would ever belong to him.

Somehow Cal remembered that the one place that made sense to him, where everything was dark and quiet, warm and safe, was in the place he had chosen to practice his profession, and one day he simply got out of the chair where he had been sitting. He returned to his darkroom and made it back into the place it used to be, a place where no screeching came, where he was protected and warm and safe. To his family, he was gone, as if he'd never been there. He stayed in the darkroom for days on end, coming home to sleep briefly, then slip away. This was the one thing June could not bear. It made the war years look easy, because at least then he was really gone. But this retreat into the womblike darkness she could not understand.

June began to behave in strange ways. She'd wander around the garden on summer nights wrapped in blankets as if she'd caught a chill. She labeled everything—shoe boxes, jars, bookshelves. Into the night she'd arrange books in alphabetical order by subject. Order was crucial. There wasn't a drawer June had not straightened a half-dozen times. The house had the feeling of efficiency of a hospital emergency room.

Naomi thought she was crazy, but June didn't care. Naomi told June to move with her back to the motel, but June wouldn't budge. She tried to create in the house a feeling of normality. Meals were served on time, whether Cal showed up or not. Even if he came in after midnight when he'd gone back to his darkroom to unravel the secrets of the universe. She waited up for him every night, sometimes until dawn. She would not give up on him. She would not let him go.

One evening she could stand it no longer. She put on black underwear and a black slip. She put on the red silk dress and wrapped herself in a shawl. It had been almost two years since he had come home bald and reclusive. It had been months since he shut himself up in his darkroom.

June made her way swiftly through the dark streets of Brewerton that led to Cal's studio. There was a chill in the air that night and she wrapped her shawl tightly around her. June wasn't exactly sure what she meant to do but she knew she had to do something. Her teeth chattered as she walked. She thought of Cal when they first met. She thought of him taking her pictures in the afternoon as they strolled through the parks of Brewerton. It came back to her then, how much she missed him.

One day, shortly after they were married, they spent the day making love while he took pictures of them in bed. She laughed as she thought of that afternoon and wondered what had become of those pornographic snapshots they'd taken on a timer of them fondling each other. Then June shuddered. She hated to think what had become of them.

When she reached the studio, June paused. She looked up at the sign. CAL COLEMAN'S FINE PHOTOGRAPHY: GLOSSY AND MATTE FINISHES. EXCELLENT QUALITY. WE DO WEDDINGS. Then she walked into the place she had never once entered while her husband was at work.

The studio itself was lit, but there was no sign of Cal. She went to the door of the darkroom and knocked. There was no answer. She knocked again. There was still no answer so she gently opened the door and slipped inside, behind the black curtain. She peered in and saw Cal bent over the enlarger in the red light of the darkroom, and June could not help thinking how he looked a little like the devil.

"Cal," June said, "we've got to talk."

"I'm busy," he replied. "I'll be home later."

She told him it was already ten o'clock and later wasn't good enough anymore. But Cal shook his head and said he couldn't talk to her now. It would have to be later. June was beginning to understand that Cal was man who would not let go of anything he needed for himself. But at this moment she needed him too.

Deep inside of her, something clicked. "No," she said. "Now." And with that she flicked on the switch and lit up the darkroom. Cal looked at her in horror.

"What're you doing?" He dashed for the light, "Oh, my God." He put the tops on the developing tanks. "You've just ruined the Goldstein wedding."

"I don't care," June said, keeping her hand pressed over the light switch. "I don't care what I've ruined. You're ruining my life."

But even as she spoke, June was shocked. She realized she hadn't seen Cal in the light for weeks now, maybe months. Now she had a chance to look at him closely. She was greeted by a pale, sickly face. His skin was pasty and what remained of his hair was plastered to his head. His arms and back slumped forward from so many hours at the enlarger and his eyes were large and beady. His body seemed to have no tension in it at all and he looked more like a victim than a veteran from the war he'd come from. As he tried to move her hand away from the light switch while covering his blinking eyes with another hand, June realized something else about her husband. Like a nocturnal creature, a mole or an owl, he was a man who could no longer live in the light.

"I'm taking you home." June removed the negative that was in the enlarger and put it into its plastic sleeve. She took the prints that were in the fixer and put them to wash in water, then in the hypoclear. Cal stood by silently, watching her, more comfortable now that she had let him turn out the light. Then she poured out the developer bath, the stop bath, the fixer, and let the chemicals run down the drain. She turned the vats upside down. She ran water over them. Then she ran water over the prints and laid them on blotter paper to dry. "Now," she said when she was done, "let's go."

Cal's head was bowed and he began to weep. "It was so beautiful from the air," he told her. He told her how things were all upside down and he didn't know how to turn them around.

"Well, you're on the ground now," she said. She spoke to him in the soft, warm voice that lured him and then she led him home.

Cal stumbled in the living room and banged into the coffee table as they made their way into the house. June went to turn on a light and he begged her not to. The light, he told her, was hurting his eyes. June went into the kitchen and got two beers. Then she led him into the garden. They sat in silence on the stone wall around the patio. At first he felt as if he were being watched, as if someone were peering down on him. "Do you think we're being watched?" he asked.

But June shook her head. "It's just the moon," she said.

Cal gazed up, then at her, puzzled, with a look of nonrecognition. "Who is this woman sitting next to me, pointing at the moon?" he seemed to be asking himself. And then his expression changed into a smile. He spoke her name out loud for the first time she could recall since he'd returned from the war. "June," he said. Then more emphatically, as if giving himself the definition, "My wife, June."

He motioned for her to sit closer to him and she did. She sniffed the air. "You smell like chemicals," she said, "and beer."

How could he explain to her, to this rather slight and practical woman, that he was discovering a way of looking at the human condition in all its multifacets and soon he would know the answer to the big questions. No, he wouldn't tell anyone, not until he was ready. But he felt he had to say something. "You smell good," he told her. It was a simple thing to say.

After a few moments June touched his arm. "Let's go." As they climbed the stairs, Cal kept his hand on the small of June's back, his finger wrapped around her waist. Once they were in their room, he pulled her to him. She felt his lips on the nape of her neck. She felt him hard against her back. She turned and kissed him as he unbuttoned her dress. Cal pushed her ever so gently onto the bed and then he looked at her. She was still a young woman, only a little over twenty-five. She was beautiful with her soft brown skin, her dark hair that fell behind her back.

Cal took off his clothes and June thought how thin he'd become. How he needed to eat. She knew she had to take better care of him. He bent over her and she brought him down to her breast. Then they made love for hours until the birds began to chirp and the sky turned a shade of pale cobalt. They made love until they heard Naomi's puttering in the kitchen and Zoe saying what kind of toast she wanted. They made love with a strange fervor, more as if they were exorcizing a demon than making contact with a human. They dozed for a few moments, then made love again. For the entire night their lips were rarely apart.

In the morning they were reluctant to slip out of bed, but finally June got up. She moved like a woman who was comfortable with the routine of her life. She went through her day confident that at last the semblance of normal would be normal. She didn't know it would never be that way again.

Badger was born the day they dropped the bomb on Nagasaki and Cal seemed oblivious to both events. During June's pregnancy he stayed in the darkroom until the middle of almost every night, making print after print of pictures no one ever saw. He stayed working with such verve and determination that once June said to him when he finally slipped into bed, "Have you discovered penicillin yet?"

At first June was patient with him, but then a great sadness came over her. As if she were already an old person, looking back on the life she'd lived, she found herself remembering the moments when he'd loved her. And then there was the baby she was carrying. She never felt him kick or move, not a stir. She felt as if she were living in a dead love with a dead child inside of her. In her sixth month she went to the doctor and told him the baby was dead and they should take it out of her. The doctor with a puzzled smile put the stethoscope to her womb and shook his head. "Just resting up before he kicks up a big storm," the doctor assured her.

The day June brought Badger home from the hospital, Cal was very busy. He was photographing all the flowers in the garden. It was the end of summer and it was a chore that had to be done. Cal was working with his camera in the backyard when June came home. He looked at his son with a look of recognition and then he looked at Zoe. "How's my little girl?" he asked. Zoe was stunned. He'd hardly ever said anything so intimate to her before and it made her uncomfortable and embarrassed in his presence now. Cal acknowledged the baby by taking his photograph half a dozen times. He photographed him near the roses. Then he took him into the house and plunked Badger down on Zoe's lap. He attached a flash to the camera and the baby blinked at each explosion of light.

"I'm going to give him his first bath at home," June said, glad that Cal was paying so much attention to the baby. "Wanta help?" Cal said he'd love to help. So, while June bathed Badger, Cal photographed each moment of the baby's first bath at home. He recorded the removal of the diaper, the bottom being wiped. He recorded the soft look as Badger descended into warm water.

And as each of these events took place, a flash went off and Badger blinked.

From that day on Zoe and Badger were never safe from a flash going off in their faces. At any instant, in the midst of any activity—in the tub, reading a comic book on the toilet, in a snuggly sleep with their favorite teddy, during the heat of an argument, even necking on the beach when they were older—Cal would stalk them down and take their picture. Just as they were about to solve some complex problem in advanced calculus, the light would flare in their eyes and the answer would be lost forever. Even the poor old mangy dog, Puzzle, who'd once been a magnificent white Himalayan, was not safe and was often captured as he tried to defecate modestly in the corner of the garden during his later years.

The Coleman children learned at an early age that there was no such thing as a private act, no such thing as a perfect moment that could exist without interruption. Badger would confess with great concern to his sister years later that once his father had flung open the door to his room and somewhere there was a negative of Badger fondling himself on his bed, his pants down around his ankles. Even as a grown man, Badger would never be able to perform the act of love without a sheet pulled across his back.

Zoe, who was an infant while her father was an aerial photographer over enemy territory, believed that she and her brother spent more time than any people in the world with little red spots in front of their eyes, with a momentary blindness that seemed able to extend itself through the years, as if they could go through life with those little spots in front of their eyes.

They had no idea what he did with those pictures. They never saw them. They never received any prints. They just knew that their father kept a loaded camera in the house at all times, the way a threatened man would keep a gun.

PART

THREE

THE MUSEUM
OF ICE

Dear Zoe, Do you know anything about bats? I've been studying them in this cave that Whittaker found. He used to be a biology major and he says bats are misunderstood. They are thought to be vampires, suckers of blood. They are thought to be drawn into women's hair. To embody demons and ghouls. But I've been watching them and none of this is true. We go into this cave and there are thousands, millions of them. You can hear their high screeching and see their little beady eyes peering at us in the dark as they flicker past.

I've grown accustomed to the darkness in the cave. It suits me. Remember that scaredy cat I used to be? Afraid of the boogie man and the Big Bad Wolf. Remember how you could put the fear of God in me just by whistling in a deep, breathy way? No more of that stuff for me. You should see me crawling around on my belly in these caves with no lights, putting my hands into cold slime, looking for a nice cozy place to sink myself into the wall. I'm good now at finding ledges and crevices. You'd be amazed at how easily my eyes adjust to complete darkness. You know that there are fish that are blind because they are so far deep in the sea that they don't need their eyes?

I feel at times as if I could live that way. But in the caves there's some light. Enough to let me find my way. There's always a twinge of moonlight, just enough for me to decipher the outlines, the silhouettes, the shadows. I'm becoming familiar with the language of bats. They have different shrieks for different things. A call of danger, a cry for food, a shout for a missing pup. They are friendly creatures, even affectionate, and it makes me sad to know how much they are misunderstood. Do you know that the females only have one pup a year and that sometimes, if the pup is lost, other mothers will nurse it? They are altruistic and kind. I could go on and on about them. I want the world to see them in a different light. Evil isn't always what we think it is. And goodness, I've come to know, isn't always what it's cut out to be.

Do you know how bats fly through their caves in the dark? They bounce sound off distant walls and it echoes back to them and tells them what lies ahead. I've thought how much I'd like that. How great it would be. To send out some signal and find out what waits for us there. But maybe we do that. Perhaps we have our own way, we just aren't aware of it. Maybe these letters to you are my way of bouncing my own sound off the wall and hoping that in some way, at some time, it will come back to me and tell me what it is that lies ahead. Much love, Badger

N I N E

Since his wife left him, Gabriel Sharp had been learning to do some basic things. He'd been learning how to live alone. It hadn't occurred to him until after she was gone that it was Marilyn who'd been responsible for coffee first thing in the morning, food always about to be served, his shirts pressed and hanging in the closet. He never thought about how these things happened. It was as if he had a silent butler who did them all.

Gabe was glad he didn't have to cook that evening because he was taking Zoe out. Most evenings he dropped his Stouffer's creamed spinach pouch into boiling water, popped a Salisbury steak frozen TV dinner into the oven. Early in their separation Gabe had struggled with broiled chicken and steak. When he got it right on the outside, it was wrong on the inside. He wrestled with fresh vegetables and baked potatoes. Like a mediocre boxer, his timing was never right. Potatoes came out hard, beans overcooked, chicken as charred as a heretic at the stake. Pancakes, dropped into greaseless pans, immolated themselves before his eyes. Coffee was indistinguishable from tea.

Laundry defied him. Socks and underwear, now the color of slush, came out grayer and grayer with each wash. He'd throw in bleach and his striped T-shirts faded, bled like broken hearts, grew smaller until he wondered if he was shrinking back to a ten-year-old. Desperate, he called Marilyn and she gave him advice. "Separate everything," she said. Separate was something he'd done a fair amount of lately. He washed only yellow with yellow, red with red. Laundry took days. His brain malfunctioned at green and white stripes. He stopped wearing madras.

He called her back. She said mix colors except those that

need to be kept separate. But how do women know what needs to be kept separate? he'd asked. What needs to be washed alone, in icy water, inside out, tumbled dry. Everything in his life was shrinking, losing its shape. The underside of his world was gray. He called her one more time, praying, if she wouldn't come back to him, she'd offer to do his laundry. Instead she conveyed to him her last piece of marital advice. "Read the labels," she said.

He grew preoccupied with his white hospital coats, how they came back spotless and starched, stiff yet smooth, with no traces of disease, decay, human frailty, tomato soup, a botched life. One day he took his laundry to the hospital with him and asked Matilda, the laundress from Trinidad, if he could pay her to do this for him. But Matilda looked with her shiny black face and her olive black eyes and said, condescendingly he thought, "I only do whites."

When it was too late to do anything about it, Gabe began to admire Marilyn, with reverence, the way you might admire Beethoven or Mahatma Gandhi. Her achievements seemed superhuman to him, almost of a mystical nature. For a brief time he missed her intensely. He missed the effortless way she performed her tasks—threading needles, scrambling eggs, serving four things hot and ready at the same moment, removing some horrible stain from a favorite shirt, making the bed smooth with two flicks of the wrist, as if no one had ever slept there.

They had known each other since they were thirteen. They had been declared "cutest couple" freshman year in high school. He had gone to the University of Wisconsin at Madison and she had gone to a small Catholic girls' school nearby. On weekends she came to his room and they made love. When she got pregnant they'd married, and when she lost the baby it hadn't mattered that much. They'd planned to marry eventually.

All through medical school, he let Marilyn work in sales or in restaurants, supporting them and taking care of the details of their lives. Gabe never had to pay a bill or wash a dish. When he was tired, she prepared his bath and gave him a back rub. When he had to work late, she never complained. If they didn't make love for weeks at a time, she said she understood. Her goodness and her refusal to want anything for herself perplexed him, but he accepted it as he had accepted her.

But as the years went by, as he grew more involved in his work, in his struggles against biological warfare, against nuclear war, as his evenings were filled with meetings and lectures he wanted to attend, he grew more and more aware of Marilyn sitting at home gluing pictures into the album.

The picture albums disturbed him. Marilyn spent half their vacations, their picnics, their outings taking snapshots with an Instamatic and then she'd spend weeks organizing them into albums. At the top of each page of the album she wrote the location, such as Disneyland, Yellowstone, Green Bay, and under each picture, in careful calligraphy, she composed a caption that was a mere repetition, a restatement of the obvious: Gabe with buffalo, Us and Mickey Mouse, Gabe and Mom eating chicken at picnic. Sometimes he'd tease her, pointing to Gabe with buffalo, "Why don't you put arrows, Marilyn, so we can tell who's who."

Sometimes he thought she was simpleminded. One night he went home and told her as gently as he could that they never talked about anything. She never did anything. Didn't she want to have a life of her own? He said he could not help but feel that she was always there, waiting for him to come home. She looked at him with angry eyes. "I'm doing nothing of the kind," she assured him. "I am busy all day long, but if you are bored, that's your problem."

Three months later she left him for a computer software salesman she had been seeing for a while. She told him on a Friday night that she was leaving and was gone two hours later. Gabe walked around the house muttering as she put her pure white, ironed and folded underwear into a suitcase, the last clean underwear he'd see for a long time. "A computer software salesman! Why?" Marilyn replied because he was good around the house.

He tried different things after she left him. He made a list of all that had ever interested him and he began to do those things. He subscribed to *Field and Stream* and to Sierra Club bulletins. He went backpacking in the north woods and canoeing on white water. He watched his clumsy, awkward body turn strong and take charge. But the outdoor life had not taken care of his restlessness.

A year ago he'd taken up the guitar. At the end of the day, if he had time to spare, he sat down and played. He had beautiful hands, the hands of a surgeon or a musician. Hands women fall in love with for their long, sleek white fingers. When he strummed with those fingers, Gabriel Sharp let hidden things come out. The rest of the time he kept everything inside. It was only in his songs that he told about his father who worked for the breweries, who'd lost his job of twenty-five years when the industry began to fail, then drank himself to death. It was a story he never told anyone, not even Marilyn, but black men in bars in Brewerton had told Gabe that he knew how to sing the blues. Sometimes late in the evening he'd go down to one of the clubs and listen or jam. It was then that he felt the most himself. It made Gabe think that if the right woman heard him just once, if she heard him sing in the right way at the right time, she would see him for what he was and she would have to fall in love. But so far no one had. So far, he hadn't had anyone to listen.

As he sat down to play, he wondered why he'd asked Zoe to dinner. It bothered him that he had. He thought he must have felt sorry for her. He wouldn't say that he liked her. Now he had to worry about making small talk over dinner with someone he barely knew from twenty years ago. He hated the idea of conversation. "So have you danced the twist since junior prom?" Or "When you saw *The Graduate,* did you think 'That's me?' " Since Marilyn left, he'd dated a nurse in the third ward and a lab technician in the annex. They knew about each other. He'd told them not to get serious and so far no one had.

He was annoyed with himself for allowing this intrusion

into his life. It felt messy, disordered. But then he thought that by spending an evening with Zoe, he'd understand her brother better. He liked Badger. There was something about Badger, once you saw your way into him, that Gabe really liked. Gabe knew that something was trapped down deep inside Badger and if Gabe could, he'd find the way to set it free.

Zoe had lost herself in the Museum of Ice. It was a small museum in a warehouse near the docks that revealed the history of ice export. Though in truth it was a fairly dreary, rundown place, it had been a favorite spot from her childhood. Outside of beer, ice had been Brewerton's primary industry. The cutting of ice chunks from Lake Michigan, the packing and transporting. She'd always loved the statistics about how many tons of ice were shipped to Barbados in the early 1900s and how many in fact arrived, and she loved the wonderful pictures of ice sculptures at the annual competition. Giant carvings of dinosaurs, mermaids, Statues of Liberty, the Taj Mahal.

She'd stayed too long in the "Believe It or Not" room. There was the tiny, hairy man frozen to death for a million years, perfectly preserved. Grotesque pictures of people whose toes, ears, noses, whatever, had fallen off due to frostbite. Famous survival stories. Tales of polar bears who'd protected men with their fur until rescue came, of men who cut holes for themselves in the bellies of horses and stayed alive in the entrails. Defrosted Ice Age fish that when broiled tasted fresh as rainbow trout caught that day. And then the stories she wanted to believe—about people and animals encased in ice, whose hearts beat and blood flowed, if only for a moment, when they were taken from the ice.

So you could be brought back from the dead, she had thought. It was a memory from her childhood, this place that proved you could be brought back from the dead. People could exist in suspended animation and then come back, almost as they were. She was pondering this when she walked into the lobby of her hotel and saw Gabe. "He looks familiar," she said to herself. And then she recognized him. "What's he doing here?" She was ready to sink into a hot tub and order a glass of wine and a bowl of soup from room service. Suddenly it occurred to her. She'd forgotten their date.

"Oh, my God," she said, walking up to him. "I lost track of the time." She apologized again. "I'm not at all ready." She hoped he'd suggest they forget the whole thing.

He frowned. "I was about to leave," he said. "Would you rather do it another time?"

"Oh, no," she said, though both wished she'd say yes. "I'll only be a minute."

In the elevator she wondered how this could have slipped her mind. As she ripped off her clothes, she thought it was not all like her to forget such a thing. I am not a flaky person, she told herself. I am a person with an excellent memory for details. I have no trouble with origins and insertions, with the names of arteries and veins. She jumped into the hot shower and ended with a cold shower to wake herself up. She dried off, dressed as quickly as she could. "This is terrible, terrible," Zoe said. "This is not like me at all. And he's been so nice to Badger." She pulled on a skirt, boots, a bulky sweater over a silk blouse, creamed lipstick across her lips, dabbed some kind of perfume on, and in ten minutes flat walked out the door.

The Lakeside Restaurant had a view of the lake, frozen over with huge ice floes as if they were dining in Alaska. They got a table by the window. Even though the restaurant was warm, Zoe felt a chill and she kept her layers on. Gabe sat across from her. She looked at him. In high school he had been the square, football type. Now he'd turned solid, like marble. His hairline was slipping back over his head. His face seemed squarer than she recalled. But he had a kind smile and she was grateful for that.

"So," he said, "tell me. What have you been up to for the past twenty years?"

She laughed. "You want the long story or the short story? I don't know. I guess the same thing you've been doing."

"Having marital difficulties?"

"Everything but that." She laughed again. He thought she looked pretty when she laughed. "That's one thing I've avoided." It occurred to her that perhaps she'd avoided it too well. "You're separated?"

He nodded. "You remember Marilyn, don't you?" Zoe remembered a rather pretty, foolish girl who'd always reminded her of a glass of champagne—tall, blond, bubbly, cold. "She left me for a computer software salesman."

Zoe laughed. "Software?"

"I know. I thought she'd prefer hardware." Zoe laughed again and Gabe said she had a nice laugh and should laugh more. "I still can't believe she left me first."

"It's always better to be the one who leaves," Zoe said, trying to recall how often she'd been on the leaving or left end of things.

"It hasn't been easy." His gaze drifted away. "On most weekends, I try to get out of town. Go skiing. Last summer I rented a cottage in Door County. But it gets lonely."

"Yes, I can imagine." Maybe he'll keep talking. She'd read somewhere that people think you are a good conversationalist if you let them talk.

"Anyway I found a place right away near the clinic, so I took it. Sometimes I think I've lived my whole life that way, taking whatever was nearby."

"It's probably time for a change," she said.

The waitress came to take their drink order. Gabe nodded. "What'll it be?"

"A glass of wine."

"Wine. You always did things with great care, with moderation."

"Make it scotch."

"I'm a little nervous. I've hardly been out with a woman who wasn't my wife in fifteen years who isn't a patient." He spoke with a teasing voice.

"I don't believe you."

"No, actually I do go out with women, but I always know them from work and we can talk about Nurse Burlington or someone or other from the hospital. I feel like I have to start from scratch."

"I can talk about Nurse Burlington. She wouldn't let me in when I got here."

"We're lucky she lets anyone in."

"I have to tell you something," Zoe said. "This whole thing with Badger is just awful for me. It's not the best time of my life anyway and now with this, well, it's awful."

"Yes," Gabe said, "I'm sure it is."

"Coming back here," Zoe mumbled, "I'm just not certain I did the right thing."

They were silent for a moment and both felt relieved when their drinks arrived.

"I was surprised when I heard you'd gone to medical school."

"Oh, I'd always wanted to go. It was a struggle. I didn't get any help from home." Outside, ice floes bobbed. A waiter took their order. Zoe ordered Lake Superior whitefish. Gabe asked for trout. "I took crazy jobs. One summer I read books to the comatose."

"Did anyone ever come out of a coma while you were reading to him?"

Zoe laughed again and it made Gabe laugh. Her face was like a different person's when she laughed. "One guy actually did. I was reading him *War and Peace* and he came out of his coma and told me to skip the war chapters."

"I thought you'd be the kind to marry early." He changed the subject abruptly.

She looked out at the lake and thought about Hunt. Probably if he had lived, she'd have been married to him by now. "You thought wrong," she said.

"I'm glad I went to Madison. It was nearby. Didn't cost too much. I got good training."

Zoe was beginning to feel uncomfortably warm. She took off her scarf and sweater. She felt as if she could just strip down. There was nothing that made her feel comfortable here. Between herself and the freezing lake was only this thin layer of glass.

Doctors had never interested her very much as people. She was bored. Robert hadn't bored her. Robert had always made her laugh. He did dumb things like make fun of people or tease her or bring home crazy things like rubber dead rats or see-through guillotines or plastic chopped-off fingers. He had a wild, crazy sense of humor and Zoe loved it and she was never bored. She was not sure she loved him, but she was sure he made her laugh.

There was another moment of silence and Zoe felt how awkward this whole evening had become. Finally, as the waiter brought their entrees, Gabe said gently, "Look, would you like to talk about your brother?"

"No," Zoe said, "I don't want to talk about him." She didn't want to, but it occurred to her that he was the only thing to talk about. What else could they discuss. The day they tore the goalposts down? Some minor high school scandal? There was nothing that was important to her in her whole life except the thing she didn't want to talk about.

"Listen," Gabe said, sounding more serious this time, "let me explain this as simply as I can and see if you can't help me. There is something wrong with your brother that I don't understand. Something that goes beyond the drugs."

Zoe sighed. "Everyone hurt him."

"I want to help him."

"I know that."

Gabe paused for a moment. "If you could just talk about

him. I think in some ways you aren't that different from him, you know."

She grew silent, trying to decide if she had anything she wanted to say, when she heard someone calling her name.

"Oh my god, Zoe." A woman's voice called. "I can't believe it." She saw a rather thin, Italian-looking woman walking her way, her arm looped through a somewhat portly man who looked as if he'd once been very attractive, but now he was bald and round. The woman looked familiar and so did the man, but she couldn't remember their names.

"It's Donna Pico and Emilio Santanelli," Gabe whispered.

Donna had been an acquaintance of Zoe's during high school, but she had been more a friend of Melanie's. Donna had been a trendsetter—the one who got the girls out of their camel-hair coats and into pea jackets. When she changed from Spalding saddle shoes to penny loafers, everyone else changed too. She and Emilio had been a kind of adorable couple, like two teddy bears, all through high school. Now, she'd heard from her mother in a letter, Donna and Emilio had been married and divorced from each other twice. He had a drinking problem and tended to hang out with young women. She had tried to kill herself on more than one occasion. They were trying to work things out.

"Donna." Zoe stood up. "Emilio. My, it's been twelve years."

"At least," Donna said. Emilio kissed her and she smelled his whiskey breath. "Just about everybody's moved away. Rich Einhorn's a big producer in Hollywood. He did *Revenge of the Killer Cabbage* and *Hot Tub Hell.* Big success. Everyone either lives in the East or the West. Only us nuts stayed around here. Right, Emilio?" She jabbed him in the ribs. He was staring at Zoe's breasts.

"That's right." Emilio smiled and Zoe remembered he had once been so handsome. "You should come by the pizzeria. We'll buy you a giant anything you want."

"Oh, sure, the last thing she needs is to come by the pizzeria. We should have a party. Invite the old gang. Have you seen Melanie?"

"Well," Zoe hesitated. "Actually I'm here to see my brother. He's a patient of Gabe's over at Heartland."

"Oh, yeah," Donna said, growing somber now. Zoe wished she hadn't mentioned it. "Yes, Melanie told me."

"So I haven't seen many people."

Gabe looked down at his plate. "But you should," he said suddenly. "We should have a dinner or something for you."

"No, really," Zoe said. "Next trip."

"No," Gabe protested. "We should have a party for you."

"Another time," Zoe replied.

Donna and Emilio seemed uncomfortable. "Sure," Donna said. "I can see it must be difficult for you. But look, come by for pizza or dinner or call me or whatever. I'd love to see you."

"Yes," Zoe said, knowing she wouldn't.

After they left, Gabe and Zoe sat in silence for a moment. "They were just trying to be nice," Gabe said.

"I know that." Zoe felt annoyed and so did Gabe. She didn't need someone being accusatory with her. And she could tell he found her unnecessarily rude.

Gabe wondered if there wasn't some way to get through to her that he could not think of. "Maybe we really should talk about Badger," Gabe said.

"Is this why you asked me out? To interview me?"

He shook his head. "I have an idea that you'll feel better if you talk about him."

"I'm not your patient."

There was something about her he didn't like. She was like a person in a capsule. He thought there might be something lovely about her. She might even have that kindness that he felt with her brother, but he couldn't seem to reach it. In high school she was beautiful and eccentric. She could have had anyone, but she'd chosen Hunt, almost defiantly, he thought.

It surprised Gabe to think of all the years that had passed, all the changes that had occurred in people they knew. The ones who turned out well, the ones who didn't do so well. Like Donna and Emilio. How everyone had thought they'd be happy. And Marilyn and himself. Now he was sitting here with Zoe, someone he hadn't cared for much in high school and wasn't sure he liked very much now. Yet somehow he sensed they were both survivors. They had this much in common.

Time in Brewerton had frozen for Gabe in a way that it had not frozen for Zoe. He still recognized people. He had had no sense of its passing, but now with Zoe sitting across from him, he did. She wasn't the same person she had been when she was sixteen. She was wilder then, more exotic. Intriguing. Now she seemed broken to him and hardened, like a woman of the world.

She wasn't making him feel comfortable this evening. She wanted him to do all the work. He knew she thought she was doing him a favor by joining him for dinner. This enraged him. He didn't want anyone doing him favors.

"I think we should talk about his case a little," Gabe said after a few moments.

"Look," Zoe said, "I love my brother. Maybe I love him more than I even know myself. If I could help him, I would. But that's not why I agreed to have dinner with you."

"But the more I understand, the more I can help him."

"I don't see what use I can be."

"This is what he's done to himself." He began to talk, naming drugs as if this were a chemistry class and not a fish restaurant. Breaking down for her the chemical compositions of amphetamines, antihistamines, atropine, ayahuasca, barbiturates, derivatives of malonylurea such as Amytal, Veronal, Seconal, Luminal, phenobarbs, moving into "ludes," tranquilizers, Valium, LSD, "shrooms," into the exotic morphine and opium, into weed and things you stick in your veins and up your nose.

He talked to her about combinations and mixings and flashbacks and psychotic seizures, while Zoe looked out at the lake.

Chemistry wasn't her best subject. She had trouble grasping how one thing bonded with another, how two chemicals, innocuous in themselves, turned into something lethal when combined. The lake was something she knew quite well, though. It was something she understood. She knew it better than any other lake in the world.

When Badger and Zoe were little, they went down to that lake together and took off their clothes and swam. They were great swimmers and they knew that lake as well as they knew anything in the world. And one day they went down to the lake at night and they swam. They'd gone into the water as children, but suddenly there in the water they both felt the water splashing cold between their thighs and they watched Zoe's breasts rise in the moonlight. They had gone into the water as children and come out as grown-ups and they never went into the lake naked together again.

But then she stopped thinking about Badger. Her mind wandered to another, more pleasant, more compelling memory. She tried to listen to Gabe, but it was useless. She was amazed at how powerfully it all came back. Some part of her that had lain dormant for so long kept coming to her in her own drug flashbacks, coming as if no time had transpired, as if nothing had happened, no loss had occurred, no scar had built up.

She saw his face. Those clear dark eyes, his dark skin. She could feel his skin against her skin, his touch to her touch. It was as if she'd been asleep all these years. It could be a summer night now when they'd gone down to the lake and stripped off their clothes, rushing into the still icy water. Even in August the water had stayed cold. How he would come and warm her with his body, rub his hands over her breasts, between her thighs. No man had ever touched her in these ways before or since. It was as if her life would always be linked to his for this and this alone.

She couldn't keep her mind from going back to those times. She was so young and he had found a million ways of touching her. Every time they were together it was different, but he was always gentle, never cruel. She thought about the child they would have had. It would have been twelve years old. But she had not been able to let the child live when Hunt had not lived. She thought how much she would have loved that child, and her body ached for the child she would have loved. Once Badger found a beach ball that contained Hunt's breath. He had blown it up one summer. Zoe had kept that beach ball for years, until all the air ran out on its own. Now she wished she'd kept the child.

She should never have come back. She should get up and walk out of the restaurant. Take her clothes off and jump in the lake, into the icy water. That would surprise Emilio and Donna Santanelli. Instead she excused herself. "I'll be right back," she said to Gabe. "I'm not feeling very well. I'll be right back."

Gabe got up to go with her, but with her arm she pushed him down. "Let me go with you," he said.

"No, please. I'll be right back."

In the ladies' room, Zoe splashed cold water on her face. The bathroom was all perfumed and as she peed, the black woman attendant sprayed deodorant. The black woman handed Zoe a towel. The bathroom was completely antiseptic, like a hospital. "Are you all right?" the attendant said. "Should I get the person you are with?" Zoe shook her head. She said it was all right. She just wasn't feeling well for a moment. She saw the pay phone in the ladies' room. Instead of getting Gabe, she made a phone call. "Hello," Zoe said "I don't know if you remember me but I'm the woman from the train."

"I remember you," he said.

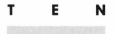
Derek kept a collection of gallstones in small vials which he showed Zoe when she arrived. It was a strange thing for someone to collect, even for a biologist, but he was proud of the collection and she admired them.

Gabe hadn't argued when Zoe said she wasn't feeling well and wanted to go home right after dessert. In fact she could tell he was glad to get rid of her. He'd dropped her off and Derek had arrived at her hotel shortly thereafter. She felt mysterious, as if she were suddenly leading a life of intrigues—strangers on trains, clandestine meetings. She anticipated the exchange of classified information.

Derek still looked good, especially in the dim light of his apartment. Everything about him seemed dark. That was what she wanted. She wanted everything to be dark. She'd have preferred to be back on the train. She wanted to recapture the train.

When Derek rolled a joint, Zoe didn't refuse. They took two puffs of the joint.

"So," he said, "what are you doing in this neck of the woods?"

"I came home to visit my brother," she said. Derek took a puff. "He's at Heartland, do you know it?"

"Sure, it's a loony bin. Is your brother crazy?"

Zoe took another toke and shrugged. "No, he's not crazy. He's just chosen not to speak, for political reasons."

"Uh-huh," Derek leaned over and kissed her again. "I suppose he thinks he's being held against his will."

"I haven't asked him."

He put his mouth back on hers. He kissed her gently, small

pecks. She held on to him tighter. Derek kissed her again. "Come on, let's go to bed."

It seemed abrupt, but since Zoe had already admired the gallstone collection and since they were already high, there didn't seem much else left to do. The house was dark and Zoe didn't notice much. She saw the mattress on the floor, the wilted plants by the side of the bed, the newspapers strewn everywhere. She glanced in the room. "I don't know," she said.

"What don't you know?"

"I don't know if I can stay here. There's something about this place, nothing personal, but I just don't know."

Derek had his hand on the back of her neck and massaged it. "What do you mean you don't know? What do you want?"

"I want to go somewhere else."

Derek sighed, leaning against the doorframe. "Where do you want to go? I suppose you want to go and see your brother, have a few drinks with him, shoot the breeze."

"No," Zoe said slowly, "that's not what I had in mind. I want to go somewhere else." It wasn't until she said it that she knew where she wanted to go.

In the arctic wind that blew off the lake, Zoe and Derek drove around the outskirts of Brewerton. They drove on a vacant stretch of highway and Derek kept saying, "Where are you taking me?" but finally Zoe said, "Here, turn in here."

"We're going to a motel?" Derek asked. "What do we need to go to a motel for?"

"I'll pay for the room," Zoe said, "I want to stay in this motel tonight."

"You really are a crazy woman," Derek said.

The Home on the Road hadn't changed much. The kidney-bean-shaped pool had the same rim of green algae around it. But now it was so dirty it didn't freeze. Steam rose from it like ghosts. The plastic deer statues still lined the front. The pink plastic lawn chairs bent in the same places as if the same people sat in them. The office was still yellow, the carpeting still blue, the walls green, the chairs still red. A small dried Christmas tree, resting in a pile of its own needles, most of its lights burned out, sat in a corner of the room, which smelled of Airwick and Martin's oily skin. He had bought the motel when Naomi went south and had done little to improve its appearance, and Zoe was relieved to find the night clerk on duty when they arrived.

She stared into the old yellow office. Before Badger was born and before her father came home from the war, Zoe used to sit in the yellow plaid office of the motel her grandmother owned and listen to her mother's voice. It came to her eight times a day. Naomi would sit, rocking back and forth, her large shadow looming against the wall, listening to the Braves or to Amos 'n' Andy, in that yellow office. Eight times a day Zoe would cease her endless restless activity and sit quietly among the alchemy jars, the objects for predicting the future, and the books with pictures of extraterrestrial life.

June's voice had a sweet and wet sound when it came over the radio. It was sultry and seemed to be beckoning as Zoe listened. Sometimes salesmen, dropping off their keys as they checked out, ready to go back to their lonely road, would pause and look longingly. Eight times a day during the war June did spot ads for Mrs. Peabody's freckle cream. June would say how easy it was to make those unsightly splotches disappear. She'd give women tips on beauty. How they should stay out of the sun. How they should put tape on their foreheads during the day or while their men were away at the war, to keep their faces from wrinkling.

War widows would write to June and say how she had given them the strength to go on. Sometimes June would read these letters on the air. They were from women whose husbands had been overseas for two or three years and they'd tell June how every night they put the masking tape on their brows, the cream on their faces because they did not want their men when they returned to think that time had passed at all.

In those years during the war when she was growing up, Zoe shaped her days around the times when her mother would come on the air and soothe her. And later, when Naomi installed radios in all fifty-three rooms of the Home on the Road, Zoe wandered from room to room trying to locate her mother's voice. But what Zoe remembered most, now, as she stood once again in this office where she hadn't been in so many years, was how many times she had come to steal the key.

The night man had seen too many nights and not enough people. His fingernails were chewed to the quick. When he ran his hand through his hair, dandruff fell to his shoulders like snow.

"What is this sleazeball joint you've brought me to?" Derek asked.

Zoe thought how easily she could reach over and just flip the key off its hook—a gesture she'd made hundreds of times. If she knew how to do anything in the world, she knew how to slip into this motel. But she didn't do it. She decided to check in in a respectable way, which was something she'd never done before. She had not been back since she was sixteen years old—since the night her father found her.

"Is Room 14 available?" Zoe asked. The nightman looked at her apathetically. He's seen all kinds. This one just wanted to hang out on memory lane. He knew her type right away. The desperate, lonely crowd. These weren't honeymooners on their way somewhere else. These two would never see each other again.

"I've got some nicer rooms, lady. That one's near the boiler."

Zoe nodded. "That's fine."

When they got into the room, Derek reached for the light, but Zoe put her hand over his. She knew where the switch was. She knew just where the bed was. She knew where he was. It was all familiar to her. There was nothing in this place she did not know. The smell of mildew, the sound of the boiler, the feel of boiler steam. It was in this room that her father had struck her across the face and for a moment when she walked in, she thought she could still hear its slap. This room was a shrine to her and she felt Hunt's presence coming out of the walls, the carpets, the bed. She could walk into this room anywhere at any time and it would all be known.

Slowly his hands fumbled with her sweater, her skirt, her layers and layers, peeling them off, removing one, then the next, the next. Until there was nothing left to remove and slowly she removed what he had to remove and when there was nothing left to take off, they got into bed.

It was not only her clothes he peeled away. It was her skin, all the layers she had built up all the years. She felt as if the clock were ticking backward at the side of the bed, as if the Magic Fingers they had just put a quarter in were a ship rocking them back to where they'd been. He reached into her and she felt as if the part of her that had stopped loving would love again. She felt Hunt right there with her. He had been in this dank room all along.

Once they were in bed, Zoe knew what this meeting was about. This man's touch will remove the old touch. It was a kind of voodoo. The removal of a curse. She imagined that someday someone would reach all the way inside and turn her around, the way faith healers could. But for now this would do.

E L E V E N

Traffic was one-way down Main Street in Brewerton and Main Street was nothing Zoe remembered at all. The Jack-O'-Lantern Candy store was gone. So were Leo's Delicatessen and Larsen's Stationery Store and Clothes for Toads where June used to take Zoe for her dresses. Heidi's Coffee Shop and Sam, the Tailor. All these stores were gone. What had replaced them on the one-way street she drove down were small shopping centers—a Burger King, a McDonald's featuring Lake Michigan whitefish sticks; a J. C. Penney had replaced the old Woolworth's. She could be driving down any street, Zoe thought. But this wasn't a street she knew.

She recalled a town where the barren ravines rolled like the backs of sleeping elephants, where the copper-based bluffs after a heavy rain looked like emerald mountains. She recalled rough woods, Indian trails, trees bent back to mark the trails, colored rocks, a turquoise sky.

There was the Brewerton of winter and the other of summer, the Brewerton of Indian summer, of a brief, transitional spring. She recalled a world of glazed ice where you sucked on icicles like teats, where your breath preceded you for months at a time. Or summer where the damp heat made you slow as a snail and everything seemed to fester. It was a world of extremes—of ice monsters and rotting plums, of trees arched with snow and purple swallowtails.

But her neighborhood had hardly changed. It amazed Zoe as she drove through the small subdivision called Deer Run how they were all still there. The Isaacsons whose heart was broken by their lesbian daughter, Michele, who'd actually bought a house with her lover on the outskirts of town. The Travinos who had spent years drinking behind locked doors and whose son, Mark, who'd gone to school with Zoe, had somehow managed to turn out all right. As had Mr. Potter, the former halfback for the Packers who had ignored his wife for forty years and then stumbled through the neighborhood, lost, when she suddenly died.

The Carpenters still lived across the street, with the same peach-colored curtains always drawn, only now Judd, who had kept birds of prey in small cages out back, was dead of Hodgkin's disease. June had told Zoe how Mrs. Carpenter had come across the street the day after Judd died and said, "Well, at least I can get rid of those damn birds." June had thought Mrs. Carpenter remarkably composed for saying that. Then the next night she woke to the tremor of the flapping of wings and in the moonlight she saw Mrs. Carpenter letting hawks and ospreys fly off into the night, her arms lifting up empty into the sky.

Now Mrs. Carpenter sat having coffee in June's kitchen as Zoe arrived. She had her hair twirled in little pincurls and blue rings of smoke engulfed her like halos. Mrs. Carpenter was a large, dark woman built like a packhorse, and it was difficult to imagine her releasing birds of prey into the night. June sat with Mrs. Carpenter, coffee cup tilted in her hand, whispering as they always had about Cal's inexorable neglect or Badger's impenetrable silence, about Zoe's strange departures in the night, or Mrs. Margolis' husband, and it occurred to Zoe that she could be walking into any day in her life.

"So," Mrs. Carpenter said, assessing Zoe without much pleasure, "you've grown up and come home."

"Yes," Zoe said, "here I am."

"You look like a real person," Mrs. Carpenter said, getting up to leave.

"Don't leave on my account," Zoe said.

"Oh, you girls probably want to be alone," Mrs. Carpenter said.

"We've got plenty of time to catch up," June said, and Zoe knew she always was nervous about being alone with her.

But Mrs. Carpenter, this now childless woman, rose and Zoe felt as if the referee were leaving the ring. Against her better judgment, Zoe had agreed to come home. She didn't want to, but when June asked her she couldn't think of a way to say no.

The house had hardly changed. It was the same house Zoe and Cal had put a down payment on when they married, and June had stayed in it all these years. What had made June feel married was less the man in her bed than the mortgage on her house. June had wanted something stable, and once she'd moved from the motel to the house she'd stayed put. Zoe thought if a tornado passed through, June wouldn't budge.

But Zoe found she couldn't stay here. In fact, she hadn't lived in the house since the year before Badger was born, when she was five, and she'd packed up her things and moved out. She'd packed her flannel nightgowns and her plastic combs, her panda bear and collection of garden spiders. She'd packed her pleated skirts and blouses, her Carter's 14 underwear, her doll's dresses, and her anthill, and she'd moved it all, box by box, into the apartment over the garage where Naomi lived. She moved in there one day when she was five years old, and she never left.

And now as she stood back in the center of her mother's life, Zoe remembered why she had left. Something was wrong with the house. It was hard to put your finger on. It was a nice house with lots of light. It had a driveway and a lawn and furniture, but it had never really been a place where Zoe wanted to live. The light seemed to come in at the wrong angle—either too subdued or too harsh, never soft and warm, not friendly sunlight. And then there were June's belongings—the dark mahogany furniture, the pale green walls, the plaid sofa and chairs.

What it reminded Zoe of, and what had always been at the back of June's mind, though she'd never been able to articulate it, was the motel. June had tried to change this over the years. She'd bought more solid chairs, an antique sideboard of great

value, more elaborate, sturdy pieces of furniture, so that one day
Naomi said to Zoe when she was little, "Your mother thinks she
can do with her house what she cannot do with her heart."

June tried to make it special and unique. She tried to make
it sturdy and safe. She had fireproof carpeting installed and the
windows sealed shut. A dustproof climate-control system was put
in. Then there was a burglar system, each room with a red panic
button gleaming over your head in the night. When the bomb
drops, Badger used to say, push the panic button.

She had made the house safe and impenetrable. No one
would break in. No one would hurt them. No one would invade
or injure. June had made a fortress of her home. And now Zoe
felt she could hardly breathe. "So," June said, "I made us some
sandwiches—salami and swiss on rye. How's that sound?"

Zoe didn't eat salami or processed meat, but she didn't
know what to say. June put the sandwich down in front of her
and watched Zoe pull out the salami. "My daughter, the health
food freak."

"You know I don't eat this stuff, Mom."

"What's a few chemicals?"

"They put hooves, noses, and lower intestines in as well."
June covered her ears.

"How was your date last night?" June said, taking a sip of
coffee.

Zoe wondered how her mother knew about her time with
Derek. Had Marvin seen them go in? Did he have spies? "My
date?"

"Didn't you have dinner with Gabe?"

"Oh yes, dinner with Gabe."

"Well, how'd it go?"

"We had dinner, we talked a little, I got home early."

"You look tired. You don't look like you slept much."

Zoe chewed slowly on what had become a cheese sandwich.
"I've got a lot on my mind."

"Why don't you tell me about it? I haven't seen you in so

long. I don't know who your friends are, what you like to do for fun." June reached across the table and touched Zoe's arm, then she felt Zoe tighten her hands around the sandwich and pull away.

"I've just been studying for exams. I'm thinking about going into dermatology."

"Well, given all the allergies in this family, I think that's a good idea. You know," June ran her hand along her cheek. "I hardly get my rashes anymore. Once in a while, if I'm tired or upset, but hardly ever."

Zoe was glad her mother had changed the subject to herself. "What gets you upset, Mom?"

June laughed. "Oh god, what more could happen to me?" She'd been heating soup on the stove and she poured two bowls. "But what about you?" June tapped her polished nails on the table. June was always good at doing small things—writing thank-you notes, arranging flowers, polishing her nails. Zoe had no patience for this. True love, immortality, curing cancer. These were her goals.

"Just give me the headlines. What about Robert?"

"What about Sam?"

June blushed and looked away. "You know Sam has always been a friend. There was only one for me . . ."

"Who was that?"

"Zoe, you know who that was. You know."

Zoe took her plate and bowl to the sink. She wanted to make a cup of cocoa and she opened the cabinets. When she was little she'd take out the milk, the spoon, saucepan, the cocoa and line them all up. Then she'd make an enormous mess, splattering milk on the floor. June loved to watch her. She'd sit and watch Zoe's tiny hands stirring, splattering. It was always that way with Zoe. She'd begin to do something neatly and end up making a mess. Then she'd get angry with herself because she didn't do it right.

Zoe felt her mother's eyes on her. When she was little, her

mother always let her do things, but she'd always stare at her. It was as if she'd read a book that told you to let children do things for themselves, but she never really could. Now in her apartment in Boston, if she was cooking a meal or ironing a shirt, Zoe sometimes felt another presence, lurking, watching her every move.

June dumped her coffee cup into the sink. "I think it's ridiculous, staying in a hotel. I want you to come here and be with me."

"I like it where I am."

"It's not normal," June rinsed a dish, annoyed.

"I'm used to being on my own, Mom. It's better that way." Zoe stood at the window, peering out. She saw Mrs. Carpenter across the street, her peach curtain pulled back, peering back at her.

"Who cares what you're used to? You should stay with me. I want you to come home."

"Mom, please, I'm happy where I am."

Zoe couldn't stay with her mother. If she did, she'd slip too easily into June's robes, into her housecoats and slippers, into her bulky sweaters. Everything that was her mother's fit her and Zoe was afraid of slipping too easily into her mother's life. Into the old rooms and cozy armchairs, into the late-night hot chocolates laced with brandy in front of the Duraflame fire. She was afraid that they'd start by trading shirts and earrings. And then end up trading confidences and secrets. It was the secrets Zoe hoarded. She knew that if they started, they wouldn't stop. And at least one secret was not for the trading.

T W E L V E

The year when June gave up on Cal, Sam Pollack arrived. He arrived from a city in the East, weighted down with gifts from his travels, with his spice clock and his Himalayan dog, his earbobs from the heart of Africa and voodoo dolls from the West Indies, his Chinese silks that Naomi would make into incredible kimonos and saris for herself. He arrived with his Tibetan blue point cat which remained his constant companion, his ancient maps of the early explorers and his tales of journeys into the Khyber Pass, through the Strait of Magellan, the alleyways of Bourbon Street.

He filled the Coleman family with the desire to go elsewhere. He made it so that Naomi, who had hardly given her ancestral home a moment's thought in fifty years, suddenly longed to return, and June began to plot extensive, impossible journeys up the Amazon and across Siberia she'd never take. He made it so that Badger would fall in love with tiny, exotic objects that he'd want to carve and mold out of wood and gold and Zoe at a later point in her life would embark upon a journey which she'd never want to stop and would not have, had not tragedy brought her home.

It was also the year when June gave up on Cal. When she stopped buying the black underwear that she'd wear beneath her dress to his studio where she'd go night after night to seduce him. Ever since he'd come back from the war, as she'd done the night she conceived Badger, she'd dressed in black underwear and a red silk dress and slipped out the door into the night, leaving Naomi at home for a while with her children, and she'd sneak to the darkroom. She'd take off her coat and her dress and for an hour pull Cal away from his drying prints that he claimed revealed the secrets of the universe. They'd touch and claw at each other and drive each other wild, until each was satisfied and spent, but it didn't matter. She never felt close to him. Nothing they did together in that chemical darkness ever made her feel close to him again.

She felt more like a distraction—like a phone call or the mailman. An interruption in the course of his work. She'd try to talk to him, make plans, but he would not be diverted from his single-minded task. It would be his loss and eventually Cal would know it. It would gnaw at him and eat away at him for the rest of his life until it finally destroyed him, but he would not be diverted. He was lost and she would not find him again.

June had it in her heart that if she could just get him out of his studio, everything would be fine. If she could just get him back into the house, into their bed, into her normal arms at daybreak, they'd return to the life they had lost when he went away. But it was impossible. He'd come home to dinner, then go back to work. He'd stumble into bed after midnight and be gone before the morning light. In bed, their bodies never touched. It was only in her nightly visits to his studio that he would pause to be with her.

She began to feel like a whore. She felt as if her own husband paid to have her. And she began to despise him and herself for it. So that year, just before Sam Pollack arrived, June stopped going to the darkroom. She stopped going for a night, then a week, certain he would notice and come for her. It did not occur to her that she was stopping forever. Rather she thought that the day when he came home searching for her, she would begin again.

While she stopped her visits, she paced. She folded her hands around her body and rocked back and forth. Her temper flared and at night her body could find no rest. She picked at the imperfections in her face, her skin. She plucked hair that didn't need plucking. She did her nails dozens of times and cleaned every drawer in the house until every piece of underwear was folded, every sock looped inside its mate.

Naomi watched. Naomi always knew where June went each evening when she'd say, "Mom, could you watch the kids for me?" She could tell during the day when June would get the misty look in her eyes and drop things in the kitchen. When she'd grow nervous and a little weary and it was clear she'd be putting on the black underwear beneath the red silk dress and heading out the door. Naomi had watched June do this for days and months. And then she watched her stop.

Naomi was surprised at her own daughter. She couldn't believe the surge of willpower June showed when she ceased her conjugal visits to the prison of work Cal had constructed around himself. Naomi was certain that at any moment, at any day, she'd put on the silk dress and head out the door into the night. But it never happened again.

June never went back to the studio. Instead, she took out the old stretchers and bits of cloth and cotton batting and began to quilt again. This time, she determined, she'd make the one quilt she hadn't made while he was away at the war. A quilt for their room, and she'd fill it with the image of the Dells, of Indians, of the parks where they'd kissed, and lakes where they'd walked, of dreams they had shared. She worked feverishly in her basement workroom, cutting cloth, stuffing cotton, hunched over. She'd hoped to finish it in late winter, but it was early spring when she was done with the thick quilt, and she laid it across the bed anyway. The room shimmered with the boat rides they'd taken, the jewels they'd exchanged, the coins they'd wished on in fountains. It was redolent with the flowers they'd picked, with the scent of their bodies after they'd made love.

Cal came home the night June finished the quilt and crawled into bed. For a moment she'd felt his body quivering at her side, as if he were waking from a long sleep. Then he mumbled to her that it was a hot night. He said it was the hottest night he could ever recall. His body was wet, his breathing short as he reached across the bed, tossing the quilt onto the floor. He said he'd suffocate under that thing.

Then June knew it was done. She knew that somehow she'd given up an addiction, the way a person who quit smoking one day forgets about cigarettes as if they'd never had anything to do with him. June woke in the morning and knew it had left her, her desire for him, and that she'd never even want to go to the studio again. Perhaps there would be moments, faint tremors, but something within her was gone.

That was the day when Sam Pollack called. June was sitting in the living room when the phone rang. She was always excited when it rang and always disappointed when she answered. She held on to a hope, a chance that it might be a surprise, that something might happen, that her life would suddenly change. But it was never someone telling her she'd won a prize she hadn't applied for. It was never a secret admirer. Everything in the world disappointed June just a little and this day she imagined would be no exception. She picked up the phone without hope or desire, and heard a strange man's voice ask if this was the home of Cal Coleman, the photographer.

Sam Pollack arrived that evening with packages tucked under his arm. He slapped Cal on the back and gave June a bouquet of flowers. He'd brought a nurse doll for Zoe with a stethoscope. Then he hugged her and said, "I thought you'd be a little girl." He handed Badger a long, cylindrical object which Badger tore quickly from the box. Badger was perplexed by the cylinder and didn't know which way to turn it. He looked in through both sides and saw nothing. But Sam explained to him that it was a telescope and that at night he'd take Badger outside and show him the sky.

He was a large man with square shoulders and limbs that seemed always to move in stride as he walked smoothly through the house, landing gently on the balls of his feet. He was so graceful it seemed as if he had no footsteps, and yet he moved like a locomotive, gaining momentum as he handed out gifts. He had a wide face with evenly set gray eyes and a husky laugh, as if he was always enjoying some private joke, and not the joke at hand.

Everything about him seemed balanced. In fact he was balanced. Sam Pollack had been working in Washington since the war with the Bureau of Weights and Measures. He was a man with a good sense of proportion.

Sam gave Cal his gift, which he opened hesitantly, and inside Cal found a photograph of himself that Sam had taken. He saw himself in uniform with a gun slung over his shoulders, his camera around his neck. Everyone bent over the picture and a kind of quiet entered the room. "Oh," June muttered, "what a lovely picture."

And everyone looked and said, "Oh, it is a lovely picture."

But it was Badger who said, "Who's that?"

Sam laughed nervously. "Why, it's your father during the war."

It was a picture of a strong young man with a glint in his eye. No one in the room could believe it was Cal just five years before. But Sam Pollack wasn't stupid. He'd been around. He was also a man with a sixth sense about things. He had stirred something up by bringing in this picture. He knew there was a great sadness that hung in the air. He looked around him and he looked at June. He wondered why Cal had never talked about her during those dark nights when they slept in the barracks or on those flights when Sam held Cal upside down by his heels.

As they walked into the living room, Sam took a good look at June. She wasn't at all what he'd expected, not what he'd thought he'd find. Her dark auburn hair lay thick on her back and her green eyes seemed misty to him. There was something ingratiating, yet distant about her at the same time. Something transient as well. She was a little too fluttery, a bit too shrill, yet obsequious as if she was used to serving others. Sam Pollack had done a great deal of traveling and he thought how June had the sad nervosity of a woman who worked in a motel.

But there was something else about her and he didn't miss it as she handed him pretzels and lemonade. He watched her rush through the room straightening magazines, making room for a bowl of nuts. He decided there was something about her which was incredibly beautiful and which had never quite been recognized.

Zoe sat on the floor with Badger, watching all of this, putting the stethoscope to Badger's heart, trying to find its beat. "So," Cal said, "it's been a long time."

Sam nodded, smiling. "Yes, a long time. So how's the photography?"

Cal smiled back and answered in a perfunctory way while trying to think of all the ways he wanted to take Sam's picture. He could photograph him from the side, he thought, looking at his profile. Or perhaps just off dead center on his face. He aimed his eyes at Sam Pollack, his friend from the war. As they talked about the brewery business where Sam had come to work, Cal kept his sights on his friend. He wanted to capture his old buddy's expression in just the right light and he found it at the moment when Sam was speaking with June about some mundane thing that didn't interest Cal. All that Cal noticed was that when Sam said something to make June laugh, Sam appeared as though he were surrounded in amber light.

Later that evening, Sam, Badger, and Zoe went outside. Sam showed Badger what to do and he fumbled, turning the focus until he landed on a star. It was fuzzy. As he adjusted it, it became less fuzzy, but it wasn't at all what he'd expected. He thought he'd be able to see fire coming from the center and he thought he'd see explosions of light. Instead he just saw stars, the same thing he saw every night without a telescope, only bigger.

Badger grew bored quickly and handed the telescope over to Zoe. Then Sam showed her what to do. He turned his hand gently over the focus. Moving the telescope across the sky, he helped her find the Dippers, the Seven Sisters, Orion. Then Zoe found a star that caught her eye. It was large and red and pulsated overhead. She focused and, whereas Badger had grown bored, Zoe was fascinated.

She moved the telescope from star to star. Badger ran around the yard and even Sam Pollack, who had great patience, wandered slowly with his drink over to the wall of the patio and sat down. What to Badger had been little fuzzy dots of small interest in the dark sky to Zoe were possibilities. They were the things beyond her reach. While Badger rolled in the grass and Sam Pollack sipped his drink contemplatively on the garden wall, Zoe stared up at the sky and fell in love with distance. From then on she would always want things that were far away from her, not near. She'd always want travel, wide open spaces, love from afar.

Sam Pollack had come to Brewerton to manage the Ferry-Hyde Brewery. He had been hired, in fact, by Walter Hyde, the idiotic father of Zoe's best friend, Melanie. Sam was looking for a change. He'd called Cal a few months before and told him he was restless and was thinking about moving back to the Midwest. Cal told him it was a good idea to work in the beer industry and he gave Sam the names of people he knew.

Sam had been with the Bureau of Weights and Measures since the war. It was a good civil service job. When Zoe finally sat down on the garden wall beside him, Sam told her that in the place where he worked before coming to Brewerton there was a large vault where the temperature was carefully controlled. He told her that inside that vault there were objects made of lead which measured exactly a yard or weighed exactly an ounce. For each measurement there was a lead equivalent. He told her that part of his job was to make certain no variable changed in the vault because then a foot would no longer equal a foot, or a pound equal a pound.

When he spoke, Sam Pollack gestured with his hands.

When he talked of an inch, he made a little inch with his fingers, and when he spoke of a ton he held his hands heavily in front of him. He was in the middle of explaining all this about the vault when June came outside. She had wrapped a blue sweater around her shoulders and she stood for a moment on the patio, watching Zoe with Sam.

"You've got to get to bed now, young lady," June said to Zoe, both of them wondering why she'd spoken like that. She'd never said such a thing to Zoe before. She always said something like, "So honey, how about bed?" But neither of them questioned it as Zoe said goodnight, slipping away.

June settled herself on to the wall and yawned, discreetly covering her mouth with her hand. "Cal wants to show you some of his pictures, Sam, but I'm going to bed. Listen, there's no reason for you to rush back to that place where you're living. Why don't you sleep here tonight? I'll make up the guest room." And Sam didn't hesitate; he was glad to stay the night.

June left Sam alone with Cal in the den and went upstairs to make up Zoe's old room for Sam. She put clean sheets on the bed and laid out towels for him. She got out a pair of Cal's blue pajamas and a fresh toothbrush she'd kept for years, in anticipation of a guest. She couldn't help but think how long it had been since she'd laid out things for a man.

Then she made a decision. She'd give Cal one more chance. She went into their room to prepare herself for him. She wouldn't go to him. She'd never go to him again. But she'd give him this last opportunity to come to her. She put on a soft pink gown and gently removed the makeup from her eyelids. She combed out her hair and put on perfume. Then she turned off the light so that only the soft blue light of the moon poured into the bedroom and she waited.

June had never consciously waited for Cal before but tonight she did. She lay there on the bed, a feeling pulsing inside of her, growing as if she were expecting a child. She felt she'd burst. She thought how it had been when she'd first met him, how crazy he'd been for her. How he hadn't kept his hands from her breasts. She cupped her breasts with her hands at the thought of it.

And then he'd gone off to war and she'd waited for him to come home. She'd taken care of Zoe and her mother and she'd waited. Then when he came back, he was different and strange and she'd waited for him to get better. And then when he started getting better, she'd waited for him to notice her again. And then from time to time, when he'd noticed her, she'd waited for him to disappoint her again, and he always had.

As she lay in bed, she could hear the voices of men coming from the living room. She heard laughter and wondered what it was that enabled Cal to give to this stranger what he could not give to her. In her mind, she willed him to come upstairs. She said to herself that now he'll stop talking. Now he'll come to her. She saw the clock glowing in the dark, the minutes ticking by. Time meant nothing. Everything seemed endless.

June felt as if she were falling into some dark hole and there wasn't anything she could grab to break her fall. When she was a little girl, there had been in the woods behind the motel a large sinkhole that had come out of nowhere and June used to go and stand by that hole, thinking about the filth and the stench and dreading the thought of tumbling in. But still she'd go and stand there, peering down.

Now as she lay in bed, drifting in and out of sleep, June felt as if she were standing at the edge of that same place, as if the bottom of the bed could suddenly give way. She had to catch herself. Break her fall. She had to keep herself from slipping down. She just had to lie there, like a person spending a night bivouacked into a mountain face.

She didn't know how long she waited for him that night, but she was patient. She was as patient as she'd ever been. But the moment he got into bed, her patience ended. Cal crawled in beside her, yawning, his breath sour with beer, and June snuggled close to him. She ran her hand up and down his chest, along his crotch. "I want you," she said to him, "I don't remember when we last made love."

"I'm tired," he groaned. "Not tonight. Tomorrow." But June hadn't told Cal that there would be no tomorrow. This was as far as they went.

"I'm going to leave you if we don't make love tonight," she spoke directly, methodically with no hesitation in her voice.

He threw back the covers. "For Christ's sake, what's the matter? I'm exhausted."

Then June rose out of bed. She took her pillow and wrapped her robe around her. Cal reached up and said, "June, come back, come to bed." But she went into the hall in the direction of Badger's room. She picked up the sleeping child and clasped him to her. Then she ran with him outside and up the stairs into the apartment above the garage where Naomi and Zoe slept.

As she rushed down the corridor past Zoe's old room, Sam Pollack sat up in bed. He sat in the cool sheets June had fixed for him, naked, the blue pajamas lying at the side of the bed. He was aware of the rush of wind, of the shadow as it passed in front of his door. He heard the footsteps, the rustling of cloth. It was a night that would make his breath stop. It was the night when he knew what he wanted.

Sam Pollack didn't live in the best part of town and it was with some trepidation that Zoe started going there in the first place. He lived off to the west, away from the lake, in the section called Industry Park, or affectionately referred to as Brewery Lane. It was on the edge of the breweries so he only had a short walk to work, but it was a long walk for Zoe before and after school.

As a child, Zoe had been warned of the dangers of the part of town called Brewery Lane. It was a tough part of town and the workers leaving the bars after a few beers were best to be avoided. And there was a smell she didn't like, something in the air that seemed foul and wrong to her. It didn't surprise Zoe, years later, when she learned of the chemicals that the Ferry-Hyde Brewery had buried in the ground or released into the air. And even now as she walked in the direction of where Sam Pollack lived, the air bothered her. It was rotten as if something large and hideous had died there. At times it felt as if it were going into her very skin.

The house was an old rooming house with white lace curtains in all the windows. It had a front porch that was somewhat battered with a broken railing and the entire house was in need of a paint job. In general it was a dreary place. Zoe was sad that a man as bright as Sam should live in a such a sad home, and she decided that when they went off to be together they'd move into something cheerier, a white house with red shutters, a rose garden, a picket fence.

Zoe was afraid Sam might find her and sometimes she tested it. She stood away from under the trees and waited until he looked out. But when he did, he didn't seem able to see her. She was in the dark. But then she wanted him to find her. She knew that. She thought perhaps if he found her, he'd ask her to come live with him right there in the boarding house. She wondered what it would be like to be with him in the boarding house. She'd lived above the garage for so long she couldn't imagine living anywhere else.

Zoe was there in the evening after her piano lesson or marching band practice. She was learning to play as many musical instruments as she could. She was learning the fiddle and the clarinet. She thought she'd learn a song and serenade him. That was how she'd let him know that she went and stood beneath his window in the evening. She planned it all carefully.

Naomi thought Zoe was acting oddly. She dropped things from the table. She didn't seem to focus. If you asked her a question, she'd start to answer, then forget what you'd asked. At night she'd sit for hours, staring at the street light outside. She was dreamy and odd, like one suffering from a lapse of memory. Naomi thought something was wrong. It wasn't the first time Zoe had acted in this way. It had happened once before. Naomi had noticed it then and had confused Zoe's first-time falling in love with an episode of aphasia.

Naomi decided that the one person who could help her was Zoe's pediatrician, Dr. Armbruster. Naomi had always found it strange, but Zoe seemed to look forward to her visits to Dr. Armbruster. Even when she was tiny and had to go for shots, Zoe looked forward to her visits and while other babies screamed and hollered inside Dr. Armbruster's waiting room, Zoe was calm as if she'd been suckled on brandy. But now when Naomi said, "I'm going to take you to Dr. Armbruster to see what is the matter with you," this time Zoe protested.

"There's nothing wrong with me," she said. "And I don't need a doctor to prove it." This surprised Naomi even more and now she knew that there was something the matter with her granddaughter. In fact, though Naomi did not know this, the first person Zoe had ever loved outside of the members of her own family was her pediatrician, Dr. Dennis Armbruster. She'd fallen in love with him when she was five and she'd contrived ways throughout her childhood to go and see him.

Most of Zoe's injuries when she was smaller were from falls. Zoe fell down a lot and sprained things. She fell down more than Naomi or June thought she should. They were sure she had a problem with her balance. And then there were always the vaccinations. Whenever there was a new vaccine, Zoe couldn't wait to get it. She was like one anesthetized in the hands of Dr. Armbruster, or like some young but worldly woman entrusting herself into the hands of a lover. Dr. Armbruster never had to promise her lollipops or shake stupid toys to distract her. He merely had to place his hands and Zoe breathed deeply.

Zoe's love for her pediatrician was of course ill-fated. He was over forty and had children much older than Zoe. He was a fat, round man married to a silly little wife. He had a huge purplish mole on the side of his cheek with hair growing out of it and he always thought of Zoe as his prize patient, never suspecting that he was the first of her many secret loves.

Zoe's early world was a world of smells. The first scent embedded in her memory wasn't the smell of milk. Rather it was beer. Whenever she'd smell beer as an adult, it would make her think of home. The first time Zoe went to visit Dr. Armbruster, she thought she was going to her father's studio. The sharp antiseptic odor of the doctor's office matched that of the chemicals her father used to make his photographs, and years later, when she was a medical doctor, Zoe always thought of her father when she went into the operating room. The scent of ether and Lysol would always be identical in her mind to the pungent smell of her father's darkroom.

Zoe always watched when Dr. Armbruster took her in his hands and felt the crack in her wrist. When she'd ask him if she could feel it, he'd place her right hand on her left wrist and say, "There, feel that," but Zoe felt nothing. She was amazed that his fingers could poke into her sides and tell her she didn't have appendicitis.

But what impressed Zoe most when she went to see him was the light he shined in her eyes. He told her to look away, and there in the darkness he shined the little bead of light deep into her pupil. And when he took the light away he didn't leave little blinding red spots in front of her eyes, the way her father did when his camera flashed.

Thinking the aphasia that had frightened her a few years ago had returned, Naomi took Zoe to see Dr. Armbruster again. But now Zoe was filled with a rehearsed, adult indifference as they drove to the doctor's office. As they walked into the waiting room, Zoe saw on the floor the children at play, serving tea at the little tables, playing nurse and doctor with ailing dolls, and she found she was bored by it all.

She sat in a corner, flipping through a copy of *Life* magazine. She liked to look at pictures now. Naomi kept sayi

"Why don't you make me a nice cup of tea," and Zoe sighed, not knowing how to explain to her grandmother that she was too old for such things.

When Dr. Armbruster came to get her, she found him ugly and old. When he said, "Zoe, you're getting to be a big girl now," his foolishness wasn't lost on her. She was revolted by the details of his person—the hair in his ears, the mole on his cheek, his warm, stale breath. Things that had not hurt before hurt now. When he examined her, she recoiled from his touch. There was nothing deader, she thought, than a dead love.

Zoe lived for Sam's visits. She'd paint him pictures she'd never give him and bake cookies she'd eat before he arrived. Whenever she thought he was coming over, she'd plan what she was going to wear, but somehow she'd always wear the wrong thing. A summer dress when the weather turned to fall, pants when he wanted to take her out for ice cream. She never looked right, never knew what to say. In his presence she was mute, stone-faced, while he'd ask her pointed questions like "Have you graduated from grammar school yet?" or "What kind of friends do you have?"

Zoe was always amazed how June never seemed nervous when Sam arrived. In fact, June never even seemed to notice his comings and goings. She'd be in her housecoat when he'd knock on the door or she'd be on her knees, scrubbing the floor. She'd just say, "Oh, Sam, what a surprise. I've got nothing in the house."

But it never mattered that she had nothing in the house because he always brought whatever was needed. He'd come with cheeses and wine and fruit and juice for the children. He came unannounced, always laden down with gifts. He'd sit in the living room and tell the stories of where he'd been and what he'd done. No one asked why for years after the war he'd gone roving. Everyone was glad for the gifts he'd brought from his journeys—the boat in the bottle, the spice clock that, when the hour struck, filled the house with cinnamon or dill.

No one liked the shrunken head, though he tried to explain that the person had been long dead and that the shrinking process was quite elaborate. They made him take it back, but they kept the masks and ornaments, the small and beautiful things. And one day he brought June a wonderful object carved out of jade, he told her, not soapstone. Jade, he said, according to the Chinese is not an earthstone. Jade, he told them, is the congealed semen that a dragon has deposited in the earth, and it has special powers.

Zoe and Badger had no idea what congealed semen was, but his explanation made Naomi blush and June turn her head. But then everyone looked at the congealed semen of the dragon, the beautiful green polished stone, for inside of it an entire world existed. There were houses and people on their way to work, pushing carts. There were goats and mules and inside the houses there were people cooking, cleaning, even making love.

Zoe loved the carved jade so much she begged until June relented to let her keep it. It was the only thing Zoe had ever begged for. She placed it in a special spot on her dresser. June said she could put it there if she never told Sam she'd given it to her. At night before she slept, Zoe looked at the jade and saw things she'd never seen before. She'd see a family all the way in China preparing their dinner. She heard them laughing. She heard them argue, though they spoke in a language she didn't understand. Sometimes the people went to other people's houses. At night on her dresser, the jade glowed and Zoe knew that the congealed semen of a dragon watched over her and that what was taking place on an obscure sacred mountain in China was taking place inside her heart.

Even though she had trouble knowing what to say to him when he was right there in their living room, Zoe loved to go and watch Sam in the evenings which she preferred to the mornings because she could see him so much better. Sometimes he'd sit in the window, reading the newspaper beneath an amber lamp or perhaps watching television. Sometimes she could barely make him out. His face was vague and distant and it was hard to see more than his silhouette from the street. But she'd watch as best she could until she absolutely had to go to home.

It frustrated Zoe that it was so difficult from that distance to make out the features of Sam Pollack's face. He seemed to elude her, even right there in the window. Every day she went and waited for the light to go on and every day she got the same results. He was too far away. When he sat beside her at dinner at her parents' house, she could barely bring herself to look at him. Yet she knew every gesture and she wanted to see him.

She wanted to see the way he nodded when he agreed with something that he heard. The way his face lit up, all coppery when he smiled. How he rubbed his eyes when he was tired. She wanted to see him relax with a book or a glass of brandy, but from where she stood for days and weeks on end, squinting beneath a cherry tree, he was too far away.

Zoe decided she had to talk to someone. She couldn't talk to her mother or her brother. She couldn't talk to Badger. Melanie she knew wouldn't understand. She tried Naomi. One night she found her in the kitchen and told Naomi how she was in love and didn't know what to do. Naomi looked at her ten-year-old granddaughter and sighed, "When you're in love," she said, "there's nothing to be done." Zoe understood that Naomi wasn't taking her seriously and that she was wrapped inside a memory of her own, but still every morning and every night Zoe went to Sam's house and stood in front of it and watched for him. She waited until she caught a glimpse, a shadow, a movement. Someday she knew he'd find her there. But he was always so far away. Zoe thought and thought about what to do to bring him closer.

Then one night she had a dream. She dreamed that Naomi stood at the sink and Zoe went to her and told her how she was in love with Sam Pollack. She dreamed that Naomi smiled and

said she was in love once too. Then Naomi turned to her and Zoe
saw that her eyes were no longer eyes. Inside her eyes was the
sky at night and her eyes were filled with the moon and the stars
and Zoe realized she had found the heavens in her grandmother's gaze.

For days the dream haunted her. She was afraid that if
Naomi turned around her eyes would be the stars and the moon
and not eyes at all. But one day as she walked home, she smelled
the lilacs. It was evening and she saw them on the wall in the
backyard, breathing in the smell of spring, and she recalled the
night when Sam Pollack had first come to them. Zoe looked up
at the sky. It was a clear night sky. Then she remembered her
dream and she knew what she was supposed to do.

Later that evening Zoe stood beneath the cherry tree and
proceeded to stare at the window of Sam Pollack the way she
always did, but this time she could watch him more closely,
sitting in his chair, walking across the room. It wasn't as if he
were far away at all, and it made her feel as close to him as she'd
ever felt to anyone. She thought how nice it had been that night
when he'd brought Badger the telescope and how gently he'd
instructed her how to focus it against the stars.

Now Zoe focused the telescope on Sam Pollack's window as
he came into view. She saw the color of his shirt, his reddish-
brown hair. He seemed more animated than usual. He smiled
and nodded. His lips moved as if he were talking to someone. At
first Zoe thought he was laughing at the television, but then she
saw that he seemed to be speaking and his hands gestured the
way they had when he showed her how an inch was an inch, a
foot a foot.

Zoe kept her telescope carefully focused on the window.
She wanted to see whom he was talking to, but she saw no one.
Sam Pollack moved from being animated to listening. Zoe saw
things on his face she'd never seen before. She saw a strange,
sad look in his eyes, and she saw the corners of his mouth turn
downward in a look Zoe couldn't quite identify, a look she'd

never seen before, but one day when she was a woman, she'd see this look again and she'd know what it meant.

Then Zoe saw a shadow moving across the room. It stayed in the background at first, but then she saw it come closer, cutting in front of the light. She could see two faces so close they were almost touching. Zoe tried to focus on the other face, but they blocked the light and for a moment she lost them. Zoe made a fine adjustment with her lens. She found a woman sitting a little behind Sam, but it was difficult to make out her features. But when they embraced, the woman turned toward the window and Zoe saw, quite clearly in the telescope, her mother's face.

That summer, perhaps suspecting that something was wrong but not quite able to put a name to it, Cal decided he wanted his family to behave as a family and so he rented a cabin in the north woods of Wisconsin, in an obscure, almost unreachable place called Deer Haven. When he announced over dinner one night that he was taking them away for a month's vacation, Zoe, who had never heard of such a thing though she was ten years old, said, "What's that?" Naomi complained that she hated the out-of-doors and June reminded Cal that his son, Badger, was allergic to every plant, spore, and blade of grass.

But Cal was adamant and so at the beginning of July on an unbearably hot day they loaded up the car with clothes and blankets, canned goods and fishing gear, camera equipment and assorted stuffed animals, and headed off to the north woods.

The cabin was a three-bedroom on a small lake, tucked at the end of a long dirt road. The nearest town was ten miles away and the nearest phone was at the general store in town. At first the Colemans didn't know what to do with themselves. Naomi sat in the rocker on the front porch and pouted while June and Cal unpacked everything. Zoe wandered to the water and back and Badger stayed close to the house, certain that some stray leaf would cause his skin to erupt in hideous sores.

But then they settled in and it became a time of berry-picking and moonlit nights. Of skies filled with stars and the air so fresh and clean that you felt as if it took everything bad out of you with your breath. Their days were spent fishing from the pier for trout or perch which Cal would clean and June would fry in fresh butter. June would take long walks while Cal went to photograph in the woods, and Naomi would sit in the kitchen making pies from the berries they'd picked or from the wild rhubarb they'd found. Zoe would take Badger down to the dark waters of the lake and let him kick and swim in the shallow water like a puppy and with great patience she taught him how to swim fifty feet into her arms.

Naomi devised a way to cure Badger of his allergies. From the woods she collected the things that made rashes on his body and she mixed them into his food in small quantities. Then a few days later she'd send him out into the woods and tell him to go get a certain mushroom or a weed and he would gather what she told him, but no hives would break out on his skin, no running sores would erupt, and slowly she began to cure him of all those things in nature that he had been deprived of all these years.

After a few weeks when he could go into the woods and come out unscathed, Badger made friends with the bears. He made friends with the deer and the swans. He went every day into some part of the forest and with his eyes he learned their ways. He studied their movements and their language. He found ways of calling to them and he learned what they liked to eat. Every day he would try to bring some small creature closer to him. He would bring food and stand still so that he could almost touch the fur of the rabbit, the nose of the doe.

Then one evening just as they were settling down to a dinner of fresh lake fish and raspberry pie, a car pulled up in their driveway and Sam Pollack appeared. Zoe looked at June in time to see her flush and Cal looked at all of them and Naomi looked away. Only Badger leaped out of his chair and rushed to Sam. No one could understand how he'd found them. "I told him where we'd be," June finally said. "It never occurred to me he would come here."

It had required a great effort on Sam's part to come all this way, but he had grown bolder lately. He found his life pointless and empty when June was away and he'd spent a fair amount of time devising a way to visit them. Since June had been coming to see him in Brewerton, it had been more and more obvious to Sam that it wouldn't be long before she would leave Cal. He had learned to bide his time. He worked in the factory and did well there. In the evenings he waited for June to call and say if she could come over. And if she could, they would sit together, evening after evening, in his rented rooms while June talked about leaving Cal and while Sam urged her to do so. But then Cal had taken June away from him for the summer and it was more than Sam had been able to bear.

He had spent weeks devising his scheme, but at last he had found the perfect excuse. First he gave them their presents which he always brought. A shell necklace for Naomi and a bracelet for Zoe, from Africa, a Chinese puzzle for Badger, a small print from Bali for Cal, and a paperweight with a house in it, a perfect house, the one Zoe knew her mother always dreamed of, inside. After the gifts were opened Sam said, "I'm sorry I came all the way up here, but I've invented something. It's going to change the beer industry."

Zoe scanned her mother's face for some trace of response. Instead June laughed and was friendly, but whatever more she felt was hidden, and Zoe kept waiting for some slipup, some small gesture that would reveal her true feelings. But she found nothing on June's face except for a warm amber glow. Instead it was Cal whose face showed his reaction. Whose mouth was tight and whose eyes were without expression.

Then Sam reached into his bag and produced a round tin can. This was not so unusual. Beer had been in tin cans for the past few years. It was in fact Sam who had shouted at the upper levels of management of the Ferry-Hyde Brewery to take beer

out of the bottles and put it into disposable tin cans. But Sam
had not rested here. He had stayed up late at night, staring at his
unblemished tin cans, smooth, impenetrable surfaces. Night after night he'd stayed up with a can opener, opening cans, listening to their vacuum-packed smoothness explode with each opening. He wanted more.

He tried to envision what was missing. He pictured the
American family on a picnic away from the world and tried to
imagine what such a family would need. He thought of June's
family up there in the north woods, and he tried to imagine what
they might have forgotten. And then one night it came to him.
"Look," he said as he peeled back the top of the beer can and
foam bubbled forth. "You don't need a can opener."

They watched with awe as he produced another can and
handed it to Cal and Cal pulled on the little nob and the top of
the can came off. Cal cut himself slightly on the edge of the can
and Sam shrugged. "I haven't perfected it yet." He had brought
several cans and passed them around and they all opened the
cans and drank the beer and had a good time.

That night Sam slept with Badger in his room and they
stayed up late, looking at the stars with the telescope and in the
morning Sam and June took a long walk together around the
lake. No one seemed to notice they were gone. Zoe and Badger
played by the water and Naomi baked in the kitchen and Cal
went off to take pictures, but something was wrong with all of
them, Zoe thought. They were out of kilter and somehow the
insulated, safe world they had known for a few days was gone.
When Cal returned from his picture taking and June and Sam
still weren't back for the walk, Zoe saw him stand on the porch
of the cabin with the telescope, scanning the horizon. It was as if
something was bothering him but he couldn't be sure what it
was, and when he didn't find it, annoyed with himself, he went
into the cabin and closed his door.

· · ·

The next day when Sam Pollack left Cal said to Badger, "Come with me into the woods. It's time to make a man out of you." There was something gruff and unpleasant in his voice and it made Badger turn away. "No," he said, "I'll stay here." But Cal took him by the arm and led him away.

He took him deep into the woods and they walked and walked. There was something different about his father now, Badger noticed, though he couldn't say what it was. Cal had always been distracted and indifferent to him, but now something harsh had entered his voice and his gait. He carried a rifle in one hand and rested the other firmly on Badger's shoulder.

At first Badger made noises, whistling and singing, warning the animals away, but then Cal told him to be quiet. They walked until they came to a small clearing by a pond and Cal told him to sit down and they both sat. From time to time Badger tried to talk, but Cal silenced him. Cal kept his eyes fixed straight ahead and Badger knew something was wrong, but he could not say what it was. Cal himself wasn't quite sure what was bothering him. He didn't know why he'd gone hunting and why he'd dragged his son along, but it was something he had to do.

Then a deer came to drink at the pond. Cal raised his fingers to his lips and slowly he brought the gun sight to his eyes. He looked carefully at Badger and Badger told himself he had to scream. He had to make a sound to warn the deer, but when he opened his mouth, no sound came. As the deer fell, Badger acquired the gift of silence.

The deer staggered, then fell halfway into the pond. Cal raced forward and walked into the water, pulling the deer out of the water. Badger came close and saw the deer, its eyes open wide, nose moist. Milk poured from its teats. "Damn it," Cal said. "It's a doe. Don't tell your mother." But Badger would never tell his mother or anyone else what he'd seen that day. He stroked the deer, then ran back to the house.

Then the rhythm of their lives changed. The berries dried up and were eaten by dark birds and no more pies came from the oven. The sky turned overcast and undefined and a mist hung over the lake so that June was afraid to let the children swim because she could not see them from the shore. The deer meat Cal brought home tasted rancid and they had to throw it away. The afternoons turned hot and muggy and brought with them an infestation of green flies and ravenous mosquitoes. Naomi complained of flashes and sudden bouts of fatigue which soon assumed reptilian proportions, and June suffered a recurrence of the hives she had not suffered in years. Badger grew wistful and his allergies returned as well, leaving him puffy and soon covered with scabs.

Zoe found herself restless with nothing to do. She watched her mother grow distracted and her father turn away, spending more and more time walking off into the mist of the morning with his camera and not returning until the flies and mosquitoes drove him out of the woods. They felt like fugitives now, running from some crime they couldn't recall. And so not long after Sam left and a week before they'd planned, they packed up the car and headed back to the life they'd known just a few weeks before.

As soon as they were home and June was back in her basement and Cal in his darkroom, Zoe returned to her habit of standing beneath Sam Pollack's window with her telescope. Zoe knew her mother did not notice her comings and goings and neither did Cal, and Naomi let her do more or less what she wanted. Sam sat by the window as usual and some nights, though rarely now, June was with him. When she was there, they moved in and out of the window and sometimes she could not see them at all. But when she could, Zoe watched with an eerie fascination, especially when she could see her mother sitting by the window moving her lips, and Zoe tried to imagine what the words might be.

Most nights June did not come, but when she did, Zoe felt a strange and protective feeling running through her and she wanted to rush and help her mother, as if June were struggling with some terrible thing, but instead Zoe just watched. Some nights after watching, Zoe went to her father's studio. She liked to watch him, now that she was older, and she liked the safe, warm darkness of the darkroom. Once she'd thought of telling him what it was she saw in the night, but now she knew she must not tell him. She knew she must not tell anyone.

One evening she went to Melanie's after having stood watching June and Sam until their bodies disappeared into the depths of the room. "What is it?" Melanie asked as Zoe came in. Zoe was about to tell her what it was she had been watching all these nights, but instead she said, "Can I stay over?"

Melanie said she could. They opened up the sofa bed on the sun porch and dragged in all the blankets. They crawled into bed, but it was a warm spring night and Melanie took off her nightgown. Zoe had worn her underwear and a T-shirt and took them off. In the moonlight Melanie looked yellow all over, like a golden angel. When Badger fell in love with her years later, Zoe remembered this image of Melanie as an angel and she'd seen why he loved her.

Under the covers Melanie said, "You're so tense. I can feel it." She drew Zoe to her and turned Zoe over with her hands onto her stomach. Melanie straddled Zoe and Zoe could feel the beginnings of pubic hair tickling her thighs. Zoe was amazed at the skill in Melanie's hands as they caressed her back and her buttocks. Melanie knew how to rub and touch her and when she was done, Zoe straddled Melanie and rubbed her as Melanie had done.

When they were done rubbing and massaging each other, they curled into each other's arms. They wrapped their arms and legs around each other so that their nipples touched. They kissed for a short while and then they fell asleep.

In the morning, Zoe was uneasy about the way Melanie's skin had felt against hers. She knew that she'd learn to say with her body what she could not say in words. She would never tell what she saw with the telescope every night but instead the secret had entered her body, dug its way deep down. Zoe knew that this had something to do with her secret and with what a terrible burden it had become to her. Zoe never returned to stand beneath Sam Pollack's window with her telescope again.

A few days later Sam came to the house, but Zoe wouldn't see him. He called up to her, "Zoe, I've got something for you," and finally June made Zoe come down. Sam said, "I've got something. Reach into my pocket." She didn't want to go near him, but he had a strange power over her and when he said reach, she reached. What she felt was wet and warm and furry and she pulled it out of his pocket. It lay there in her palm, flat, thick and white as snow freshly fallen, and it was moving. "Oh," Zoe said, "a polar bear."

"No," Naomi said, "God help us. It's a pure white dog." Then she spit into the air as if warding off a curse. "I've never seen anything so white," Zoe said. But it would not remain so white for long. It was a purebred Himalayan from Nepal and it would turn into a creature as large as the Abominable Snowman and impossible to keep clean in the sooty air of Brewerton. Zoe looked into its face and saw that it had an odd, questioning look, as if it was trying to grasp something it couldn't understand. She gave it a name that captured that look, a look that would stay in the dog's face for almost two decades, even until it became an old, mangy thing. "I'll call it Puzzle," Zoe said as she cuddled it in her arms.

She was about to forgive Sam everything. She was even about to forgive her mother everything, when Cal walked into the room. He had been at his studio, working, when suddenly, like some volunteer fireman who'd just been signaled for duty, he was alerted. He had no idea what moved him or why he had stopped working, but he hung up his prints, leaving them to hang wet, and closed up the studio at eight o'clock at night, something he hadn't done since he returned to it after the war, and he went home.

As he walked into his living room, he knew he'd done the right thing by coming, but he also knew he'd been drawn by an emotion he couldn't clearly recognize. It had a name, but he'd never experienced it before. In fact, he would not have understood it at that moment if Sam had not described it to him years ago in their barracks in France—the palpitating heart, the shaking hands, the seemingly endless pit in the stomach.

With one glance he took in his daughter nestling a snowball in her hand, his wife laughing wildly, his son making the spice clock go around, and Naomi dancing across the living room wrapped in ancient Chinese silk with a dragon embroidered on the back. Like a great hibernating beast, he woke in his den. He grew territorial as he named the emotion that was gripping him and he knew for the first time in his life he was experiencing what others had described to him as jealousy.

"What is going on here?" Cal asked.

"The same thing that goes on every night," June replied nonchalantly but not without bitterness.

Sam and June glanced at each other in a way that made Cal's recognition instantaneous, only many months too late. "I said," Cal repeated more slowly this time, "What is going on here?" He spoke in a way that made Zoe tremble and Badger stop the spice clock and Naomi cease her twirl in green silk.

"Sam brought us gifts," Badger said, for he had grown fond of Sam and did not see anything wrong. The presents Cal could see, but there was something else he saw. He saw that he had lost them all. He had lost them all, but he resolved to set himself upon the task of winning them back. He pointed to the door and told Sam to leave. Sam nodded, said goodnight and without another word walked out the front door. He would never return through it again in all the years he loved June and saw her and tried to win her over. They would meet in restaurants and cafés and bars and movie houses, but never again inside the house from which Cal Coleman had banished him.

Then Cal set upon the task of reclaiming his home with all

the fervor he had thrown into reclaiming of his darkroom years before. He began by throwing out all the gifts of Sam Pollack. The spice clock, the silks, the earbobs, the magic carpets. He made them get rid of everything, except for the dog, Puzzle, at which Zoe balked. She hid him in her room, beneath her bed, until her father's rage subsided. She watched as the dog grew bigger and bigger, as his paws flattened and his thighs thickened so much that she thought she could put a saddle on him and ride him to school. It was the dog she'd loved dearly. She'd keep him as white and as clean as she was able in the filth and grime of the city where they lived and she always believed he came from the foothills of Annapurna, and not the local kennel where in fact Sam had procured him in order to win Zoe back.

After the elimination of the gifts, Cal embarked upon what became his sudden and primary preoccupation, the passion of his life—the effort to win back his wife at a time when it was already too late. His great problem, his terrible blindness, would be that he thought that what had occurred between himself and June was concrete and that he could remedy it with something concrete. He could not understand how June, now suddenly faced with more possibility for happiness than she'd seen in years, had a hollow spot that had been within her for so long and now she filled it with her own indifference. A hardness came into her and what had mattered so much for so long didn't matter to her anymore. In all the years of waiting and wanting, June's heart had acquired the strength and density of lead.

But Cal failed to notice. Instead he came home for dinner and spent the evenings with the family. He'd sit in the living room and smoke a pipe near June. Or if she was in her basement, working on her star maps and her quilts, he'd read a book in the dank, mildewed basement until the cold entered his bones.

Though June slept in the spare room, she did not lock her door and Cal could visit when he wished. He would make love to her all night. He'd satisfy her, but he'd never win her back. His jealousy would drive him wild. He'd say, "Just tell me. What did he do to you? Did he touch you?" Some days he wouldn't be so patient. He'd shout, "Tell me, what did he do?" He'd demand, plead, threaten and cajole. But June wouldn't reply and her refusal drove him mad. "It's not your concern," she'd say. "It is none of your business." Cal did everything but strike her. This he would not do. He would die gnawed by jealousy and grief, without knowing that the closest Sam Pollack ever came to June's skin was in the comforting embrace he'd provided in the late afternoons while Zoe watched from the street below.

It would be years before he'd grasp the futility of his gestures. On his deathbed he'd realize what an utter fool he had been. For he had returned to her not out of love or even loneliness, but out of jealousy and rage. And that jealousy came to him not as she was leaving, but after she was already gone. If he had come to her a month earlier, a week, or that night when she had waited up for him in their bed, it might have made all the difference, but June, once she was gone, wasn't a woman to be won back.

And so it would be Cal's curse to want her when she no longer wanted him. He'd be doomed to touch her, to touch himself, to touch other women, all in an effort to win her attention, to get her back. He'd make love to her night after night in ways that would drive them both wild and then he'd withdraw for weeks at a time. He'd tell her he loved her, and then say he didn't. But none of it seemed to matter to June. The only person it affected was Cal, and it drove him crazy.

But the fact was, June was a different person. The woman who'd spent so many years quilting in the basement, who'd planned trips she'd never take, dreamed of a love she'd never have, had somehow left this world. She entered the realm of the spirits. This world, having disappointed her, lost her interest. She found her connections in the stars, in the lines of her hand, in the tales told by the cards, in the Ouija boards.

Zoe tried to understand. At night she curled up in her bed with Puzzle as he grew bigger and bigger, so that his paw would cover her entire face as she slept and his bulk weigh down a side of the bed, and their bodies, girlchild and dog, would roll against each other like lovers in the night so that Naomi worried that the child was destined for unnatural acts. Zoe tried to forgive Sam, but found she could not. Even at the age of eleven, Zoe understood something about herself. She understood that, as with her mother, when she was through with someone, she was through.

Zoe was the kind of person who'd never go back. Men and clothes, she learned, were two things she never went back to. When Zoe cleaned her closets, it was for good. Nor was she the kind to confide. She spent her days and nights with Puzzle, the dog given to her by Sam Pollack, but she never told anyone what she'd seen on those nights when she'd stood beneath his window.

It would shape her life more than anything she could imagine. It was the secret she'd always keep. Like the pure white dog that slept at her side, it would be entirely hers.

PART

FOUR

STREET
OF DREAMS

Dear Zoe, I have this memory of you, but I don't know what it means and wonder if you remember it as well. I am sure you don't and maybe it never happened. But I'm lying face down in the snow and I'm wrapped in this snowsuit—blue I think—and I remember I have to go to the bathroom, but I am lying there, like somebody frozen. I'm little, tiny in fact, and you are trying to arouse me. You shake me and try to drag me like a dog, but I play dead and don't move. You grow panicky and shake me more and more, but I still don't move and I learned this is the way to drive you mad. I know now that I was only testing you that day. That I wanted to prove you care for me. I want you to prove it to me again now. I have other memories like this as well that are so alive in my mind, so clear that I don't know what to say about them. I see you all the time in my dreams as if you were my lover, not my sister. But I carry this rage inside of me and it's as if I'm playing dead with you again. Because you drove me across this border, for which I am grateful, but then you didn't look back. And in a way it is as if I am dead, as if all of us on this side of the border just don't exist anymore, and I keep thinking you're going to shake me and drag me home. How could you let this happen to me? How could you never turn around? If there's one thing I'll never forgive you for, that's it. Badger

THIRTEEN

Zoe was living with Robert when the letters started to arrive again. They were living in a small two-room apartment in Lechmere not far from the MTA tracks. Zoe was washing beakers in a pathology lab at M.I.T. where she had no idea what was in the beakers, though she feared some form of biological warfare or something with recombinant DNA, but she was willing to do anything then to get herself through medical school. And Robert was working as a production assistant on a series of animal documentaries for WGBH. It was clear to Zoe that they were both going somewhere and she assumed it would be together.

Robert was into animals. He'd crawl on his belly through slime to look at a gopher. Zoe figured after they'd been together for a while that anyone who was into animals couldn't be that bad. Robert wasn't all that bad. He just wasn't into people very much and it took Zoe a while to figure this out.

Robert was working on a special on snakes when the first letter arrived. Night and day he talked about different snakes, including the Ouroboros—that mythological serpent that eats its own tail. One night he brought home a medieval drawing of this creature devouring itself, foreshortened and crazed. Zoe had difficulty concentrating on the picture of the Ouroboros. Her first letter from Badger after a hiatus of two years had arrived that day. When Robert was in the middle of a series on alligators of the Everglades, the second letter came.

Zoe didn't show anyone the first letter. But she showed Robert the second because it was about bats. Robert read the letter and shook his head. "He's on drugs," he said.

"Maybe," Zoe nodded. She folded the letter and tucked it back into its envelope. "But at least he's writing."

Robert saw things differently. "He's losing it. You'd just better learn to accept that."

But Zoe wouldn't let it happen. Not her father and then her brother. In one letter Badger sent Zoe a cartoon he drew. It was Humpty-Dumpty with her brother's face, smoking a joint, while a bunch of marines tried to keep him from falling off the wall. But she didn't show these letters to Robert anymore. She just tucked them away in a drawer.

Robert had always been a great realist. It was what had drawn Zoe to him in the first place when they met. "Don't believe everything you read," he said. He saw things for what they were. He was no moper-around-the-house the way she was. He was no looker-back, no past-obsessor. He had no love he'd never gotten over, no memory that wouldn't leave, no incident that had changed his life irrevocably.

Time for Robert was present time. Here and now. That's why television was his medium and he planned to devote his life to it. He liked what was happening before his very eyes. He couldn't stand complexity. As long as he and Zoe were happy, they'd be together. As soon as they began to drift apart, Zoe knew—the way animals know things from a deep place of instinct—that he could leave and never look back. She used to say, "If I got run over by a truck, Robert would have a bad week."

But Zoe had incidents, accidents, memories, losses, a past, hopes, failures, disappointment, secret loves, fantastic dreams. Things that had happened to her she'd never forget. And now she had letters from her brother, wild, crazy letters. And she kept it all to herself, while Robert told her about the alligators of the Everglades, as he weeded his herb garden and cooked his gourmet meals. He took pleasure in the simplest of domestic chores, in making love, in going for a run along the banks of the

Charles, while Zoe buried the letters from her brother deep in her lingerie drawer.

Zoe did have a great capacity for disposing of bodies. She was amazed at how she could do things in medicine, things she could not do with her life. Tear somebody's guts out. Chop people up. Remove their eyes. Toss away their diseased hearts. Stuff them into body bags, tag them, put them away. That was how she felt about her letters from Badger. She knew he was in trouble, but then he'd always been in trouble. He was after all only her brother. Not her lover. She was happy in her life now. She'd made her peace. She was content, having picked herself up and gotten away. She wasn't on drugs. She wasn't doing anything wrong. She was in love, on her way to becoming a doctor. And so for a long time she didn't give Badger much thought.

Then Robert went to the Grand Canyon to shoot a film about wild donkeys. The producer, Eileen, was an acquaintance of theirs, and she and Robert had worked on several films together in the past. But this film they planned more carefully and Robert spent many late nights at the studio, going over each shot.

Each night Robert phoned from the Grand Canyon. He'd tell her what they'd done that day, what was on for the next. After three days, Zoe began to miss him and then another letter arrived. Normally Zoe didn't miss him, but after the letter came, Zoe decided to call. It was too late to phone that evening, so she waited and decided to give him a wake-up call before she left for work at nine.

It was five-thirty in the morning at the Grand Canyon and there was no answer. She couldn't see how this would be possible. How could he not be in his room, she'd asked herself. In her mind she ran through what was possible. He was in Eileen's room and she couldn't call Eileen's room. She knew how crazy this was, that he would be there, but she couldn't bring herself to call. Instead she panicked. She called in sick to work. She left emergency messages for Robert all over the hotel.

At noon the phone rang. "What's all the excitement?" he said. "What's wrong?"

"Oh God, I don't know. I don't know what's wrong with me. Where were you? Where have you been? I just felt like something was wrong. I can't describe it. I was just sure so I started calling." She caught her breath. "Where were you?"

"Out filming the sunrise. It comes up at about six around the rim of the canyon. We went out to film it." He laughed softly into the phone. "You silly thing."

Zoe laughed too. "I don't know. I miss you. Oh, honey, I'm so dumb. I don't know what's wrong with me."

When he returned, he wanted her to see the rushes. He always liked her to look at everything he did. They went to the editing room one night and he showed her the footage on the wild donkeys, every inch of it. She watched numb as the film rolled by. When he finished he said, "So what do you think? You think I've got a film?"

"Is that it?" Zoe asked. "Is that all?"

"Isn't it enough?"

"Yes," she said, "it's enough." But there was no sunrise.

FOURTEEN

Memory is stronger than anything, Zoe thought as she took the lake road home. It is stronger even than the present. Stronger than love. She knew the lake road better than she knew anything. She knew every twist and every turn. A block away from the lake were malls, subdivisions, movie houses with sticky floors. But here was the lake, and its road, an old Indian trail, followed the lake as if somehow they were meant to be. She'd spent much of her youth on this road. It was the road, for instance, that had taken them to Canada, when she'd driven Badger. And it was a road that could take you to Florida. Or just down to the beach.

When Zoe picked June up, it was a cold gray November morning. "I'm going to buy you a coat," June said. "You can't possibly be warm enough." The car fogged up right away. Zoe fiddled with the defroster. Her hands were numb and she felt the warmth from Derek's body quickly leaving hers. June had taken the day off so they could go shopping. She'd called Zoe just as she got back to her hotel and said, "You need a coat. You need a winter coat."

It was very cold that winter, Zoe had to admit to herself. She could use a coat. She had been cold last night and she had been cold this morning when Derek dropped her back at her hotel. When he dropped her off she said, "I'd like to see you again."

He'd smiled. She'd seen the space between his teeth and his face had looked older to her. She'd thought for a moment how the difference between love and lust wasn't who you wanted to go to bed with at night, but rather who you wanted to wake up with in the morning. Still, she wanted to see him again. "Why don't you meet me tomorrow night," he said. "We could have a drink at the Packer's Pub."

In the car her body still felt warm from his touch. He had touched her everywhere and everywhere felt warm. She thought she was falling in love because someone had touched her everywhere. June said, "I don't remember a winter so cold. I hope it means we'll have an early spring."

They drove through gray Brewerton to the mall downtown. June took the road along the lake and Zoe saw that the lake was steaming and ice moved in large floes. Zoe was suddenly struck with the fear of a giant snowfall, one of those paralyzing blizzards that could leave her snowbound for weeks. She wanted to go back East. She wanted to go back to Boston and to her friends, but there were things there she couldn't go back to and there were things here she couldn't live with.

At the Rue des Rêves Mall all the stores were connected so you could wander from Bonwit's to Korvette's to Field's to Saks to the Rise'n Shine dress shop. It was one giant store, occupying a huge section of the downtown part of Brewerton now. This mall was new. It came under a program called "urban revitalization." Zoe thought it was ridiculous for a mall in Brewerton, Wisconsin, to have a French name.

She had never seen so many coats. As they moved from store to store, all she saw was coats. There were too many kinds to choose from. She might as well have been looking at space suits, they felt so foreign to her. Car coats and winter coats, raincoats, transitional coats. Coats of different colors. Powder blue, baby pink. And fur coats. Coats from animals. Little animals clubbed to death, tiny beavers, foxes, wild animals, beautiful animals, rabbits. She thought of Derek. She didn't want a coat. All she wanted was a body to keep her warm.

In the mall she was too far away from his body. Among the coats, she felt him drifting away. June ripped coats off their hangers and handed them to Zoe. Zoe tried on a bulky flannel, an expensive cashmere. Raccoon. Then June saw a coat she liked. It was a fake fur, huge like a polar bear, only dyed red. "Oh, look at this," June said, "isn't this adorable?" Zoe thought it was the most grotesque coat she had ever seen. It looked like an animal on fire. It looked like a bathroom rug.

"Well," June said, "I like it for myself." She slipped it on. She looked like an orangutan.

"Mother," Zoe said, "you look ridiculous."

But a salesman who'd been observing them came forth. "Oh," he said, "that looks simply marvelous on you. It's you. It is absolutely you."

"Mom," Zoe said, "that coat's not anybody, except maybe the Abominable Snowman."

"It's a fun coat," the salesman said. "It's for when you feel flamboyant." He raised his hand in an arch. "When you feel wild, and crazy and free."

Zoe realized his hair was dyed yellow. Everything was fun fur around here, she thought. "Something more conservative is better for you, Mom."

"Anyway," June said sadly, "it's not my size. It's too small. I need a twelve, do you have a twelve?"

"Oh, it's on the mannequin in the window."

June wanted to try it on, so as the salesman left to search for another twelve, Zoe and June divided ranks, headed in opposite directions, like trackers stalking their prey. June headed in the direction of dress coats. Zoe stuck with more relaxed camel hair and flannel.

Zoe went into sports clothes, a section she gravitated to naturally enough. She preferred to look at ski pants, casual slacks, bulky sweaters. June moved into cashmere. In sports clothes, Zoe ran into the salesman who was waiting on them. "Did you get my mother that twelve she asked to see? Like the one on the mannequin?"

"Oh, I was going to," he said, "but she said she wants to think about it."

"Oh," Zoe said, "I see."

"She said she wanted to come back tomorrow with her husband."

"Oh . . ." A chill ran through Zoe. Whatever heat Derek had given to her was gone now. "That's a good idea."

"She said she wanted your father to see it."

"Yes," Zoe said, "he should see it." She turned and looked for her mother.

June was nowhere to be seen. She had disappeared among the racks. As Zoe wandered the maze of coats and clothing, that twist and turn of dresses and skirts and blouses, she thought she saw her mother turning a corner, disappearing around a bend. It was like June to wander off in parades, to disappear in stores. Zoe followed the person around the bend. An old woman turned and Zoe saw that it was not her mother's face. Zoe cut through shoes and purses, into sweaters and jackets. She made her way into accessories—scarves, gloves, gold chains. Her mother wasn't in gloves. She wasn't in hats or bags. As Zoe turned back toward fun fur, she ran into Melanie.

Zoe had not seen Melanie since Badger left for Canada and she did not recognize her at first.

But Melanie recognized her. "Zoe, it has been so long. I can't believe it. How are you?" Melanie hugged her.

"I'm all right." Zoe kept scanning the store. "But I've just lost my mother."

"Oh, I'm so sorry," Melanie said, her face dropping. "I've been out of touch. I didn't know." And she offered her condolences.

"No," Zoe said, "I lost her in the store."

FIFTEEN

More and more of Mrs. Margolis' predictions were coming true
and her credibility was growing at the clinic. She had predicted
Sunday's victory of the Packers over the Bears, down to the
point spread. She had predicted the last major snowfall. And
that morning she had told everyone that Badger would have
more visitors than he'd know what to do with. "Three women,"
she'd said. "All hungry for love."

"What women?" Gabe asked, surprised that there was one
he wanted to see.

"The one who waits for the person who will never return,"
she'd said.

"She's crazy." Nurse Burlington shrugged, turning away.
But she was on duty when the three women arrived. Zoe didn't
expect to find Nurse Burlington working the day shift. In fact,
Zoe hoped never to see her again, but Julie had the flu and so
Nurse Burlington was covering for her. Zoe was surprised to see
that in the daylight she wasn't nearly as old as she'd seemed
before. Zoe placed her now at not more than fifty. Zoe tried to
imagine the private life of this matron, this aging spinster. A
lover in her teens or a brief marriage to a lab technician. Whatever it was had ended in grief and led her to what else Zoe
imagined for her—cat-clawed chairs, lamps lit with sixty-watt
bulbs, open cans of sardines and creamed corn.

"So," Nurse Burlington said, glancing at Mrs. Margolis
who stood with her walker in the doorway of the waiting room,
gloating. "Lots of visitors today." Zoe was disturbed by this
display of enthusiasm. "How's he doing?"

"Fine," Zoe said.

Nurse Burlington laughed. "Fine? I'm sure he isn't doing fine."

"Well," Zoe replied defensively, "he's not doing worse."

"Well, worse isn't fine." She smiled. There was the yellow stain of coffee and cigarettes on her teeth. Her hair was a faint shade of blue.

As they went upstairs Melanie said, "I used to go all the time. I'd go and sit there and nothing would happen. I'd say, hey Badge, it's me, remember? The love of your life. But nothing would happen."

No one said anything, so Melanie went on. "I used to go every day. I'd sit and sit, but nothing ever happened. He never said anything to me. I'll always love him." Her voice was shaking now. June looked away. "I'll always love him, but I just have to do something else with my life."

Melanie was blond and thin and young. She should have no trouble doing something else with her life, but so far she hadn't. She sold wedding rings in the mall and that was what she'd done with her life. She said to Zoe, "You managed to get out." She wiped her hand across her eyes. "But I'll never get out of here."

They went upstairs and sat for an hour without speaking. Badger ignored them. At last Melanie got up. "What's the use?" She was crying. "I can't come anymore."

As they left, they ran into Gabe. He overheard what Melanie said and he frowned. "He has good days and bad days." Gabe looked at Zoe intently. "Just like the rest of us."

As they left, Mrs. Margolis still stood at the waiting-room door. June stopped to say hello to her and she caught her by the arm. "Your mother lived a secret life. And now all of you, your whole family, everyone lives a secret life."

After dropping June off at the radio station, Zoe drove Melanie home. Melanie still lived in the big house by the lake with her father. When they got to the driveway Melanie said, "Why don't you come in?"

The big moosehead still hovered over the landing. They went into the den and sat down. "You want a drink?" Zoe asked for a Coke. Melanie poured herself a scotch. "My afternoon drink." They sat down on the leather chairs of the den. "You should have let me know. I was so surprised to see you."

"I know," Zoe said, "but you know, I haven't been here in years. I thought I could just slip into town and slip out again."

"Well, you can't. You should forget about some things. It was all a long time ago."

"My brother wasn't a long time ago. He's now."

Melanie nodded. "He is now."

"Why didn't you go and see him, Mel? You know, that Christmas in Canada when he was expecting you?"

Melanie took a sip of her drink. "Because sometimes you have to save yourself. Do you know what I mean? I think if I'd gone, I would have stayed. And I'd be just like him."

Zoe nodded. "I guess there's some truth in that."

"I'm not sure anyone could have helped him. I think he was bent on doing himself in."

"Maybe. Anyway, what's with you? You aren't married? No major changes?"

"I keep thinking he'll get better. That he'll change. You know, when he was good, your brother, he was the best."

"I believe you," Zoe said. She looked at her watch.

"I had to save myself," Melanie said. "Or I'd be just like him."

Zoe nodded. "I've got to get going. I have to be somewhere." Zoe thought about saving yourself. She looked at Melanie. She thought of the night when they lay together in Melanie's bed on the sun porch with their breasts touching and she thought how then Melanie was capable of anything, though now she supposed from looking at her that she had changed. There was something about Melanie that still made Zoe nervous.

"Maybe another time, all right? Why don't we have dinner or something?"

"Sure," Zoe said. "Another time." Melanie walked her to the door.

SIXTEEN

Packer's Pub was located not far from the main brewery district of Brewerton and it wasn't the safest part of town. It wasn't the worst part either and it certainly wasn't worse than parts of Detroit where Zoe had worked and parts of the Amazon where Zoe had traveled, but still it wasn't the best part of town to go to. The pub was dedicated to football and in the evenings after the factories closed the workers came and hung out at the pub and watched TV sports. There was a woman with long blond hair at the bar, but she was clearly a bar hanger-on, and there was a priest. But the rest of the people in the place were men and Zoe didn't feel so easy when she walked in.

Derek wasn't there, so Zoe took a table in the back. The bartender came over and she ordered a local beer. It wasn't like her to be on time, but tonight she was. She was very much on time. She wished she'd brought something to read or do until Derek arrived, but for a while she just looked into her beer. She looked at the foam, like puffy clouds, and took a sip. Then she looked around the pub. It was filled with memorabilia from the time when the Packers won the NFL. Signed pictures of Vince Lombardi, Bart Starr. The headlines from Super Bowl I.

The bartender came over. "You want another?" Zoe shook her head. She didn't want another. She hadn't even wanted the first. She wasn't going to want the third, but she ordered another. While he was bringing it, she went to the bathroom. The bathroom was coeducational and it had all kinds of graffiti written on it. "Moby Dick is not a social disease." "If you have something, let it go. If it comes back, it's yours. If it doesn't, get a gun and track it down."

She didn't know how long she read the graffiti, but when she came out the men at the bar looked at her. A few of them shook their heads. One smiled. She found an old copy of the *Brewerton Times* on the bar stool and took it back to her table. But the beer went right through her and it wasn't long before she had to go to the bathroom again. This time when she went back, she put on lipstick and powdered her nose. She said, "I'll count to ten and he'll be out there."

When she left the bathroom again, all the men looked up. A few of them made comments under their breath. Zoe said to the bartender, "May I use your phone?"

He said, "Of course, it's right on the wall."

She decided to call, just to make sure he hadn't forgotten. She called and the phone rang a dozen times. Good, she thought, he's on his way. She smiled at the men at the bar and went back to her seat. He was on his way. It was cold out, it was difficult to get around. Derek was only twenty-five minutes late. After all, she'd kept her own mother waiting for twenty minutes just the day before.

Zoe remembered once reading about what people did with those spare moments in between the events in their lives. What some people did while waiting for a bus or in line for a film or for a friend to show up. One woman learned Japanese at her bus stop in the morning. A man stayed in shape doing isometric contractions in between business appointments. A mother wrote poetry while sitting in the car when it was her turn at carpool.

The important thing when waiting is to have something to do. Zoe looked around the bar and thought about what she could do while sitting here. She'd read how Anwar Sadat once said that the years when he was in solitary confinement were the most educational years of his life. That was when he really learned things. So, given the constraints of place and time, Zoe thought about what she could do with herself until Derek showed up.

You could study the place where you're sitting or make a new friend, she told herself. You could do stomach contractions or help somebody in need. You could count the number of cars in the parking lot, the number of headlights that passed. Study the walls. Study the faces. Study the types of beer. Or count the number of people who come through the door. Do a study on what they look like, what kind of people they are. Increase your powers of observation. Pray. Renew your belief in the divine. Try to invent relationships, lives, situations for all the people in the room. Tear your napkin into paper snowflakes or small animals. Make a pile of napkin shreddings. Have a martini. Imagine you are in Afghanistan caught in crossfire. Think about what you would do. How would you react? Tell yourself that if he's not the sixth person to come in the door, you'll leave. Count the number of cars that pass. Count the headlights.

Practice deep breathing. Plan the conversation you'll have with him when he arrives. Think of the number of times you've kept other people waiting and feel contrite. Make a resolution. Think about hobbies you'd like to take up, like learning to knit with a stitch counter. Collecting matchbooks. Imagine yourself in solitary confinement in a Turkish jail on a false drug charge. Tell yourself if he's not the tenth person to walk in, you'll leave.

Use your time very constructively. Try to recall favorite passages from the Tibetan Book of the Dead. Try to recite verse you had to memorize in school such as Laertes' advice to Polonius or "Daffodils." Imagine yourself in solitary confinement in a Mexican jail. Increase your word power. Do yoga breathing. Carry needlepoint with you at all times. Make eyeglass cases and small-change purses for friends. Make your Christmas list. Tell yourself if he's not the fifteenth person, you'll leave. Make an alternative plan in your head. Be sure it is constructive, not destructive. Learn to increase your options. Have a backup. Life is not an either/or. Think about writing a book on this very topic. Turn pain into art. Turn suffering into work.

Go to the bathroom again. Comb your hair. Sit down and have a good cry. Get it out of your system. Set yourself a series of acceptable goals. Cry. Order something to eat. Collect crumbs.

Make drawings on the napkin. Write down your feelings. Have a conversation in your head with the person you are angry at. Think of the way out. Think about how you got in. Analyze your dilemma. Don't make the same mistake again.

Imagine yourself on Rikers Island, too poor to afford bail for a crime you didn't do. Or trapped in a small elevator. A subway. Develop empathy for those who are trapped. Quit feeling sorry for yourself. Imagine an earthquake victim under the rubble, awaiting rescue. Feel what it feels like to be really trapped. Think about how lucky you are not to be. You have the power to change your life. Change it. Imagine yourself waking up in Kuwait in the middle of a revolution with no way out of the country and your embassy in flames. You have feet. Move them. Imagine yourself in a loony bin on a permanent drug trip, thinking you are playing third base for the New York Yankees. You have legs. Stretch them. Think of yourself as a grazing animal, as a house plant, a bookend, any object with nothing but time. Imagine how it feels to be your own brother sitting in a stark white room. You have power. Use it. You have legs. Use them.

SEVENTEEN

Zoe drove. She drove the streets she knew well. She drove out of the factory district toward the center of town. She drove past the old red brick schoolhouse where her science teacher, Mr. Berkley, had given her his love of cells and protoplasm and microscopic organisms. Mr. Berkley had the word WHY? over the blackboard and whenever anything happened, whenever anything went wrong, Mr. Berkley told them always to ask themselves WHY? Why did your ink-distilling experiment explode? Why did the frog you just pithed jump off the table? Why haven't things gone according to plan?

Zoe had loved Mr. Berkley with his big ears and his thick glasses and his gentle way. He had taken a tiny bit of blood from her finger and put it on a slide under the microscope. "Look," he'd said to her, "you're alive." But Mr. Berkley wasn't alive. First he'd gone blind from a terrible disease of the blood. Then he'd died slowly and, she'd heard from Melanie, alone. She wondered if he'd kept asking why to the end.

She drove past the library where every summer they had a bookworm contest and every time you finished a book you got to color a joint on what was really a caterpillar dressed in a mortarboard. She was a mere child as she set out on her drive through these streets she knew so well, picking up horse chestnuts, cracking them out of the spiny shells. Or skating on the streets after the ice storms. A child with her taut little girl's body.

She passed Leo's Delicatessen where she used to take Badger after school with her friends and she'd make him sit there, staring at her with his big dark eyes while her friends ate french fries and sipped Cokes. He would never ask for anything and she'd found that odd even then. She'd say Badge, don't you want something? A soda, a lemon Coke, but he'd shake his head. He didn't want anything. He never did.

She hated having him around, but there'd been times when she was nice to him. Times in the winter when she'd brought him inside, made him sip hot chocolate. Times when she'd taken the chill from his body with her very hands. Why couldn't he remember those times? "You're my little baby," she'd say, rubbing his limbs, "and you are so very cold."

But now as she drove she wasn't a child any longer. She was older, a girl of sixteen. Driving for the first time. Driving down to the high school parking lot or to the lake to meet Hunt. He was always there. Now she was driving to all the places they went to hide and to all the days when they kept the heaters in their cars running. She was driving to everything they'd done to be together.

She drove back into summer when a warm night was upon them and the northern sky filled with the brilliance of stars. And she felt it now, her back pressed to the tree, the fresh lake breeze, the warm, warm night, and Hunt with her, his mouth pressed against her thighs while she ran her hands through his hair, and she drove into the air and the warmth and the sky above the lake and the ghostlike icy streets of Brewerton were gone.

She drove until she came to the clinic and there she stopped. She knew that they would not refuse her and when she went in, she walked right past Nurse Burlington who rather than attempt to stop her pretended not to notice. Zoe walked the stairs to his room. Badger was resting and Zoe went in.

She knelt by the side of his bed. "Badger," she whispered. "Remember, when we were little, remember how you came to me then?" But his eyes told her she had betrayed him. She'd driven him to the border and never looked back. She had made as much space as she could between herself and them. But now Zoe reached down deep inside of herself and found him pulling at her as he'd pulled at her once when he was a little boy.

Once when he was crying and she couldn't get him to stop —he was just a little thing of two or three—she had taken him into the cedar closet and taken off her shirt and there she had held him to her breast. She had seen June do this when Badger was very little and June had said to him, "Don't cry. Go to sleep." So Zoe had done the same. She had put his lips to her breast and felt him clamp down and begin to suckle. Not for long, but for a moment he had suckled. He had tried to drag the milk out from deep within her; she was just a child, but still she had felt it, his deep suck, and it had sent her into a quiet place that she almost would have called sleep.

Now she let her body drop onto his bed beside him. "Please," she said. She let her head rest against his shoulder. "Please, say something. Do something. Please."

He felt her there, but did nothing. Still, he didn't push her away. And for a time they lay there in the dark of his room, neither of them aware that Gabe had paused in the doorway and stood staring at them. He was working late and hadn't expected to find what he saw. He wanted to look away, but couldn't turn. He saw Zoe there, curled against her brother. And all he could think of—and this was what surprised him—was how he wanted to be where Badger was.

Gabe's place was done in neo-American hippie with some early bachelor style. All red-and-black leather chairs and sofa. The bed was a kind of army cot stuck in the middle of the living room with a plaid spread thrown over it. There was a huge TV and a small bar. All the furniture, he explained, came from Rent-A-Room. He took this place because when he stood at the bathroom window he could see the hospital. He wanted to be a stone's throw from work.

Zoe opened the refrigerator and found three beers and a

dozen bottles of all kinds of vitamins. She opened the freezer and found frozen spinach, hamburger patties, and assorted TV dinners, mostly Salisbury steak. She slammed the icebox shut. The signs of a personal life were negligible. A drooping spider plant, an old football team photo, a guitar case in the corner, a poster from the 1960s, "War Is Unhealthy for Children and Other Living Things," back issues of *Field and Stream,* an ancient University of Wisconsin bedspread flung across the bed.

"I don't know what I'm doing here," she said.

"You needed to go somewhere." He stood there in a T-shirt and jeans. "You're shivering cold. You look terrible. Why don't you tell me what's been on your mind? And where you've been."

"I've been driving."

"You want some coffee?"

Zoe shook her head. "Tea. Do you have any tea?"

He put a kettle on. Then he turned back toward her, arms folded over his chest.

"I guess I want to apologize."

"For what?"

"For being an impossible person."

Gabe shrugged. "No more impossible than the rest of us."

She looked at him in his T-shirt and jeans. "I should go. You have to work tomorrow."

"I'm used to not getting a lot of sleep." He sat on the unmade bed, patting a place for her. "Why don't you sit here?" Zoe hesitated. "I'm not going to try to seduce you, I promise."

She laughed. "I don't think that's possible."

The teakettle whistled and Gabe got up to make a pot of tea. "I guess I'd like to talk," Zoe said, looking down at the floor.

He came back with the tea. "I'm listening."

"You see," she muttered, "it's all coming back to me. I thought it was gone, but it's there."

Gabe nodded, sitting down beside her. "And you want it to go away."

She was going to cry. "I hardly know you."

"Well," he put his arm around her, "you may as well start somewhere."

EIGHTEEN

Cal was a man who had no use for the seasons. He did not seem to know if summer followed spring, if fall preceded winter. He never seemed to know if he was hot or cold. He could leave the house in a raincoat on a beautiful day or put on a Hawaiian shirt in the middle of winter and June would have to rush after him with a sweater. He'd sit under a maple tree as autumn leaves fell golden and orange on his head or as seedpods, like little paratroopers, spun to earth around him. Millions spinning, landing around his head, but he never noticed. He never noticed the snow or the sun. He knew no dates. He remembered no times.

He brought chaos with him into the house. Papers he didn't touch were moved. Rooms he simply passed through grew messy. Food he passed by spoiled. June scurried around whenever he was home, trying to make order. But he didn't notice. He was ensconced in his life's ambition—to make a photographic record of the meaning of life. He never noticed how as he moved from room to room, from place to place, disorder grew. Shirts wrinkled, beds unmade themselves, weeds sprouted where he stood, moths appeared and gnawed their way through winter clothes.

In her efforts to comprehend, June turned to the astrological relationships of things. Her destiny, she determined, was in the heavens. The basement workroom, where she'd made the quilts from the war years, she now turned into a den of scientific inquiry. On the wall she put up maps of the signs of the zodiac, the phases of the moon. She purchased sextants and compasses and books on the history of the locations of the stars.

She studied the impulses at work in the universe at the time of Cal's birth. She charted paths, she determined courses. She understood the troubling aspect of double Scorpio rising. She persuaded her radio station to let her begin a morning horoscope program and she turned her latest passion into her work while her husband wandered about oblivious to time and the seasons, attempting to photograph the meaning of life, and Naomi declared that the curse on the family had been activated again.

In the midst of all this, Zoe fell in love.

When Zoe turned fourteen, she was so beautiful she could have any boy she wanted. Zoe, who had been a terror and a tomboy in her early youth, turned into a spectacular beauty at the height of adolescence. Her green eyes deepened to the color of secret pools and her auburn hair fell in long tresses down her back and it always caught the sun. The bones of her face turned sharp and the freckles disappeared, turning her skin to the color of fresh peaches. Her breasts grew, her body expanded, stretched itself. Her mouth grew wide, her lips thicker.

It was a beauty that would not endure. Naomi knew that, and so did June. It couldn't. It wasn't that she would age badly. Like an athlete or a child star who has had a great moment early on, and never again has been able to repeat it, Zoe would have to learn to live with herself as someone who would never again achieve the same heights, in the same way, again.

But she was privileged to have that one moment. The problem was, she was unaware of it and in the end her beauty never mattered to her. Boys could have been falling dead at her feet, turning their bodies into bridges over puddles, falling off cliffs, and she would not have noticed. They could lie down in her path or give her their football jerseys, but it simply did not matter to her.

She could have had the football heroes, the math whizzes, the debaters, the class presidents, the prom kings, the richest and the wildest. She could have had the leader of the band and the best dancer, the valedictorian, the salutatorian, the class clown, the most likely to succeed, the best actor, the smartest, the dumbest, the ones with cars, the ones with bicycles, the ones who started food fights, the best kissers, the ones with sloppy lips, even the class revolutionary, and even, they said, Mr. Greenspoon, her guidance counselor, who was happily married with four kids, yet was rumored to be mad for Zoe.

But Zoe didn't care. She focused her attention on scientific inquiry. She drew blood from rodents and examined it under the microscope. She collected beetles and bits of soil and wrote extensive charts as to her findings. She kept little fuzzy hamsters with pink paws and tame white mice. She kept them all in cages and recorded every phase of their behavior. Though Naomi said it wasn't right for a proper girl to collect horrible creatures, June said it was all right. "It's better for her if she's interested in something."

Eventually Zoe turned her scientific study to the huge white Himalayan dog named Puzzle that Sam Pollack had given to her. Puzzle had grown to unexpected proportions, his bulk filling the house, so that at times guests thought he was a polar bear.

Zoe began to measure the dog. As he grew older and moved into infirmity, she measured him and invented slings and splints, hip supports, corsets, assorted elastics, such that the dog would look like a victim of foreign wars. And one day June came home and found Puzzle slung in a hammock in neck traction. Only then did she decide that Zoe's future lay in veterinary medicine.

Zoe's interests expanded to everything—to the wings of butterflies, the composition of stones, the origins of pigment, the shattering of the atom, the fate of the whales—everything, except boys. They could get tickets for concerts no one could get tickets for. They could spend hours playing with her dog. They could drive off the bluff into Lake Michigan and Zoe would not have noticed.

Then one day she noticed Hunt Fisher.

It was the summer of dead fish and green flies, the summer of a heat that would not lift and a stench of rot and death that hung over the town, the summer when the woods were filled with biting insects and the air in the houses never cooled. It was the summer when Zoe went with Badger and Melanie to the beach where Melanie stretched out on the sand and tried to attract boys. Melanie would say, "Hey, Zoe, what about that one?" But Zoe never looked up. And Melanie, who would let the top of her bathing suit droop so Badger could see, and Badger, who already could not take his eyes off Melanie, laughed and teased her.

Then Melanie said to Zoe, "What about that one?" and Zoe sat up and stared. She looked straight ahead, right at him. In the distance, a young man of about sixteen was collecting trash in a garbage satchel. She watched as he dug and found things. She saw his thick, dark shoulders as he reached for a glass shard. She said to Melanie, "Who is he?"

Melanie shrugged. "I don't know."

Badger, taking his eyes off Melanie for the first time all day, was startled. His sister had never shown interest in a boy before. But Badger knew who the collector was. He said, "That's Hunt Fisher. He's famous for collecting things."

Zoe kept looking his way. "What's he do with them?"

"Makes funny things he calls sculptures," Badger replied.

Perhaps it wasn't a coincidence that Hunt was the only boy in all of Brewerton no parents would allow their daughter to see. He did strange things. He combed the beaches and the garbage cans, the dumps and the lots that were between demolition and construction. He dug for what he found. He collected the usual glass shards and pottery pieces, the pebbles and shells. But then there were the other things. The bones of birds, tufts of hair, broken shells, useless metal objects, bits of cloth, junk, trash, bottles crushed at the dump, the soles of shoes. Then he took all these objects and attached them to giant mesh wire that sat on the front lawn of his father's house and that made the neighbors try to have the house condemned.

Hunt came over to where they were sitting, his pack slung over his back. When he looked at Zoe, he thought how her eyes were like bits of Coke bottle he'd just found, how her hair was

like rusting iron. How she was the most beautiful statue he'd
ever seen.

And Zoe was drawn to the wild, disheveled hair. To the
dark, wandering eyes. She was like someone who had just discovered a hidden, secret world and, as with her mother two
decades before, somehow her fate was sealed.

Hunt came literally from the wrong side of the tracks. In
fact, he came immediately from the other side. No meal he ever
ate, no night he ever slept occurred without being punctuated by
the sound of a train, carrying beer or cattle or cheese to all the
parts of America he longed to see, but never would.

His family was very poor and his father worked in the
canning section of the biggest brewery in town, the Ferry-Hyde
Brewery that Sam Pollack managed. Hunt Fisher was the kind of
boy any young girl would fall in love with. He was sleek and tall.
He had jet-black hair and he wore white duck trousers with
black T-shirts in summer and black trousers with white T-shirts
in winter. He was a bad boy, not because he'd ever done anything bad but because he looked bad. He was a genius at frac-
tions, a great basketball player, and official class truant. Everyone loved him, except for the parents of the girls who went to
Brewerton High.

When Hunt asked Zoe out on her first date, Zoe didn't
know what to do. Dozens of boys had asked her out before, but
this was the first time she was planning on going. She was more
than planning on going. She was delirious. She was so delirious
she forgot to ask her parents if she could go out. So when Hunt
arrived for their date, Cal opened the door, surprised. "Good
evening, sir," Hunt stammered. "I've come to see your daughter."

"Oh, well, I'm sure she doesn't want to see you," Cal said
and he closed the door.

But just then Zoe came downstairs in a new blue sweater
and a straight gray skirt. Her hair was pulled back and raised on

top of her head. She wore green eye shadow and red lipstick and on her feet were small black patent-leather shoes. Her father looked at her, stunned. His daughter was transformed, but to what or why he wasn't sure. It took him a moment to make the connection between the boy standing outside in the white shirt and his daughter who came down the stairs. "You're going out?" he asked.

"Yes," Zoe said, nonchalantly. "I have a date."

"Over my dead body," Cal said.

Zoe looked perplexed. "Dad," she said, "please open the door." Cal opened the door and found Hunt still standing there, not having moved from the spot.

"We're just going to a movie," she said.

"Fine," Cal replied. He had grown astute in the ability to sense a rival. "I'll drive you."

Zoe and Hunt didn't know what else to do, so they got into the back seat of the car while Cal got into the front and chauffeured them. First he took them to McDonald's where they sat in the back, silently munching on hamburgers and french fries. Then he drove them to the movie and sat in the back row, watching not the screen, but the slightest movements of his daughter and her date. And as Hunt tried to put his arm around the rim of Zoe's chair or hold her hand, they'd hear a deep cough coming from the dark recesses of the theater, and Hunt would retreat again.

Cal had no idea what he was instilling in his daughter by his presence that evening. But he had imbued her with a sense of danger she had never experienced before. He had let her know, through his ludicrous protection, that she had found a way to the place where danger begins, where anything can happen. She knew when she reached across Hunt's leg and clutched at his fingers, as she let her fingers grasp his, that she was doing something wonderful and that it was wrong.

Zoe and Hunt continued to go on dates with Cal driving them. Sometimes Hunt came by the house and they'd go for a walk, but Hunt kept looking over his shoulder. "I'm sure," he said, "we're being followed." Finally one night they spotted Cal driving down the block behind them, his headlights off.

They began inventing ways to meet on the sly and Zoe thought they could perhaps meet just before and after her piano lesson. Zoe studied piano with Mr. Zeckler, who had a glass eye that roved in its socket as she struggled through Chopin preludes or a Beethoven concerto. Cal always dropped Zoe off before her lesson and picked her up afterward. One evening Zoe said, "Dad, can you get me to piano earlier? I like to practice for a few minutes before my lessons." And her father—pleased that she was becoming more interested in music, though puzzled when he saw no improvement—would drop her off earlier and earlier.

Every Tuesday night Hunt hid in the dim light of the stairway of the first floor corridor. He'd get there well before Zoe because he didn't want to risk being seen. She'd always find him, hands in his pockets, back pressed to the cinder-block wall. Then he'd hold her to him and as she felt her body pressed against his, it always amazed her. It was a feeling she'd never grow used to.

They'd stay in this embrace for five or ten minutes until the pimply-faced boy who had lessons before her came clomping down the stairs, gazing at Zoe in disgust. Then she'd dash to her lesson, flushed and breathless, and play for a miserable half-hour while Mr. Zeckler's eye roved around until he dismissed her and she could run down the stairs and slip back into Hunt's embrace for a few more moments until her father arrived.

While Cal didn't seem to notice that his daughter's piano lessons were extending themselves into an all-evening affair and June didn't notice because she had discovered the mysteries of the stars, none of it was lost on Naomi. The scent of strawberry lipstick, of jasmine perfume, the bleary look in the eyes, the way Zoe tended to walk with a bounce on the balls of her feet, the way her breath came too shallow and too fast—all this let Naomi know that somehow her granddaughter had at last entered the realm from which there is no return, a realm Naomi herself had once been privy to, before life had jettisoned her back to the arid desert of the once-loved. Zoe would return home from her piano lessons hot and impassioned like one possessed, and if Naomi said, "How was your lesson, dear?" Zoe would mutter something, disappearing into her room like a ghost.

Naomi also understood how, while her granddaughter had left behind the mundane responsibility of this world, Cal suddenly began to take an interest in her. He had ignored Zoe for years, except to come into her room at night and sing old army songs to put her to sleep. But that had stopped long ago and since then he had scarcely noticed her. But now a kind of rage seemed to have entered him. He'd come and pound on her door and say, "You'd better clean up that room, young lady," even though he hadn't seen the room in weeks and had no idea if it was clean or not. Or he would say, "Change that blouse. I don't want you wearing a red blouse," even though she'd worn it for the past year without his saying a word.

Though Naomi told him her room was clean and June said to leave her alone and Badger ignored them all, sitting in a corner drawing pictures of imaginary beasts, Cal went on pounding on Zoe's door, complaining about things he'd never even noticed before. But Zoe didn't care. She'd open the door and show him her tidy room, hand him the blouse he'd forbidden, and he'd leave in a huff. Then she'd close the door and return to the dream she'd dream for a very long time.

Badger was the only one who really knew what was happening. He'd been with Zoe when she met Hunt and he had seen the change come over her. And whenever he could, whenever they'd let him, Badger tagged along. He'd go with Zoe to the place where the rivers met and often Hunt would be there, collecting his bits of tin and glass for the sculptures he made. And the three of them would walk around and collect together. Some-

times Badger went to Hunt's house alone and he sat with him for
hours while Hunt glued bits of glass to wool and glued the wool
to metal to make his giant animals and decorated automobiles. It
was Hunt who taught Badger how to shape and carve.

But sometimes when Zoe was going to meet Hunt, she'd say
to Badger, "I want to go alone," and Badger, though he wasn't
much more than ten at the time, understood. And at those times
Zoe went and met Hunt at the tree and they'd spend hours with
their backs pressed to the tree, kissing, until Zoe had to wrench
herself away to go home.

Then Hunt got his driver's permit. In the evenings he'd
borrow his father's car and say he was going to practice his
driving while Zoe would slide down the drainpipe, clanging all
the way with Puzzle howling behind her, and she'd meet him at a
corner. Sometimes they'd drive to Tornado Memorial Park. It
was a lovely park set near the lake where there had once been a
little town, but a tornado had passed through and now there was
just this little park. But mostly they just returned to the place
where the two rivers met, high above the lake. They'd take a
blanket here and lie down and kiss and touch under the stars.

They weren't aware of the leaves turning overhead or of the
orange and yellow leaves that fell on their heads and buried
them. They brushed them aside and continued in their embrace.
They didn't notice when the leaves had fallen and the trees were
bare. But one night, when they found themselves buried under a
light layer of snow which they hadn't even noticed as they
kissed, Hunt was concerned. He thought that winter would set in
and they'd fall asleep in a frozen embrace and not be found until
the spring came and crocuses sprouted around their bodies.
"We've got to find another place," he said, brushing the snow
from her cheeks.

For weeks Zoe thought about it. She kept to herself and
planned. Then one night she did it. When Cal had gone to his
studio after dinner and June went downstairs to study her maps
of the stars and Naomi was dozing in a chair, Zoe walked out of

the house. She walked past Badger who was building a model city in the living room and who knew, just by looking at her, what she was doing, but averted his eyes. He'd never tell. She walked out of the back door and turned the corner. She walked for two blocks until she found Hunt waiting in his car.

They drove to the Home on the Road and parked along the side entrance and stole the key to open number 14. She slipped the key easily. She had been doing this all her life. She knew how to reach over and flick any key off its hook. She had spent a long time thinking about which key to steal, but Room 14 was the best.

It was the room no one used very much because it was at the bottom of the back stairs, near the parking lot. It was near the boiler room and the laundry room and it always had a hot, steamy air about it. It was the room you gave guests when you were full or if they were black. Zoe knew the way into the motel and she knew just how to get to Room 14. As a child, it was the room she used to hide in because nobody would ever think to look for her there.

When they got into the room, they made sure the shades were drawn and there was no sign of a guest. Zoe could tell by the pulse of the place that it hadn't had many guests. They lay down on the bed together and Hunt put his lips to hers. For a long time he kissed her. Then he let his hand slide under the back of her blouse and she stopped him. "I'm not ready," she said. "You're much older than I am and I'm not ready."

Hunt pulled away. He said, "I loved you for six months without touching you. I can wait a lot longer." Instead they switched on the television and watched old movies until they thought they had to leave.

At night whenever they could, Zoe and Hunt sneaked past Marvin at the reception desk, slipped the key to Room 14 off the hook, and went to the room for a few hours. They'd put the television on ever so low and they'd stretch out on the bed. Hunt would reach his hand under Zoe's shirt, each time try to maneuver his hand a little farther around her breast. But each time Zoe stopped him and Hunt said he could be patient. And slowly she began to give more and more of herself to him. She loved him. She would always love him, she thought. Zoe found herself clutching at him, in a way she'd never quite clutch a man again. She'd give herself to him in a way she'd never give herself again, slowly, a little bit at a time.

But somehow she left the room a virgin every night and went home. When she was dropped off, she felt her body hot and red and she wondered if there was a smell about her. Without saying goodnight, she climbed the stairs to the small apartment over the garage and slipped into bed.

One night Zoe woke and found Naomi standing at the foot of her bed, spitting into the air. She drew a deep breath, mumbled something, and then spit over Zoe's head. "Grandma," Zoe said, "what are you doing?"

"There's an evil spirit," Naomi said, "and I'm keeping it away."

"Grandma, forget it. Go to bed."

But Naomi shook her head. "The ghost of my mother came to me in a dream. She said to protect you from the cossacks when they ride through the town." And Naomi sat at Zoe's side for the rest of the night and for many nights after that, spitting into the air.

Zoe and Hunt were asleep, wrapped in each other's arms, looking like pale blue angels in the flickering light of the television the night when Cal opened the door and walked in. When he woke them, they were startled, but they had nothing to hide. They were dressed, but sleepy and ashamed. The worst for them was the knowledge that came over both at the same time—that never again would there be an easy way to see each other.

Her father grabbed her by the arm and dragged her across the room. Hunt reached for her, but Cal shoved him away. Then he raised his hand and brought it flat against his daughter's face.

The sound of the slap reverberated through the room and it would continue to do so for many years and generations to come.

When her father struck her, Zoe knew that at this moment she was as close to her father as she'd ever been. She also knew that somehow she was through with him. He would find no other way to hurt her. She tightened her face. Her lips were resigned. She accepted whatever was about to happen to her with cold defiance. Cal still clasped her by the arm, but he felt her go icy in his hand. Then he turned to Hunt. Raising an index finger to the boy who scrambled toward Zoe. "You will never again, do you understand me, never again see my daughter," and he dragged her from the room, past the desk where Marvin sipped a Coke. When Cal slapped the key to Room 14 on the desk, Marvin just smiled and Zoe knew who had betrayed her.

When they got to the parking lot of the motel, Zoe broke away. She ran across the main highway and into the side streets of Brewerton. Cal watched her disappear down the snowy streets. He went looking for her, but at last he gave up. When he got home, Badger stared at him as if Badger already knew what he'd done. "You know where she is," Cal said. "You find her."

She always went to the same place—to the confluence, to the place where the waters gathered. When Badger reached the spot he found Zoe facing the lake, her head resting against the tree. She was crying and shivering in the cold as she waited for Hunt. He would not be far behind. "It's just that we could never be inside," she said as Badger wrapped his arm around her gently, pulling her from the tree to him.

Zoe had no doubt what her punishment would be. Like some princess from a fallen regime, she was locked in her room in the evenings. During the days her movements were monitored. Someone had to go with her to the movies. Though once in a while Naomi forgot to make her call when she went to a friend's or June ignored it when her daughter slipped out in the evening if Cal was working late, mostly Zoe had no freedom in her life. Her father's rage seemed bottomless as the days and weeks went by.

But it made no difference to Zoe and Hunt. A pact had been sealed between them. A pact that would last for years, that would be the last thing Hunt would think of as he died, that would never leave Zoe's mind even as others entered it. They simply loved each other. They knew they could not be together, though they had thought that later, after high school, perhaps they could; they knew they might have to wait a decade, but it did not matter to either of them.

They saw each other when they could. Sometimes Zoe went to the place where the waters met and Hunt came and they'd kiss and hug each other. But Hunt never came by the house and they never spoke on the phone. It was just the understanding between them. That this was where they'd meet.

Then Zoe went off to college to study botany and French and the history of the world. She wrote to Hunt about the courses she was taking and he wrote her about the brewery. He had gotten a job, shortly after graduating from high school, at the Ferry-Hyde Brewery, the one that stood at the edge of the lake at the place where the Chippewa burial ground used to be so that the Great Spirit could easily find his way across the lake to the land.

Hunt worked in bottling. He worked the night shift, and while Zoe pulled the all-nighters that would help get her into medical school, Hunt watched beer bottles go by. He watched as one hundred and twenty bottles a minute passed his inspection, to be certain they were full of beer before being capped. He watched as beer sloshed out of the bottles, dripping over the sides, covering his legs, a smell that would enter his skin and which Zoe would smell when his body was close to her. It was a smell that he carried away with him when he left and brought back with him when he returned. It was a smell that would accompany his coffin and Zoe would never know, even though she was so sensitive to smells, if it was embalming fluid or the beer that clung to his flesh.

For three years Hunt worked the night shift, soaked and miserable, bottling beer, and by day he continued the collecting of bits of glass and tin cans and bottle caps. He constructed giant cows and decorated automobiles he found in junkyards with rhinestones and sequins and bits of glass and whatever he found as he combed the garbage dumps and the beaches and the reject area of the brewery. He worked at the construction of remarkable works of sculpture that would one day stand in sculpture gardens and in a major museum. For three years he slept only in snatches and dreamed of the day when he would be able to ask Zoe to marry him.

Finally, one day when he knew he could not stand it any longer, he joined the Seabees, the naval reserve, for two years of active duty, and then he'd be home free. He joined with the understanding that they would put to use his skills as a collector and that he would work in inventory in an office in Virginia and at the end of two years he would be sent to college on the G.I. bill. He wrote to Zoe and told her what he had done. He wrote and said he had just completed his basic training at Fort Benning, that he would soon be designing all kinds of sculptures out of army ration cans of soup and instant pudding, that in two years he would be sketching nude models in art classes in New York.

When his orders came, he found he was assigned to the MCB 53, the Mobile Civil Battalion. He would work in inventory, but in Da Nang. So he wrote and told Zoe his orders had been changed and he was to go overseas. He was being sent to a place where he would still work in inventory, only in munitions. Hunt would write to Zoe every day from overseas. On rainy days he wrote twice. He'd describe how the rain fell. Not like at home, where you could see the drops, but here it came in sheets, long and straight for days on end. And he'd describe the heat after the rain stopped and the sun came out and everything was wet and baking. He'd write these long letters of the people he talked to, of a highstrung people with a great capacity for living, but mainly he wrote about the weather which wasn't like any weather he'd seen or imagined before. And just when Zoe began to grow weary of these letters, when the monotony of his life was beginning to wear on hers, the letters stopped. They never came again. For days until Zoe received word, she'd pray. "Please," she'd say to herself, "send me the weather. Tell me if the rains have come again."

The last time she saw him it was a hot summer's night and he'd just shown up at her door. She knew he was going away and she'd expected him to show up before he did. She'd taken a job as a lifeguard that summer and each night after work she showered and put powder and cream on her skin and waited for him. Each day while the sun beat down on her already wrinkling and freckling skin she scanned the beaches, expecting to see him somewhere on the dunes, picking up tin cans as he always had.

Zoe knew it was Hunt when the doorbell rang. They were having dinner and Cal went to open the door, napkin still in his hand, and his mouth gaped when he saw Hunt standing there. "I've come to see your daughter." Cal didn't move. "I am going away, sir, and I have come to see her."

It was apparent to everyone that Hunt wasn't asking for permission. He was simply telling Cal what he intended to do. Zoe got up from the table and walked over to him. She had changed, he thought as she approached. It had been some months since they had seen each other and she was not as beautiful as she had been. The sun and her intense capacity for study had diminished her. Something about her had hardened, but he was glad to see that she was growing older and the time until they could be together was less. They went into the living room and spoke for a time in whispers. Then Zoe came out and said, "I'll be back later." And she added to her father as an afterthought, "Don't bother following us."

They drove to the bluff above the place where the rivers

met and there they pitched a tent. In the morning Hunt would leave Brewerton for a training camp in the state of New Jersey and from the training camp he would be shipped to another place from which he would not return. But for that night they were together. She felt him rise within her, there on the bluff above the lake, and she felt him in a way she would never feel again. Everything would happen to both of them at once. It would be her first time and his last. They studied and memorized each other in the moonlight as if they were learning some ancient text. And he carried this away with him when he went.

I grow mute. It is odd. I try to speak but I cannot find my voice. Or I speak and it makes no sense to anyone but me. It is not what I really want to be saying, and yet I understand what it is I am saying. It's just that nobody else does. I try to think what is the worst kind of loneliness. I used to think it was not having someone you wanted to say something to, but now I think differently. Now I think it is having someone you want to say something to and being unable to say it.

You are my sister, so I write these letters to you, because I cannot think of anyone else to write them to and because I know, practical and organized creature that you are, you will keep them for me. You will guard them in a safe place so that I may try to decipher my state of mind at a later date. They are my voice. I do not know what is happening to the voice in my throat, but now these are my voice.

I have stopped moving. That is, Whittaker decided we had to stop. We were in the middle of maybe our fifteenth trip across Canada and Whittaker said he couldn't take it any more, so we stopped. We got work at an Indian trading post with a guy named Lanyard Three Lives. It seemed like better work than a road crew or pipeline or some lumberjacking we were doing before. Lanyard does just about everything. He makes lanyards. He can stuff a moose, cook a beaver. We get along all right. He is an Indian, a Chippewa with a little bit of Inuit thrown in.

He was the first one to notice I wasn't making any sense. He said to Whittaker, "Your friend, he doesn't talk in a way that makes sense." Whittaker was too far gone to notice. Lanyard put me to work, doing what I like. I carve animals for him and he sells them to the tourists. He says I have a gift for little animals carved out of bone. He also says a sadness has entered my voice and it has made me give up. Lanyard has tried various remedies. He has mixed tree bark solutions. Lanyard knows more about tree bark than anybody I ever met, but nothing has helped.

Except Jessie. I think it was Lanyard who brought Jessie around. She is part Inuit and she reminds me of you. Jet-black hair and incredible green eyes. And silent. Not a word out of Jessie. We make a great pair. We used to watch each other in this town with our silent eyes and one day I followed her down to the river and I took her into the river with me and we made love like fish.

She is all that is keeping me sane. Nobody knows the depth of my grief. With her I don't have to talk. With her, it is all with the eyes. Lanyard says that love could be what will cure us both.

NINETEEN

Death's Door is a strait at the tip of Door County where the ships often failed to make their passage. Lake Michigan is famous for its shipwrecks. This is because the middle is so deep and the edges are so shallow. Storms come up when you least expect them. There are dangerous shoals, treacherous straits. There is danger where you would not imagine danger to be. Where it looks peaceful and calm, it is not peaceful or calm at all.

At the McDonald's just outside of Green Bay, there is a wall and on the wall there is a map of all the famous shipwrecks in the Great Lakes. Most of them took place near Door County. Zoe examined the wall of the shipwrecks, finding herself preoccupied with irrelevant facts. She studied the number of shipwrecks and remembered the names. The *Edmund Fitzgerald*, the ship where all the sailors disappeared, the *Monte Cristo*, the ship that sank in a storm and reappeared, crewless but intact, ten years later, sailing as if she'd just been launched.

It was difficult to imagine this could happen on her lake. Zoe was amazed at how easy it was, how much easier than she ever thought, to run amok. Zoe and Gabe stopped for coffee before continuing their drive north. They were at the entrance to Door County. The road north was a road Zoe knew well. It was the road she and Hunt took when they used to go find a place to be. It is the way to Tornado Memorial Park.

It is also the way to Canada—the road she drove Badger when she took him north. It is a neat, straight road that leads to the place where the weather comes from. The day was cool and crisp with a certain clarity that once made Zoe love to live in this part of the world. The water steamed off the lake as they crossed the bridge at Sturgeon Bay and entered Door County. They planned to drive all the way to Newport Beach State Park. They wanted to stand and look at the Porte des Morts Passage. They wanted to go all the way to the strait called Death's Door.

Gabe had taken the afternoon off and they were heading toward the tip of the county. They drove past the town where the hot fudge sundae was invented and past the town where the ice trade flourished at the turn of the century. She knew this part of the state well. Summers she used to come here with her family. They would spend the day at a resort that had Astroturf all around it and piped-in music even outside. Gabe and Zoe drove slowly. They were in no hurry as they stopped to buy cheese curds, salami and ham. They stopped at an Indian trading post and bought knickknacks they didn't need—lanyards, key rings, plastic placemats with a map of the state of Wisconsin. They went inside the tepee. The tepee felt damp and smelled of skin. She picked up gemstone nuggets, turned them in her hand. They had names like Mexican lace, rattlesnake, moss and blue heaven. Zoe bought strung beads for good luck and Gabe got a pair of moccasins to wear when his legs could stand no more.

They drove to the town of Ephraim where there was an ice-skating rink and a Swiss restaurant with goats grazing on the grass roof. Gabe pointed to the roof. "The food's not so great," he said, "but I love the goats."

They took a small table in the back and ordered cheese fondue. Zoe found herself drifting into a bad mood. She'd been home too long, and nothing had happened. There was no sign of anything. "I'm exhausted," she said. "I think I'm going to go back East soon. Maybe next week."

Gabe reached across the table and took her hand. It was a gesture he didn't expect from himself, but he did this. He wanted to comfort her. She looked at his hand, examined the skin. In the freckles and the moles she saw small animals, a baby giraffe, rainbows, sunsets. She saw a lovely spring day and saw herself laying her head back in the grass, resting, sniffing the air. The smells of summer. Long life.

Gabe's face didn't look like a geometry problem to her anymore. His squareness was rounded, his flatness given shape. "I want to tell you something," she said. Gabe raised his hand in protest, as if to say she didn't have to reveal any more than she had already. But Zoe gently lowered his hand. "I just wanted to say," she said slowly, "you have been extremely kind."

After lunch they continued their drive north, and on the way to Death's Door they saw a sign: TODD'S TAXIDERMY—YOU SHOOT IT, I'LL STUFF IT. Todd sat at a bench, stretching skin over the Styrofoam image of a deer. A sign over the door said what he'd stuff. Antelope, beaver, bison, caribou, cougar, moose, mountain lion, polar bear, squirrel, wolf. They walked among wild animals, stuffed heads, glassy-eyed moose. The walls were lined with rifles, bows and arrows, sabers. They passed a shelf where the taxidermist had stuffed his own pets. Parakeets, two dogs, assorted cats, a goldfish. All with little plaques with their names. Simon, the Persian, Foxy, My Little Terrier. Stuffed to perfection. They passed a strange animal perched on a log, teeth pointed, tail raised.

"That's a badger," the taxidermist said proudly. "State animal of Wisconsin." The taxidermist's skin was a pale shade of green and Zoe wondered if he was stuffed. She moved closer to look at the animal with the fangs and the glazed look of the eyes. She'd never really seen a badger up close, but she thought how this animal had nothing to do with her brother. Then she turned away.

As they wandered through the rooms of the taxidermist's workshop, past dead birds and bears and moose and family pets and state animals, Gabe wanted to reach out across all the dead raccoons and chipmunks and touch Zoe. To feel her hand, her arm, not as he had in the restaurant, but in a different way. He had touched many women since his marriage broke up, but this

time what he felt was different. This time he wanted to. He
hadn't really wanted to, not like this, in a long time. But he
checked himself. He had checked himself for years now, so he
checked himself again. He knew how easily he could take a fall.
And he had no time for such things in his life. He had time for
work, but not for love and certainly not for getting hurt.

Gabe understood that in order to touch Zoe he had to reach
out across all the dead things and find her hand and then both of
their lives would be different. He knew he could hold back and
not touch her and their lives would be the same. But he wasn't
ready for anything to change. He wasn't ready for the unknown.
He took a deep breath, like someone who had escaped a near
collision. He held himself back until the moment passed.

Zoe was aware of something. Her head felt tired, her limbs
weak, as if the weather had shifted, the air grown heavy. A storm
could be brewing. Her blood sugar dropped. But she attributed it
to the smell of formaldehyde, to the embalming of dead things. It
weighed her down. Fatigue settled in. She had never felt so
fatigued, not even during her internship, not even when she'd
worked thirty-six straight hours. Nothing had ever made her as
tired as she felt at this moment.

She felt the weight of love passing over her head, but it was
lost on her. She looked at the animals. The polar bear seemed to
be watching. The deer looked sad. The badger was about to cry.
She didn't know that among all the animals and the green-faced
taxidermist, something alive was about to spring at her, but it
hadn't. If Zoe had been more aware, she would have felt the
spark of life come from all this death, but it had been too long.
She mistook it for something else. For the weather, for the embalming of the dead.

They never made it to Death's Door. At about six Gabe
looked at his watch. "I should be getting back." He said he had
an early call. They drove with a sadness between them that
neither could name. It was late when they reached her hotel.

"Do you want to come up?" she said. "Would you like a brandy?"

"No," he said, "I need to get some sleep."

"I had a wonderful time," she said. She wasn't ready to be alone. She wanted to go somewhere first. "I'd like to go and see my brother," she said. Gabe looked at her and agreed. It made sense somehow.

The night nurse with the bad breath, Nurse Burlington, was on duty as Zoe defiantly passed her station. They went up to the room where Badger was and tiptoed in. Badger's head was tucked into his chest like a bird's. His hands curled around his face. They watched as if he were their child and for a short time they admired his sleep.

The next afternoon Gabe phoned Zoe at her hotel and asked her to come with him that evening to get a pizza. Zoe said she had planned on staying in or going over to see June. "You don't want me to eat a pizza alone, do you?"

As they walked into Donna and Emilio's pizzeria, a big banner stretched across the entrance way read, "WELCOME HOME ZOE." She looked at Gabe, stunned, and he shrugged. "I'm as surprised as you are." But there was a twinkle in his eye. "You planned this," Zoe said. She laughed as she walked into the pizzeria, surrounded by a few of her friends from Brewerton High. Melanie wore a turquoise blue jean suit cinched tight at the waist, and Sally Baxter came up to her in a pink jumpsuit. There was Robbie Carter, captain of the football team, who now worked in his father's valve company, and Annie Joffee, divorced with two kids. "Surprise," everyone said. "Surprise."

Zoe took Gabe by the arm. "How did you do this?"

"Oh, I just thought you needed a party."

Tears came to her eyes. "I had no idea . . ."

"Save it," he said. "I just had to make a few phone calls, that's all."

"I've been away such a long time."

Emilio and Donna had closed the place down for the night and they had pizzas going in the oven. They kept coming out, with anchovies and sausage or cheese and meatballs or vegetarian, and everyone stood around the bar and ate and drank free beer. Donna grabbed Zoe by the arm. "See," she said, "you can always come home. You can always come here."

Melanie took her aside, ready to provide her with some gossip. "Here's the scoop," she said. "Robbie's been having an affair with Annie Joffee since he married Linda Levy, but everyone knows. Don't mention Sally's brother, Donald, remember him? He killed himself and his girlfriend in a hunting cabin up north two winters ago. Drugs, they say. Annie Joffee's husband left her for Donna, but Donna won't have anything to do with him since Emilio's been on the wagon. Anything else you want to know?"

Zoe laughed. "I think that just about covers it."

"What's with you and Gabe?"

"We're friends, that's all."

Melanie rolled her eyes. "I wouldn't count on it," she said.

"What do you know?"

"Oh, I've known you for a long time, remember."

Emilio clanged on a glass. "A toast," he said, "to the one who got away."

Donna said, "We love the ones who made it to the coasts."

"Yes, Rich Einhorn and 'Hot Tub Hell'."

"Oh, and to Susie Wasserman." Gabe whispered to Zoe that Susie had five holes in her ears and a baby she was raising alone in a loft in Manhattan and a few hundred thousand dollars in the bank from some photo-realist canvases she'd done.

"The ones who get away do well," Melanie said, hands on her narrow hips.

There was a small pond out back and Donna and Emilio kept about a dozen pairs of skates around for anyone who wanted to skate. Others had brought their own. "Come on,"

Gabe said. "We're all drunk enough and the moon is high. Let's go skating."

"Skating?" Zoe laughed.

Gabe handed her a pair of figure skates, size 7. "These should fit you."

"I'm putting hot chocolate on," Donna said. "There'll be hot chocolate waiting when you get back."

They trudged out into the snowy night, lit by a moon that shimmered like a coin. Gabe had brought his own skates and Zoe sat on a bench putting on hers. It gave her pleasure to see that she could still cross-lace them. She remembered how to pull the laces tight across the ankle, how to walk on her tiptoes as she headed for the pond.

"Where're the others? Aren't they coming?"

"They may be too drunk." They watched as Melanie ran outside, shivered. "Brrr," she said, rubbing her arms, then disappeared back inside.

"I'm going to kill myself," she laughed as she slipped onto the pond.

"I'll be right behind you," he said.

Donna and Emilio put on a floodlight and the pond was lit. Over the loudspeaker came a tape of Barry Manilow, Johnny Mathis, and Strauss. "Oh, no," Zoe laughed. It had been years since she had skated on water. On a pond like this. But now she let herself go.

The pond was bumpy and at first she stumbled slightly as she tried to remember how to let her feet glide, her arms sway before her. Gabe watched her skate ahead. He watched as she skated off, wanting her to circle back to skate with him. He knew that if he was patient, eventually she would. He wanted to go up, slip his hand through her arm, and skate in circles with her around the pond. Instead, he let her go.

It was a beautiful night and the moon was high. It all came back to her now. Skating, Zoe thought, it's one of those things you never forget. How to cross over on the turns, how to set your balance forward on your skates. Now she let her arms swim through the air and held her shoulders high. And so she skated. She went around and around, feeling wild and cold, her face stinging in the wind. She skated forward and backward, doing crossovers and small turns.

As she took the curves of the pond, she loved the feel of the wind on her face. She had grown up with this cold and it was familiar to her. She recalled the pleasure she'd once taken in simple things. A walk home in autumn leaves, a cloud of breath before you. A piece of gossip whispered in halls. The changes of season, the simple rhythm of their daily lives. Life had taken her then and she'd moved with it. Glided from moment to moment as simply and swiftly as she glided now.

PART

FIVE

RAINBOW'S
END

Zoe, things aren't so good. It's hard to say how this is all happening to me, but Whittaker has taken off and I think Jessie went with him. It's the dumbest thing, let me tell you, getting left like this. I mean, I thought Whittaker and me were good friends, but it shows to go you who and what you can and cannot trust in this world and I never should've trusted someone named Whittaker Jameson Peters the Third. I should'a stuck with the simple people, the little people, like me. Now Jessie, she is another matter. I loved her dark skin and her dark hair, but all she really did was make me long for Melanie. You know, Melanie was so incredible to touch, to feel, to lie next to. Melanie was like a kid with her giggly face and her freckles and the way she always chewed gum. I loved to watch her dance around just acting crazy, dancing around a room just for the hell of it. But Jessie was my friend here, my companion, and it is terrible to have no companion, no one at all now. Except Lanyard Three Lives. It's all so crazy up here. There's a bunch of draft resisters and they hang around and we get high and talk to Lanyard, but none of it makes me feel too good. In fact I don't feel very good at all. I wish you'd come and get me. I wish Melanie would come and marry me. I write her all the time, but she never writes back. Nobody ever writes back. I don't get it. Where do your letters go? I have gone from general delivery to general delivery, but nothing comes my way. I have the worst feeling, the most awful feeling that if somebody doesn't come and get me soon, I'll never get out. If somebody doesn't come and get me, I'm going to have to burrow back in for the next coming winter, and all those to follow that.

Some things are happening to my mind. I have flashbacks, see things. I see Mom at the sink as if she's really there and then she turns into some kind of worm crawling on the floor. I know these things are crazy, so I can handle that. But one night I opened the door and there was Melanie, standing right there. I said, "Oh my god, Melanie, why didn't you tell me you were coming?" And she said, "Let's go to a movie. I want to see a show." Just like she always did, so I got my coat and went to the door, ready to go to the show, and I reached for her hand and came out with nothing at all, with the air and cold breeze.

The animals howl at night. I hear things, see them. I watch the news and see what is happening in the world and whatever is happening in the world starts to happen to my own skin. Some nights I burn as if on fire. Other nights I am being tortured, encaged, strung up from trees. I am completely fucked up. I am clean. I went cold turkey, but it doesn't seem to matter. It's all being done to me. Love, Badge

TWENTY

Naomi Daring was manager of the Sea'n Surf Motel on Route
A1A in Boynton Beach, Florida. In private she referred to her
motel as the Undertow because it was dragging her down. This
was the place where you come for your last swim, she'd say, with
a sweep of her hand as she pointed to the withered old bodies
turned to the sun like raisins laid out to dry. As she pointed to
the sagging breasts, the varicose veins, the shriveled faces of the
once beautiful, the once sensual, of former playboys and lovers,
of women who'd been lovely young things. Naomi had no illu-
sions about the state of Florida. It's not a state, she'd say emphatically. It's God's waiting room.

Naomi wandered around the deck of the pool of the Sea'n
Surf. She told Beverly, the enormous blond lifeguard who used
to be a diver for the navy, to be sure and bring Mr. Samuels a
big towel when he came out of the water, and to watch Mrs.
Letterman because of her broken hip. She waved at Mr. Samuels
as he dog-paddled in the shallow end. Why did he always have to
swim in circles around the whole perimeter of the pool, endless
circles that made her dizzy? And Mr. Winchell in his red-
checked Bermuda shorts, his golf cap and cigar, doing his one
hundred walking revolutions around the pool, nodded good
morning and Naomi said hello, making a face, as she did every
morning, when she sniffed his cigar. She checked on all of her
patrons. There were the ones she liked and the ones she didn't
like, but what she liked was that mostly they were regular and
they came back year after year until they were dead.

Of all the motels Naomi had run this was her favorite because it didn't try to be anything more than it was. A pool, a few

deck chairs, a view of the sea, a place to come and die. After leaving the Home on the Road, Naomi had tried out a few other motels. Before the Sea'n Surf she'd run a place called the Madonna Motel where all the rooms were theme rooms like Merry-Go-Round with its circular bed or Spaceship with its round room or Cowboy with its Western motif of spurs and whips on the wall. And then there were the strangest rooms like Crucifixion where the bed was in the shape of a cross or Immaculate Conception where the room was made to look like heaven with little angels all over the room and the bed decorated like a cloud.

Naomi circled for the second time before retreating back into her office. It was not so easy for her to make these circles that she called her rounds as if she were running a hospital and not a motel. Her bones were bent like wishbones and her blue eyes more white now than blue, like a fish tossed on land. The sounds she heard seemed to come from overseas on a faulty cable. Her hair was like the hay animals eat, her skin as spotted as a leopard's hide. She was almost a hundred years old and had not had a period since before World War II, a fact that even amazed Naomi, who could barely remember World War II.

The worst had been the eyes. Over the last decade Naomi had been going blind. Slowly, in the cruelest of ways, the light had been going out. God knows how many times she phoned the electric company to say her lights were dimming, to say she was losing power. How many times they had kindly sent the technician to placate her. First she lost color and the world became an old forties film, playing over and over—grainy and old-fashioned. She'd confided in June how she hadn't minded losing red, the first to go, because for a while the world came to her in shades of violet and blue. But then she lost the peripheries and her vision narrowed until life came to her through a dim, unreachable tunnel of light and all experience, everything she had known, was out there beyond her grasp, until the present was lost to her and all she really saw was the past.

But she hadn't minded this, for what had come to her had

been pleasant enough. She'd seen, for instance, through her tunnel of light, her mother come dancing out of the house, holding her in her arms. And she had seen her beloved Ivan walking up the front steps. And so when she saw the car pull up and her daughter and granddaughter, wearing sundresses and carrying small duffels, emerge, it took her a while to understand that this was happening now, not a quarter of a century before.

It had been three days since Zoe had woken in her hotel room in Brewerton, lethargic and at peace after a night of skating under a winter moon around a frozen pond, to find June at the foot of the bed packing Zoe's suitcase. It had taken a moment for Zoe to assess what was happening, but once she did she saw June, with her suitcase opened, carefully folding sweaters, pants, shirts. "Mother," Zoe said sleepily, "what are you doing?"

"I'm getting you out of here," June replied. She had finished with the drawers and was going on to the closets. Zoe's head was groggy. The night before Gabe had escorted her home, kissing her on the lips, and now here was her mother, packing her things. Her mother had always been an excellent packer and Zoe was impressed with her efficiency.

"Where am I going?"

June handed her a letter. "Here," June said. "This came for you. I opened it by mistake."

Zoe knew her mother never did anything by mistake, but she said nothing as she opened the envelope. It was a letter Zoe had written two weeks before she traveled home. Her roommate in Boston had forwarded it. She had sent it to the address Badger had given her for Whittaker Peters the Third's family and now the letter had come back to her. She read once again what she had written, "Dear Mr. Peters: My brother is insane and I understand you are not. He is on a drug trip from which they say he may not return. Could you perhaps help explain to me how this occurred or what it was that transpired while you were with him in Canada? Sincerely, Dr. Zoe Coleman." It was the first time she had signed her name "Dr."

At the bottom of the letter was a one-line sprawled reply, written in a childish hand. It read, "Your guess is as good as mine." The return address was the Rainbow's End Bait and Tackle Shop, Key West.

Zoe watched as her mother closed her suitcase. "Get dressed," June said. "We're going."

"Where? To your place?"

June snapped the suitcase shut. "To South Florida. Come on, I'm double-parked."

Zoe had been about to protest, but then she looked at June and understood. Her mother had come to claim her back.

They had driven down through Illinois, past Starved Rock, into bluegrass country, Missouri, Kentucky, deeper into the South, to where the Derby is run, where they'd paused to admire horses, and then had driven on to where cotton is grown, to a land of former slaves and too much heat. They had sweated through the humidity of the lower states, past the small plots of land in retirement towns, on into Florida, into old-age and nursing homes and the sounds of ambulances and radios. They had driven barely speaking, but Zoe did not once question her mother's right to take her where she pleased, nor did she ask where they were going or why. She felt this journey was in her stars and for once she gave herself over to destiny and let her mother take her by the hand.

They alternated driving and stayed in motels where they slept in the same bed like sisters and where Zoe kicked her mother in the leg when she snored and put a pillow over her head when her mother would turn on the TV and watch the news at six in the morning. June did not know herself what had moved her. She did not know what it was that made her pack the car and decide she could no longer sit around at the Heartland Clinic while her son had good days and bad. She had to do something.

All June knew was that she had suddenly and inexplicably

taken charge and that Zoe had somehow permitted herself to be taken charge of. Zoe had never let anyone run her life since the day her father put his hand flat across her face when she was a girl of sixteen, but now she gave herself over willingly. June was simply in charge and Zoe watched with amazement as her mother drove the twelve hundred miles and never once asked their destination until they pulled into the Sea'n Surf and Zoe said softly to herself, "So this is where we're going."

As June's blue Chevy pulled into the parking lot, Naomi sat in the chair at the reception desk in front of the mural of palmettos and egrets and waterfalls, trying to decide what room to put them in. Once she realized it was really them and not some game being played on her by the tunnel of light in which she dwelt, she had no idea what they were doing here, so she could only assume they'd come to watch her die. She greeted them with a sigh as they entered through the double doors. "What took you so long?" she said.

The small apartment Naomi gave them had a view of the ocean and June told Zoe to take the bed near the window. "The sound of the sea keeps me awake." June put a face mask and earplugs on the end table. Then she took a deep breath. "So," she said, "here we are." There they were, but now it occurred to both of them that they had no idea what they were doing there. "Well," Zoe said, "I guess I'll go to the beach. I'm going for a swim."

Zoe slipped on a black suit with a white stripe like a spinal cord down the middle and June admired her daughter's body. Her sleek long legs, her full breasts and thighs. Zoe had always looked good in a bathing suit and she always looked better with a tan. June thought how in a few days Zoe will look good, very good, with a tan. Zoe dashed downstairs, towel in hand, heading for the ocean. "I'm going for a swim, Grandma."

"You just got here," Naomi said. "Sit down."

"I want to relax."

"Here," Naomi said, "relax with this." She handed her a glass of fresh-squeezed orange juice. "Sit down, there's no rush. In Florida nobody rushes." Naomi rubbed her neck. "I want to relax too. But I can't. Everything hurts. Everything aches. Look at this toe. Look at these knuckles. My eyes see like I'm flying through the clouds. Like I'm a train in an endless tunnel. My heart behaves like a cage with a bird locked inside. My joints are coated with rust. I go from doctor to doctor. Nobody finds anything wrong. What good can doctors do?"

Zoe shook her head. "I guess not much, Grams."

"Old age is a disease for which there's only one cure," Naomi muttered.

Zoe thought about what she knew. She couldn't help her grandmother's toe. She couldn't help her brother. She couldn't help herself. What really matters, no one can help. She gazed at the mural of egrets, palmettos, pelicans. On the mantel Naomi still kept the bone of the woolly mammoth and the fistful of soil from her native Russia. It was almost dusk and Zoe wanted to get into the water.

Naomi sat very close, so that her nose was almost to Zoe's face, and she stared into Zoe's eyes. "So tell me. What's new?"

"Not much," Zoe said.

It was just like her granddaughter to say that after three years. "Not much. I haven't seen you in years. I'd forgotten what you look like. Now I remember. You look like me. Except you're tall and skinny. I bet men like you but you chase them away. Something must have happened to you in three years."

Zoe felt the plastic straps of the beach chair bevel into her skin. It had not occurred to her for some reason that in the years since she'd seen her grandmother Naomi would have changed. To Zoe, Naomi had always seemed fixed in time. June had changed and her father was dead and her brother had certainly changed, but Naomi wasn't supposed to change.

Now Zoe watched as her grandmother stared out the window at the pool, at the orange trees, the bougainvillea, at all the old people who sat like sunflowers, faces turned to the sun. It had never really occurred to Zoe that people grew old, just as it had never occurred to her that her parents had to make love in order to make her. Some things just happened to other people.

It was not for her to grow gray and lose her teeth, to lose circulation and limbs and short-term memory and let herself drift deeper into long-term memory. But now as she looked at her grandmother sitting there, smaller than Zoe remembered her, frail, her blue eyes almost too clear, her face withered like a pug dog's, Zoe knew that growing old is something else and that it would happen to everyone, even to her. It is wanting everything just a little bit less than you wanted it before. That imperceptible lessening of desire, until it is gone without your ever having noticed its leaving.

June seemed content, going to stores and coming back with plastic flamingo lamps, jars of orange marmalade, coconut candy. "I'll give them away," June said, "as gifts." She sent Badger a box of citrus fruit. "Mom," Zoe said, "what do you think he's going to do? Peel a grapefruit?" But June just shrugged. "Fruit is good for him."

Zoe watched as they drifted under Naomi's spell, each reverting back a generation while Naomi told them what to cook at night, what chores they needed to do, and each one obediently listened to the next. Zoe watched her mother shop, cook, and help Naomi out. By the time she had been in Florida two days, it felt more like two years. It felt longer than anything in her life had ever felt. But in truth she was not in a hurry to push on, not because she enjoyed relaxing—Zoe was not a person accustomed to having time on her hands—rather, she was afraid of what awaited her at the journey's end. She was afraid of what she might find.

She watched Naomi, almost a hundred years old, running the motel, puttering around. Zoe prayed silently, "Please don't bequeath me the Sea'n Surf." She listened to her grandmother recounting the history of the flying machine. Zoe tried reading around the pool, but each morning Mr. Winchell, puffing on his cigar, said, "Nice day, isn't it?" with each of his one hundred rotations. And then when Zoe was ready to swim her laps, Mr. Samuels, a shrunken prune of a man whose age no one could guess, got in and swam endless circles in the middle of the pool.

She read medical journals. She wrote letters to people she hadn't written to in ages. To Robert she sent pictures of Everglades wildlife, to Alison a postcard of astronauts, to Melanie she sent the Daytona Speedway. She treaded water in the ocean, her head tilted back like a lily pad, and took long walks along the beach where she poked Portuguese men-of-war with sticks and gazed into their rosy-blue jelly, until at last it occurred to her what it was she wanted.

"Grandma," she said, going into the office, "I want to make a phone call."

Naomi looked at her askance. "So, you know how to dial."

"It's long-distance."

"You mean you want to call a man."

Zoe laughed. "Yes, I want to call a man."

Naomi passed her the phone. "Calling a man never got a woman anywhere. I've never called a man in my life—not even the butcher. Look at your mother. Look what it got her. A broken heart, that's what it got her."

"I want to call Badger's doctor."

Naomi shrugged. "You don't need to call the doctor. You're a doctor. What good's it doing him? You don't need a medical report. I can give you the report. It's no report. You're calling for the wrong reason."

Zoe laughed. "I think I'm calling for the right reason."

"Write him a letter," Naomi said. "Send a card. Here." She handed Zoe a postcard of the palmetto and egret mural of the Sea'n Surf. "Mail this. Then see what happens."

"Grandma, what did all that waiting ever get you?"

"Ten years of happiness," Naomi said. "That's more than most people can say. I had ten good years."

But Zoe could not explain the torment that had entered her soul. The shells on the beach left her dreary. Mr. Samuels' swimming around made her depressed. Life seemed pointless, and the image of her brother languishing came back to haunt her. She had not doubted herself in a while, but now suddenly she doubted everything. You couldn't heal life. Nothing was adding up to anything.

Whatever had mattered seemed out of reach. The healing of the sick, her plants, her work, her few friends in Boston, the men who drifted in and out as if passing through a revolving door, but what it all came to she really couldn't say. She felt as if she had never really loved anyone or anything, not even Hunt, no one because she had never known how to let anyone in. There had always been this thing—whatever it was—that separated her from the world.

But now she found herself thinking about Gabe. In fact, she found she could not *not* think about him. Don't think about a pink elephant, Mr. Berkley, her science teacher, once said and then of course she could think of nothing but pink elephants for days. Don't call him, Naomi said. Now what choice did she have? But perhaps he wouldn't want to talk to her. She had treated him poorly. She hadn't said good-bye.

Like a teenager, sneaking away, she went to the pay phone on Ocean Boulevard across from the pharmacy and placed her call. She asked for Gabriel Sharp and to her surprise she was connected quickly. "Gabe," Zoe said, "it's me. Zoe."

"My god, where are you? You just disappeared."

Cars were passing by swiftly on Ocean Boulevard. Old people walked hand-in-hand. An old couple tottered by. She watched the wife help her husband down the curb. "I guess I did. I disappeared. But I'm alive. I'm in Florida."

"Florida? How can you be alive in Florida?"

"Well, I'm half-alive," she said.

"I could use a vacation," he mused.

The old couple had reached the other curb and now the husband helped his wife up. That was what she wanted, Zoe thought. I want to help someone down so they can help me up. "Wanta come for the weekend?" she said.

There was a pause. "No, I can't. But will you be back?"

"Yes, I think so. I think I'll be back." She thought for a moment how much she would like to be back now. But wanting anything made her uncomfortable, so she drifted back to what she knew. "I'm sorry I've been out of touch, but I was just wondering—how my brother is doing."

Now his voice grew professional, detached. "Your brother has a new green sweatshirt Melanie brought him and he wears it every day. He looks better."

"That's all?"

"He says there're buds on the tree so spring training must be underway."

"Are you very angry with me?" she said softly, surprised at her own words.

"I went looking for you. They said you'd checked out. I thought you'd leave me a note."

"I've been confused. I made some mistakes."

"You looked beautiful when you were skating on the pond."

There was a pause. "Why don't you come down? There's room at the motel."

"I *could* use a vacation," Gabe sighed. "It is awfully cold here."

"Well, then, why don't I just send you an electric blanket," she paused, "with a long cord."

Gabe laughed. "I guess you didn't hear what you wanted to hear."

"Guess not."

"Well, I'd like to see you—when you come back."

Zoe smiled, looking around at the street, the sky. The old couple had made it across the street and were approaching the next corner. The wife was about to help her husband down the curb. The palmettos swayed in the breeze. "Yes," she said, "I'd like to see you too. Look, I'll call you in a few days, is that all right?"

"Yes, it's all right." He said that anytime she wanted to call, she should feel free.

Zoe felt better, more at peace, when she returned to the Sea'n Surf. The pink beach chairs, the plastic flamingo, the green algae ring around the edge of the pool didn't bother her so much anymore. She did her laps dodging Mr. Samuels' circles and ignoring Mr. Winchell's cigar. Naomi dozed in the office while June sucked on a pencil, going over the books. "Ma," June kept saying, "how can you run this place like this?" But now it was all very amusing. Zoe thought it was very amusing indeed.

When Zoe finished her laps, she tapped Naomi gently on the arm. "Come on, Grandma," she said, "I'm taking you to the beach. It's right over there, just a hundred yards."

Naomi opened her eyes, wondering what decade this was, and gazed skeptically at her granddaughter. June shook her head. "Given your expenses, that's not a bad idea." But Naomi frowned. She envisioned spinner sharks and men-of-war, sting-rays, manta rays, undertows, barracuda, and all the denizens and dangers that could drag her down into the dark mysterious waters, into that place she'd been resisting for so long.

Naomi had lived near the sea for almost five of her hundred years and had never so much as stuck a toe at the water's edge. But because it was Zoe who was asking, she could not refuse. She made her way upstairs and returned in a bathrobe. Underneath she wore a bathing suit with palm trees and coconuts all over it, a modest skirt, the large bodice to accommodate her sagging breasts. She wore a bathing cap with a big yellow flower on it. Her legs were so veined they seemed blue. Her belly stuck out of a mass of flesh and sitting on top of this mass of flesh was a tiny head. This woman who had traversed the Russian steppes, gone through pogroms and men and children, through motels, through the invention of the light bulb and the airplane, had emerged from it all to look like a brontosaurus.

She let Zoe lead her by the hand as they walked to the seawall, to the place where the concrete ends, and gently Zoe guided her grandmother down the steps to where the beach began, and there, for the first time in her life, Naomi's feet touched wet sand. Seaweed crept between their toes. The ground was unsure. Naomi hesitated. She wrinkled her face. "This is enough. I think this is far enough."

But Zoe said no. "You'll like it. Water's good for you. You know, the Fountain of Youth."

Anything but that, Naomi thought, but still she followed. First a foot, then an ankle. The waves swept over her feet. The feet disappeared. Zoe held her tightly. She got her across the dip in the sand, the waves. Zoe helped her onto the sandbar where they both easily stood. "Here," Zoe said, "lie back. I'll show you how to float."

Naomi shrugged, trying to be philosophical. What's the worst thing that could happen? A tidal wave will come. A shark will eat me. But Naomi entrusted herself into Zoe's hands. She leaned back like one about to be baptized, head in Zoe's hands as her long silver hair came undone, floating out like octopus tentacles. Naomi closed her eyes and folded her hands across her chest as if she lay in a warm coffin, cradled by the one whom she'd once cradled.

Zoe loved the feel of her grandmother's body, her soft, wrinkly skin. She had never touched this skin before, never felt the silken texture of her grandmother's flesh, and felt as if she could spend her life just touching this skin. She'd thought old age would feel like an elephant's hide, like horse's hair, harsh and rough, but it did not. Zoe wondered how it was possible, from all her years of training, that she had never felt skin this old before.

It seemed as if she could just pluck her old grandmother out of this skin and a new grandmother would emerge, young and buoyant, ready to begin again. As if Zoe could just shake her like salt out of this old skin. For it no longer belonged to the body. It was ancient, a skin that had long ago left behind its connection to sinews and ligaments, a skin ready to be shed.

That night Zoe slept fitfully, aware of the sound of the ocean. Of a door opening and closing in the night breeze. June snored beside her and Zoe had to say roll over many times to her mother, and June obeyed like a trained pet. But still Zoe couldn't sleep.

She rose and went to the window. She saw the waves, white, coming out of the sea in the warm Florida night. She saw the coconut palms, the water lapping the shore, and there in the moonlight at the edge of the concrete walk, which was as close as Naomi would ever go to the ocean until that morning, Zoe saw her grandmother.

Dressed in a white nightgown with her long silver hair streaming down her back to her waist, she seemed to be staring at the moon. She stood there for a long time, just looking, but after a while she approached the steps of the seawall and disappeared onto the sand.

Zoe slipped on a robe and went to the seawall where she saw Naomi, the ocean lapping at her feet as if she was about to enter the sea. "Grandma, what're you doing? You should be in bed." But Naomi just stood, like one bewitched.

"Grandma," Zoe said, frightened now, "what're you thinking about?"

Naomi shook herself as if waking from a dream. "I'm thinking about Houdini," she said, but Zoe didn't understand. Naomi sighed. "I'm thinking about my old lovers," she said.

Zoe tried to take her by the arm and lead her back to her room, but Naomi shook her head. She said she'd lost the taste for sleep.

TWENTY-
ONE

Several times in the past million years or so, the Florida penin-
sula has been submerged in and then resurrected from the sea.
This is not caused by land shift. It is caused by the great conti-
nental glaciers which spread from the poles to the equator and
which melt from time to time. The glaciers never reached South
Florida, but in their advance they drove down to the tip of the
continent various prehistoric animals—the mammoth, wolf,
camel, bison, bear, saber-toothed tiger. South Florida remains
one of the most prehistoric places on the earth.

U.S.1 is the road that will take you from the tip of Maine to
the Rainbow's End. To get to the Everglades, you take it straight
to Homestead. Zoe drove as the road flashed by. The stores of
America. Gun & Pawn Instant Cash, Parrot City, Orchid Exter-
minators—America's Most Trusted Termite and Pest Control,
Waterbed City, Waterbed Outlet, Cafe Cubana, Monkey Jungle,
Live Worms and Night Crawlers, Shiners, Nude Review, Total
Nolan—I hate Creepy Crawlers, Miami Beach Casinos, auto
parts, aluminum siding, cold beer and cigarettes, more auto
parts, Aunt Jemima Pancakes, spare parts, Caribee Muffler, more
spare parts, another Waterbed City.

In the back of the car sat Naomi with June in the passenger
seat. They were all going to Key West to meet Whittaker Peters
and it was Zoe's idea to go via the Everglades. They stopped at a
fruit stand after an hour and bought star fruit, mangoes, avoca-
dos, strawberries, sapotas. Then they drove on, deeper into
America. They drove past a trailer park surrounded by barbed
wire, in which the trailers were all white and nothing green grew.
Outside, gangs of kids stood on the sand behind the barbed wire

breath. Good-bye, he said. Then he turned swiftly. "Come on." He picked up his knapsack and tossed it over his shoulder. "Let's get out of here."

For the first hour, Badger was quiet. He had carefully worked out the details and he went over them in his mind. He'd made his contacts and he'd give Zoe all the information once they were at the border. He promised her this. He'd figured it out. He'd made up his mind. He knew what he was doing. He was confident, sure of himself.

He had wanted to be a builder of great cities, but now he knew he was going to be a carpenter. It was something he could manage. Something he could do. It wasn't what he'd planned, but none of this was what he'd planned. He had never been a carpenter before, but he thought he could be one. He liked wood. He liked building things. He'd enjoyed building that log cabin.

He was going to work with his hands. He didn't want to work with his head for a while. His head needed a rest. He wanted to touch beams, wood, solid things. Tangible, permanent things. He'd only packed solid, simple things. His guitar. His tool kit. Two shirts. Her brother, she thought as she drove him north, was a simple soul.

They drove due north all night, for six hours. It was cold and the driving made Zoe sleepy but she drove on. They didn't say a word as she drove. Pine trees guarded the roads, keeping a cold vigil. The moon was silvery above and they drove swiftly on the road north.

An hour below the border they stopped and checked into a motel. It had been agreed upon that they would do this. Stop, rest, have a meal together. Then she'd drive him to the border and she'd go back. When they checked into the motel, the owner looked at them suspiciously, then smirked. "You want a double bed?"

Zoe laughed. "He's my brother. Two beds will do."

Badger nudged her. "Sister my eye. Give us a double, man."

Inside the motel, Zoe laughed. "How could you do this? How could you do this to me?" They flopped down together on the double bed. For a moment they lay there side by side, then Zoe put her head on Badger's shoulder. He stroked her hair gently, then clutched her to him. The last thing she remembered before she fell asleep was Badger's lips kissing her hair.

Zoe had no idea how long she slept, but when she woke she knew he was gone. She felt it in the room immediately. In the bathroom she found the note, stuck to the mirror. "Now I owe you one. And I promise you, my very own word, that one day when you least expect it, I'll do something for you."

Zoe got up and checked out of the motel. She knew, because she knew motels, that these people felt sorry for her. She watched the slight snicker in their faces; they knew she'd been jilted. Zoe said nothing. She just turned and drove away. She drove for six hours straight back to where she'd come from and when she walked in the door she found her mother, her grandmother, and her father sitting in the living room. No one said anything until her father cleared his throat and rose. "Tell me, where did you take him?"

Zoe shrugged. "I don't see what that really is to you."

Cal cleared his throat again and said in a barely discernible whisper, "It is something to me."

"You should've thought of that before," Zoe said.

"That's probably true."

"You always think of things when it's too late to do anything about it."

Cal raised his voice now. "You just keep your opinions to yourself, young lady."

Zoe kept her opinions to herself and went about the business of creating as much space as she could between herself and where she came from. She had had enough of the magic, the premonitions, the photographing of memories and ghosts, the walls of the basement turned into maps of the stars. She had had enough of Naomi's prophetic dreams, of her father's living burial in the darkest of all darkrooms. She recalled the wondrous journeys of Sam Pollack, his tales of the Gobi Desert and the South Sea Islands, and with what little she had saved, upon graduating from college Zoe became a drifter.

She worked her way from place to place. She went to Japan where she taught English to bankers' children, then worked her way to Australia where she mined opals for a time. She went to South America where she took railroads through the Andes and slept with men she met on those trains. She wandered until she came to a clinic in Brazil where a doctor who was a friend of a friend she'd met on a train somewhere in Peru had invited her to visit.

The doctor's name was Jorge Rodriguez and he had one continuous eyebrow that was always arched. He had deep dark eyes that never seemed to sleep. He worked in his clinic outside of Rio night and day. He told Zoe she could stay in his house for a time if she would help with housework and cooking, but Zoe found she grew bored in the house, and while she cooked and cleaned she found herself drawn to the clinic.

She would wander among the children with diseased eyes, spindly legs, the women whose stomachs ached with parasites, the men whose parts were missing from one industrial accident or another. She saw eyes so swollen they would pop and bellies so distended that men looked like pregnant women and after a few weeks she asked Dr. Rodriguez if she could work in the clinic instead.

Dr. Rodriguez was thirty. He was a small, slight man, but his body seemed incredibly powerful and every night Zoe thought he would take her to his bed, but every night they returned from the clinic exhausted and spent, and they would eat a small meal together and go to their separate rooms. Still, Zoe knew she had come to stay for a while. For the first time in almost two years she cabled her parents to say where she was.

Then she set about the task of the care of the sick. She

found she could touch sores and not cause pain. She had a gentle, caring touch. She cleaned wounds. She bathed diarrhea off the buttocks of men and took a diseased baby from its dying mother. She could do things that would make other people cringe and grow ill, but somehow she had a gift for this. She knew it was within her, but she didn't know it yet in a way that she could tell herself that this was what she would do with her life.

Though she sensed it, she did not know for certain until one day when Dr. Rodriguez said, "It is your destiny, to heal the sick. I will teach you what I know." She was not surprised. He taught her all he could of the illnesses of the tropics and of the poor. Of the diseases that came from hunger and malnutrition. Of the worms and bacteria that could burrow into the skin, make their way to the eyes or deep into a person's brain, causing a pain no morphine could stop. He taught her how to suture and how to cut, how to cure and how to wash. She watched as he soothed the ill and comforted those who hadn't much time.

He taught her everything she could learn by watching. And then one night he taught her how to let go. As they turned to go to their separate rooms he said, "Why don't you come with me?" For three years, since Hunt was killed, Zoe had lived as if she kept a hard nut inside her, but now he took her to bed and she let go of it. First he undressed her. He took a sweet almond oil and rubbed it into her skin. He massaged her arms and her legs, her breasts and her groin. He did not even make love to her that night because he sensed she was not ready, but she felt the tightness in her tendons soften. And that night she slept as if all her restlessness had left her body.

At night they left the clinic and went home. If they were too tired to make love, he rubbed her body with oils and she did the same to him. When they were not exhausted, they made love. At the clinic he taught her what he knew of curing the body and at home he taught her what he could of curing her soul. They hardly spoke and Zoe knew that what she felt for him was not the kind of love she was capable of, but she felt an enormous closeness to him. He would touch her gently and for as much time as she needed. And she learned to touch him back in gentle ways. She felt she was being healed from a deep place within her and she did not question the passing days or weeks. She understood that this was the time of her rehabilitation.

For three months they lived this way and then a cable came. At first Zoe said nothing about it, but walked around with the cable in her pocket. At night when they made love she would think about it, there in her white smock. And finally one night Jorge said, "I don't know where you are, but it is not here."

"My father is dying," she said. "I don't even know if I care."

"Then you must go home to find out."

It took her a week to get her papers in order and two days to fly home. She cried bitterly when she left Jorge and his clinic and he told her that when she could, she should come back. But somehow as she touched the small, slight body that had taught her so much, she knew she would not. She knew this was the end of her journey.

When she arrived home she found a shrunken, yellow man who could barely breathe, buried under piles of quilts he'd once tossed off, now trying to keep warm. He had refused the hospital and June, who had nursed him when he came home from the war, nursed him again, but she was relieved when Zoe arrived and somehow knew what to do.

Zoe took one look at him and did not regret coming home. With a sweep of memory she did not see this wasted man whom disorder had followed, who could make the leaves fall, the seasons change. Instead she saw the man who had tossed her into the air where she had remained suspended since childhood, dangling in the trees with the birds, waiting to come down.

Zoe rolled up her sleeves, and with the skill and confidence Jorge had taught her, she nursed him. She bathed him and made him comfortable. She turned him from side to side and brought him what he needed. Then he lapsed into unconsciousness and for five days he tossed and turned like one adrift at sea. Then on the fifth day he opened his eyes. He sat up in bed. There was a look of terror in his eyes and Zoe saw he was struggling to get away from something.

He reached out, beckoning to her, and Zoe reached down to comfort him. He pulled her to him and held her with a strength that surprised her and she allowed herself to be folded into his arms. He tried to tell her that he had been frightened by the screeching halt of a freight train and the sound of metal crushing that had run screaming through his dreams and he had reached his arms out, crying into the night.

When he released his grasp, his eyes were closed as if in a gentle sleep. Then she noticed what she thought at first was a halo, a thin golden band of light coming from around the rim of his head, which she understood in a few moments to be amber fuzz, like that of a peach, encircling his head. His hair was growing back and it would continue to do so, despite the under-takers' efforts to trim it. The undertakers said they had little embalming to do, for a harsh, briny substance ran through his veins, but there was nothing they could do about his hair. Cal was buried, without great ceremony or mourning except by his wife and by his daughter, with a full head of hair that kept growing and eventually made its way through the cracks in the coffin into the ground until it strangled the roots of the young tree beneath which they had buried him.

After the funeral June handed Zoe a packet of unopened letters from all over Canada that Badger had written, each with a different postmark, and Zoe sat down and read the letters which told how in the kingdom where he dwelled there was too much space between the trees, too little between the people. How he had learned the language of bears and been touched by angel wings. He said he had loved a gypsy girl and that once while carving wood he'd heard it cry. She read these letters five or six times before concluding her brother was on drugs or insane, or both. She decided she had made the right decision a few years before when she tried to create as much distance as she could between herself and the rest of them, and without responding or writing back, without answering a single word he had written, she put the letters in the same drawer where the letter about Hunt had once been and headed east to medical school.

This was the same week that Naomi bought a motel in Florida, saying she'd had enough of the arctic freeze and headed south. Only June was left in Brewerton.

After they left, June thought back over her life. "What have I done," she asked herself, "to deserve this?" The failure of her marriage, the death of the only man she'd ever really loved, the loss of her son, her daughter a stranger to her—what had she done to bring all this down upon herself? And as she scanned her memory and searched back into the darkest recesses of all that had occurred, she only saw one face, one person, one event, but she knew that it had somehow colored her entire life. She saw the embittered face of her brother who had been left behind, neglected and ignored, even in his death. She saw his thick, soft body as he shattered the glass, pinioned in that hideous web for an instant which would last forever.

June then set upon the single purpose of bringing about Badger's return. She consulted oracles and psychics. She wrote to presidents, requesting amnesty. She wrote to the Canadian authorities. She had waited all through Cal's funeral for her son's return and she had prayed that he would find his way. She told Sam Pollack that she would marry him after all these years if he brought her son home to her and Sam devoted months to the investigation of the whereabouts of Badger in his final attempt to procure the bounty to win June's heart.

But two more years went by. And then one day Badger appeared. He had come staggering back into town, aged and thin, covered with mud and filth. June speculated that he had simply walked across the border and wandered home. He had arrived on her doorstep with a wild, crazed look in his eye and mute as a giraffe, the same way his father had once come home to her.

PART

SIX

WHERE THE
WATERS MEET

Dawson Creek
April 24, 1972

Dear Z, Sometimes I wonder if I shouldn't have gone to jail. I wonder if I wouldn't have been better off there. I try to imagine guards. I try to imagine some guys trying to fuck me and me having to fight them off. I can imagine all of that. I can imagine the slop they serve and the stink of toilets. I can imagine no heat and only a thin blanket to keep me warm. What I try to picture and can't is me, sitting alone in a dark, windowless cell, locked up, enclosed. Sometimes I try to imagine that, the dark, windowless room, but this isn't easy to do in spring when the weather is beautiful and I can see the hills, but Dawson Creek is far north. I seem to be traveling farther and farther north. I'm moving east and west, but also north. I'm a moving target, you see. Anyway, try to picture this. Me in that windowless cell. Perhaps you feel responsible for my being here in the first place. That's why I keep moving. I don't want you to take any chances. I want you to finish school and do what you're supposed to do. You shouldn't feel guilty or bad about my being here. If you want to know why, try sitting alone in a room with no heat and no windows and no one to keep you company for a week or so, which I've done, and you'll see how I'm much better off here than in jail. You'll see how much better it is for me to be here than there. Love, B.

TWENTY-THREE

Zoe watched the seasons change as she left behind the palmettos, the magnolias, and the citrus orchards. Summer became spring, spring turned to fall, fall into winter until somewhere in northern Tennessee ice glazed the trees like frosting on sugar cookies and the cows froze standing in the fields. They prayed the car wouldn't give out, crossing the frozen tundra of the Midwest as they drove back to the arctic part of the world from which they'd come, Brewerton, home of the ice manufacturing industry.

They returned to a mid-March blizzard that made them pull over to the side of the road until they could see again, but for a time the car was ensconced in snowflakes and Zoe found herself traveling through the center of them. Then, as they drove on, Zoe had to admit to herself, even as they approached the familiar roads to Brewerton, that she was traveling a way she had known before, and she let herself be rocked into the frozen days, until at last they came to the house, now surrounded by drifts, except for the neatly shoveled walk and driveway that led to the front door which they opened and found, before a fire blazing in the fireplace, Sam Pollack, sitting in the middle of the living room, where he had passed the last two days archiving the photographic works of Caleb Coleman.

It had been almost twenty years since he'd set foot inside June's house, but now he was back, older, eccentric, hair gone white. He had trembled as he walked inside and laid down his gifts of a leather backpack for Zoe, an exotic plant with tiny red flowers from Bali for June, and a small keepsake box from Africa for Badger. He followed June's instructions exactly and let himself in with the same keys she had given him when he was allowed in the house so many years before. After June called from the highway, somewhere in the middle of Tennessee, he had gone to prepare the house. He had dusted and cleaned and cooked a capon and wild rice in the house from which he had been banished so many years before when Cal had come home to find Badger with a spice clock and Naomi dancing in a silk dragon kimono and Zoe cupping a small white dog in her hand.

After struggling to comprehend the dustproof climate-control system, the burglar alarms, and the red panic buttons June had installed over the years, Sam, not knowing what else to do with his idle time, set about the chore that would occupy him for the next few days. After cleaning and cooking, he found in a corner of the room the cartons and boxes of photographs that had stood stacked since Cal's death and he began to sift through these, slowly at first. But then he began in earnest, pausing only briefly to shovel the front walk, then returning to what would be his work for the two days the storm delayed June and Zoe and what would be his work for years to come. When June and Zoe walked in, they found Sam, hunched over, intent, putting together the first posthumous and major exhibition of the photographer who would, years after his death, thanks to his archivist, achieve acclaim as a social realist, a photographer of American life in the Depression and war years, and a foremost capturer of the American family.

Zoe and June had left the Rainbow's End the week before and driven the one hundred and sixty-odd miles back to the Sea'n Surf. When they reached Naomi, they'd found her despondent. She had seen her granddaughter call a man on the phone and she'd seen her own face reflected back at her from the great swamp of the Everglades and that was enough living for her. She said, "There is nothing for you to do here anymore." And she went about the business of putting her things in order.

But Naomi was always putting her things in order so June and Zoe decided this time was no more serious than the other times and began the journey north. June thought she'd have to persuade Zoe to return with her, but Zoe was willing. She navigated and drove most of the way and did not notice when June got out of the car to make a phone call somewhere before the climate shifted from spring to fall before the palm trees and the magnolia disappeared and the scent of gardenia and blackened fish left the air. Something more powerful than she'd known before was bringing her home.

After they greeted Sam, Zoe looked down at the work he had spread out all over the floor—the photographs he'd put in some semblance of order that for years had sat in their boxes, awaiting the snowstorm and the right moment for their sorting and sifting through. She saw Black Thunder, that dust-bowl disaster, rolling toward Cal's aunt's house, and she saw her great-aunt on her deathbed, chalk-gray with circles around her eyes, like a raccoon. The Oklahoma countryside and the pictures of Europe, the war years, the record of aerial reconnaissance missions in some of whose blurry images the earth looked more like another planet, like the moon, complete with rings and comets. She saw to June's horror the pictures of her parents in a nude, breathless embrace, and the pictures of tiny children holding hands as they played in the backyard, the pictures of the small private invasions to match the large—her baths, her toilets, her brother's adolescent erection. And she saw a picture of the back of Badger's head as he left for Canada, turning away from his father forever, knapsack on his back, heading out the door—the last picture her father ever took.

Sam gave her a big hug. "Look, for you, for the world traveler. A leather backpack." It occurred to Zoe as he handed her this that Sam seemed rather foppish and silly to her and while she had adored him when she was a child, she wondered what it was her mother had ever seen in this man.

She took the backpack, which felt heavy as she slipped it on and so she took it off and opened it. Inside, Sam had put a thick envelope and Zoe opened this to find a packet of photographs of herself as a mere child really, in the back seat of cars, at her piano teacher's entrance way, on the bluff, on the bed at the Home on the Road—pictures of herself in places and situations she thought only known to herself, all in the arms of the boy she had loved.

How could he have done this? she wondered. How could he have followed her all those times? Aghast, she put them away. "Thank you, Sam," she said. And muttered, "I had no idea."

"Oh," Sam waved his hand, "don't thank me. I didn't even open them." He pointed to her name on the packet. "That's not my handwriting." Zoe examined her name and the word "Personal," recognized her father's shaky scrawl, and realized that the grouping of these pictures was one of the last things he had done before he died.

Since before his death, Zoe hadn't set foot in her father's studio, but she knew that if she were to confront him, it would have to be in the only place where he'd ever felt warm and safe. June had left it intact, never selling it but using it instead for storage for all the furniture she kept buying, growing dissatisfied with, then putting away. Now in the dark hours before dawn Zoe, who had hardly slept, took the key she'd found in the kitchen drawer and let herself in.

She made her way into the studio, past the piles of furniture June had left, where she walked among the backdrops of cherry blossoms where lovers had gazed into each other's eyes, past the thick quilt with giant bears where babies posed in the buff, past the settings for Paris or Rome, the old-fashioned street, the Western sky, Niagara Falls, wondering where was the funereal sadness, where were the backdrops of loss and despair?

Then she wandered into the darkroom, where nothing was changed, where all was as he'd left it; even the wash trays were still turned upside down and a few yellow and wrinkled prints hung on clothespins to dry. She put on the red safety light, and out of the backdrops and the darkness she felt him come to her as she knew he would. "I know you're here," she said. "I came home. I've done what you asked. I've seen him." The cherry-blossom backdrop fluttered. The room felt warm, even though she saw her breath before her. "I've had to be too strong," she went on. "I don't want to have to anymore. It's your turn now. Go make your peace," she said. "And then you can rest."

Zoe wrapped herself in the quilt of the bear blanket and curled into a ball and stayed there with cherry blossoms behind her until the moon had set and the darkest night filled the room and she left the studio, locking the door, knowing it was for the last time.

June sat in the living room, a cigarette lighting the darkness, watching as Zoe walked in the door. Zoe didn't see her as she walked in and was startled. "I'm sorry," June said. "I didn't mean to frighten you. I wasn't sure you were coming home."

"Here I am. What're you doing up?"

"Why don't you sit with me for a while?" June said, knowing this would probably keep Zoe from doing so. Then she added, "I don't feel like being alone."

Zoe thought about it for a moment. "I guess I can sit down."

"How about a brandy?"

"It's almost dawn, Mom."

"Just this once won't hurt."

Zoe nodded. "I'll get it." In the dark she fumbled for glasses and the decanter. She poured two glasses of brandy, handing one to June.

"We hadn't talked really since yesterday. Were you surprised to see Sam?"

"Yes," Zoe said, sipping, "I was surprised."

"Did you think I'd marry him? After your father was gone?"

Zoe shrugged, feeling uncomfortable. "I thought you'd marry him before."

June sat forward, lighting another cigarette. "What do you mean? You know, I've tried to understand you. Believe me, I have, but you've always been a mystery to me."

"Some things get in our way, Mother. Some things keep us from happiness." Zoe knew she should keep her mouth shut—that it wasn't the time to speak. She didn't know why, of all the times when she could have said something, she chose to say it now. "It's not a great mystery really, Mom." Zoe felt all the pressure of all the years build up inside of her. She didn't have to hold on to it any longer or be special in that way anymore. "All right," Zoe said. "It's just that I saw you."

Zoe was amazed at herself. It was her secret, her small secret, and now it was out. It was out and she wasn't special anymore. Now there was nothing entirely hers. "I saw you."

June had no idea what Zoe was talking about. "I'm sorry, but what did you see?"

Zoe continued, her voice trembling now. "I saw you in the window." She muttered and June could barely hear her. "I saw you with Sam."

June sat back. "What are you talking about?"

Zoe spoke louder now. "You were there, by the window. I used to go and just watch you." She could see her mother staring at her from across the room. "And I'll never forget it."

"What you saw isn't what you think," June said after a long silence. "There's only one person I've loved. There wasn't anyone else. No matter what you saw."

"You were with him, that's all I know."

"You don't know anything," June said. "You think you know, but you don't."

"You're not the only person who loved somebody you lost. You're not the only one."

June was silent for a moment. Why can't you understand? June wanted to say. What child who has never had a child of her own can understand? If June could have any moment back, it would be those first years with Cal. It would be when Zoe was so small she'd lie beside June, just watching her as she read or sewed, never taking her eyes away. How I ached for you, June wanted to say. The others, I know why they went, but you, how I ached for you. How I longed to hold you. "The only one I really lost," June said, "was you."

Zoe said nothing, so June went on. "You'll never know how much I've wanted you near me. I've tried to figure you out. So you saw me with Sam. So you've kept your distance from me because you thought you saw something you can't even begin to understand."

Zoe kept her eyes on her glass which she turned in her hand. She was older now. Things were behind her. "No," she said, "I can't. You're right."

"You've lost someone you love too. I know that. We made a mistake about you and Hunt. We should have let you be together. Maybe you would have gotten it out of your system. Maybe it would have been the right thing for you. Whatever, we made a mistake. I know you lost someone and this isn't to belittle your loss. But it's different when you lose someone all at once, and not every day a little bit more. Because when you lose a person all at once, in your mind you can keep him whole. But when you lose someone the way I did, it's like something rotting and turning bad. And there comes a time when you can't remember the good anymore."

"So you think I'm lucky." Zoe sipped her brandy.

"No, darling, I don't think you're lucky. I just think you've still got a chance."

"A chance at what?"

"At finding what you want. At going after it."

They sat in the dark for a long time, then Zoe got up. "I'm going to bed now, Mom. I'll think about what you said." June reached her arms out and Zoe let herself be brought in. June kissed her on the head and on the cheek and for a moment once again pulled her daughter to her, had her there back in her arms, then slowly released her daughter again back into the world.

After Zoe went upstairs, June stayed in the dark, then lit another cigarette. She lay on the sofa and thought of all she'd tell Zoe when the time was right. She'd say that she knows more about life now than she did a few years before, that she knows love isn't something you sit around and hope will come to you. How it isn't something you wait for. It's something you do. Then she'd tell how she learned it. Tell about all the time on her hands —all the hours, all the days, all the hours of night and darkness, all the time when there was no one to turn to. She'd tell her about how at night she'd fluff up the pillow beside her and talk to it as if it were her husband. She would tell Zoe how at night, before she fell asleep, she kissed a pillow goodnight. She would fluff the pillow and put her mouth to the pillow. She would say goodnight, dear, to feathers and foam. She would tell Zoe about all the years and all the times love came right up to her, so close it was within her grasp.

Zoe couldn't sleep. She was aware of every sound in the house. Every movement of the boards, every creaking, every time the dust-control system went on. But mostly she was aware of the fact that June was staying downstairs and it would be hours before she'd hear her come upstairs.

It would be a long night if Zoe thought about it, but she didn't want to think about it. She was tired, but she knew she wouldn't sleep. When she was younger and couldn't sleep, she used to sit in the dining room and count the headlights that shone on the stop sign across the street. She'd say to herself, "I'll wait for six headlights and if Hunt isn't here by then, I'll go to bed." But six would come and then she'd wait for another six, and then another. Sometimes she'd sit for hours, staring at that stop sign, wondering when his lights would appear and she could sneak out of the house.

But now she sensed that a certain phase of her life was

over. It surprised her that this had occurred, that she had moved from one phase to another. As she lay awake, Zoe thought of her mother and where she had been. She thought of what had happened in her mother's life and how she hadn't understood it at all, even though June's life had shaped hers in ways she could only begin to discern.

It was strange how notions about the world enter you. When she was small, Naomi had told her things. How she came from the land of the firebird. There was a czar and his soldiers rode through the town and stole children for the army or speared them with their sabers, hurling them out of the way. When Naomi told Zoe these things, her breath smelled of cabbage and she spit into the air to keep the devils away.

How was it possible, Zoe used to ask herself, that her grandmother came from a place where you had to blow the devil away with your spittle, where soldiers speared babies into the air. It was as if Naomi had come from a made-up place that wasn't real at all. But Naomi always said the name of her country with a sigh as if it somehow broke her heart, the way Zoe thought only a man could do.

When Zoe thought about Russia, she envisioned a small village, the Asian steppes, the face of the Tartars, horses pulling wooden carts. But impressions came to her as if in a dream. She could be driving down a road or eating a hamburger and it would come to her in snatches. A taste of sweet tea and dried bread, cabbage soup, a recollection of the dirt in her mouth from burials alive, even though she'd never been there at all.

As Zoe grew older, she'd dream about the place where her grandmother came from and she could see it—the mud-covered streets, the wooden carts, dolls inside dolls, as if memories were built inside memories, and it amazed her how what even another person remembered could take root inside of you as well.

TWENTY-
FOUR

Mrs. Margolis' husband returned. He came back to Brewerton a
wizened old man. He tracked her down at the Heartland and
though thirty-five years had elapsed, she recognized him right
away. "That's him," she said to Mrs. Alexander whose son had
plucked out his eye. "That's him," she said to Nurse Burlington
who sucked on the eraser of a pencil. He was old, bent over, his
face white and wrinkled like an unmade bed. What amazed Mrs.
Margolis wasn't his arrival; it was that she hadn't predicted it.
"What are you doing here? Where have you been?"

He sighed, clutching his hat in his hands while she anticipated stories of Swiss bank accounts, tales of the sea. She
awaited a saga of romance and the wonders of Arabia. "I've been
in Detroit," he said.

"Detroit?" Mrs. Margolis said.

"I worked for a car dealership. I sold factory rejects. Good
cars, but they never got approval. I lived in a small apartment in
the downtown. I learned how to do my own cooking."

"That's it?" Mrs. Margolis leaned her bad hip against the
wall.

"I made some investments, but I lost it at the track."

"That's all?" He smelled old, as if he'd been hanging in the
closet too long. He smelled tired and old and he reminded her of
her own death, which she had not thought about in quite some
time. The banality of it humiliated her. "Why did you come
here?"

"I missed you," he said, dropping his face to his hands.
"I've missed you."

"That's all?"

"You look good, Jean. You don't look bad. You always were a good-looking woman."

"You want something?"

"Perhaps you could help me a little. Let me stay at the house for a while. I want to call the kids. I'm old. I could use a hand."

She softened to him. He was old and he looked as if he'd been alone too long. She was about to say yes, stay at the house, call the kids, but then she saw herself standing in the window, her oldest boy dangling in her arms, hour after hour, day after day. She saw her little girl every evening at five o'clock, clutching the doorknob to the garage. "Is it time to go?" she'd say. "Is it time to get Daddy at the train?"

"Get out," she told him. "Get out of here." She made a scene. She shrieked as loudly as she could. She shrieked so loudly that Mrs. Alexander stood up and Nurse Burlington lifted her eyes. And she sent him away, wishing he'd never come— that he'd remained in her mind as he'd been the day she'd kissed him good-bye, a man upon whose mystery her own life had been built.

Zoe watched from the window of the waiting room as the old man hobbled down the marble steps, back out into the cold, and Mrs. Margolis joined her at the window, preparing to tell her story. Of white-collar crime and hidden identity, of money he'd put aside, of how he pleaded for her forgiveness and said he'd never stopped loving her. "He begged me," she told Zoe as they both stood at the window, watching Mr. Margolis pause, his shadow thin in the now murky snow. "He wanted my love. But I've got my dignity," she told her. "I've got my pride."

The old man, bent and saddened, turned the corner. Just then Nurse Burlington came into the waiting room. "Your brother asked for a knife this morning," Nurse Burlington said. "We have him under surveillance."

For a moment Zoe was taken aback. Then she thought

about what Nurse Burlington had said. "Is that all he asked for? Is that all he said?"

"No, he asked for something else, but no one could understand what he said."

Zoe got into her car and drove to the nearby lumberyard where she purchased some blocks of wood. Then she went to the hardware store and bought a carving knife. She returned to the clinic, walked straight past Nurse Burlington, told the nurse who was keeping an eye on her brother to get out of the room. Then she pulled off the covers he'd pulled over his head. She dragged him by the arm so that he was sitting up. "Here, is this what you want? Is this what you asked for?"

He gazed at her stunned, as she dropped blocks of wood onto his bed, poured them at his feet. "Here," she said, "which one? Take the one you want." She watched as his hands fumbled with the wood. "Here, this one?"

She thrust the knife into his hand and watched as he turned the blade over and over. Then he set the knife at his side and fondled the wood. He did this for a long time, it seemed to her. Whittling, quilting, making a surfboard—these are three activities, Zoe read once, that make memory return.

Now she watched as he took a piece of wood, felt it carefully in his hands, then went back to his chair. At first he made senseless strokes, but then he ran the knife over the wood with a more assured stroke, as if he were petting a cat. Soon he began to drift into the dark forests, farther north than any could be, into the place where nothing could grow, and from there he began to shape the wood with his hands into the magical creatures of his own making.

Zoe had no doubt that she was being watched. She felt the eyes upon her and she felt whatever had passed over her head at the taxidermist's a few weeks ago hovering again in the air and this time she could not mistake it for embalming fluid or a change in the wind. She turned and saw Gabe standing there, watching the small procession of animals growing on the side of Badger's bed.

"So here you are," Gabe said to her.

"Here I am," she replied.

They stayed until Badger grew weary and put the knife down. Until he picked up the shavings with his own hands and piled the wood in a corner of the room. Then Gabe gently took the knife and folded it into his own pocket. "Let me know when you want this," he said. Badger took one of the pieces of wood he'd carved and put it on the table. Then he seemed tired and he curled up on his bed. Gabe watched for a moment. Then he took Zoe by the elbow, leading her away. They walked down to the lobby where he glanced at Nurse Burlington who frowned. "Let's get out of here," he said.

They drove over to Emilio and Donna's where they ordered a "Slice of Life," a pizza with everything on it, including a few secrets neither Donna nor Emilio would name, and discreetly took a seat in the back. "It's good to see you," he said.

"Yes, it's good to see you as well." Zoe was amazed at how empty she felt, as if someone had drained all the fluid from her limbs, and she ate ravenously as if she had to fill herself up again.

"Well," Gabe said, "things are better here. Your brother is talking more. He thinks he's being traded to the New York Mets and that he's a winner on an underdog team."

"Sounds like an improvement."

"He also says the world is going to end."

"That doesn't sound so good."

Gabe shrugged. "Maybe he's getting realistic, that's all."

As he ate, he spilled tomato sauce on his tie. He groaned as he looked at it, having no idea what to do with tomato stain in his laundry. "I'll never get this out," he said. But he watched as Zoe dipped her napkin into cold water, gently rubbing at the spot until it began to disappear. "Shout," she said.

He looked at her oddly. "Shout?"

"It's a stain remover." She rubbed at the stain with her napkin. "Try Shout. It works on this kind of stain."

They drove together in her car back to the parking lot where Gabe lived. "Well, you probably have an early call tomorrow," Zoe said, "so I won't keep you."

"Yes, I do have an early call tomorrow. Otherwise I'd ask you up." She turned to get into her car. "But on Saturday morning I have no call. So why don't you come by tomorrow night? I'll take you to dinner." He hesitated. "No, on second thought, I'll make you dinner. I have mastered lasagna."

"I'll be there at seven," Zoe said.

He cupped his hand around her chin, kissing her ever so gently on the lips. "Are you sure you can remember?"

Zoe nodded. "I can remember."

Things come back to you in strange ways, Zoe thought as she made her way home, recalling something she hadn't thought of in years—the note Badger wrote to her, the last sane and sensible thing he ever said to her, which he'd left on the mirror in the motel room on the border of Canada. "When you least expect it, I'll do something for you."

With a bottle of wine and a plastic container of Shout, Zoe
arrived at Gabe's at seven o'clock to the smell of burnt lasagna
and an apartment full of smoke. They were going to go out when
the wind shifted and the sky burst. They both knew it was early
for this kind of a storm, and all night long it would batter the
shore. It would melt the snow that had fallen just a few days
before and crack the deep ice on the lake. It would turn the earth
to slush and make the earthworms and spring flowers come
abruptly out of the ground.

   She had been to his place before and had noticed the guitar
propped in the corner against the wall. "Do you play?" she
asked now as she flopped onto the bed.

   Gabe shrugged. "Not really." He poured them two glasses
of white wine. "I sing. I just play to accompany myself." Zoe
picked up the guitar. It felt warm and sleek in her hands, like an
animal she liked to touch, not like a thing made of wood. "Would
you sing for me?" she said.

   First he played old folk tunes, songs from the 1960s, songs
of protest. But then he stopped. He said, "I don't know what you
want to hear."

   "What do you like to sing?"

   "Oh, I'll sing anything. There are songs I've made up. Do
you want to hear one of those songs?" And Zoe said she wanted
to hear a song he'd made up.

   She listened to his voice as he sang. It had a soft, sweet
sound as it rose and fell, like wind chimes. But then it deepened
into something more solid and substantial. She had learned to
listen when she was young. She'd listened to her mother's voice

on the radio and to the sound of Hunt coming to the bluff to find her. She thought of all the things that had taught her how to listen and now she used that knowledge as she heard the sound that came from Gabe's voice.

He sang to her like an angel of his own private sorrow, of what he had endured. He sang to her of his drunken father, his broken home, his unhappy marriage to the girl everyone said he was made for. But it was not the words that came to her. He conveyed the meaning with his voice, and it was through his voice that she came to care for him. As if he were speaking in a secret code, a private language, like the secret language of beasts that can speak across the miles and find each other through a sound no one not attuned can hear.

Zoe wondered how this was possible. How can I love someone with my brother the way he is? How can I love someone with everything that has happened to me? But the answer kept coming back: How can I not?

Then he stopped playing and at first she didn't notice he had stopped. She didn't hear the silence in the room, but it seemed to her that the music went on and on. Then she realized he had stopped and was looking at her. "Come here," he said. Zoe tried to move but her body wouldn't comply. "I can't," she said. Gabe put down his guitar. "Then I'll come there," he replied.

He wasn't even sure that he wanted to, but because he said he would, he got up. He walked to her. With his hand he gently lifted her face. His gesture surprised her. It was steady and sure. Gabe expected her to pull away, but she didn't. He bent over and kissed her on the lips, but the room felt too bright. He turned and flicked out the light. It took their eyes a moment to adjust to the darkness, but then they found each other easily. Zoe felt as if she were reeling, staggering through the night, though in fact she hardly moved from the place where he held her.

·   ·   ·

In the morning they drove along the lakefront. The storm had broken and the air felt like spring, the way it can in Brewerton. It was the dead of winter and then the breeze shifted, you felt the thaw, and it was spring. They were driving to nowhere in particular and suddenly Zoe asked him to pull over. "I want to look at the lake," she said. It was mid-morning and the sun shimmered on the water, on the breaking ice floes. He pulled the car over and Zoe realized they had stopped at the confluence, the place where the great waters met.

They stopped for a moment, not knowing what to do. The windows steamed up with their breath and Gabe reached over. He bent across and kissed her. The night before he had been tentative, and even as they'd made love he had been so delicate she could almost not feel him at all, but now he was surer and she found herself stunned, like a sparrow who strikes the glass and for a moment at least is unable to fly away.

She opened the door. "Let's take a walk," she said. And she felt as if she had to get out and stretch her limbs, as if it was all too much for her to sit still. "Can we go for a walk," she said, "down by the lake?"

In Brewerton everything can change in an instant. The minute the wind shifts from the south it enters another season. They went to the top of the bluff, to the place where Zoe used to wait for Hunt, but the place felt different now, not like before, and she didn't feel drawn to it as she had before. They took the stairs and went down to the water. The sand was moist and they held hands as they walked on the shore.

They paused for a moment. Zoe faced the lake and took a deep breath. Suddenly she felt something racing through her. June said it would feel like an arrow starting in your gut. But it would also be as if someone had shot warm water into your veins. A warm rush moving through you. It came over her fast, traveling through the veins, the arteries, into the tips of the fingers, the capillaries.

It was as if a child began to grow within her, even though

she knew no seed had been planted. But inside her something grew, something she had formed on hope. It would not happen right away, but she knew she would feel it when it did. She felt a tiny round turning inside of her as if her own brother were beginning again.

Zoe closed her eyes and the world went away. Now it was her own self she found in water, swimming through space toward a beam of light before her, a tiny speck of emerald light. She tried to open her eyes, but found she could not open them as she cascaded toward the light.

It was like a memory, only it came from a more distant place than memory. A place she had been to before, but could not recall as she closed her eyes and swam, more patiently now, in a steady breaststroke, crawling through water. Nothing stood between herself and the world, only the liquid she moved in, and she knew that this was something she'd wanted for a long time.

One day when Badger was little, Zoe took him for a walk in the snow. She put him in a red snowsuit and galoshes and she told Naomi, because June was at work, I'm taking him for a walk in the snow. Zoe was perhaps seven and Badger was two, but in her memory she was much older and more mature. "You are my child," she told him as they headed out into the snow. "I am your mother. You must do as I say." And they trudged out.

They walked to the edge of their property and down the road toward the woods near the lake and in the woods they went off into the snow and it grew deeper and deeper. It was difficult for Badger to walk, but he did. He pulled his legs up as high as he could and struggled against the rising drifts. Zoe wondered why she'd taken him on this trek, but she had. She said, "It will make you stronger. It will give you good legs."

He did not protest, even as the snow reached his waist. He kept on and Zoe, proud because her legs were longer and she could go farther, pulled him along. But finally he could take no more and he looked at her without a word. He stopped. "You must do as I say," Zoe said, but Badger stopped. "It will make you stronger." She tried to pull him, but he lay down in the snow. He extended his arms and legs wide into a snow angel and buried his face deep. Then he just lay there, stubborn, without moving.

And then it was, and this was the part Zoe had forgotten, the part that came back to her, that she picked him up in her arms. He was heavy and even now she did not know how she'd done this, but she picked him up. His face was white and cold and tears came down his cheeks, but he was silent. "I'm sorry," she said as she kissed him lightly on the cheek. "I really am." And she carried him in her arms all the way home.

ABOUT THE AUTHOR

Mary Morris was born and raised in Chicago. Her previous books include *Vanishing Animals and Other Stories,* which was awarded the Rome Prize by the American Academy and Institute of Arts and Letters; the novel *Crossroads; The Bus of Dreams,* a book of stories awarded the Friends of American Writers Award; and a work of nonfiction, *Nothing to Declare: Memoirs of a Woman Traveling Alone.* Having traveled extensively, Mary Morris and her daughter now reside in New York City.